THE RED MOUSE

" 'DID YOU PUT *HIM* IN THAT FRAME?' "

Frontispiece, The Red Mouse

The Red Mouse

A Mystery Romance

By
WILLIAM HAMILTON OSBORNE

ILLUSTRATED BY
THE KINNEYS

A. L. BURT COMPANY

Publishers   New York

To

L. G. S. O.

I

For years—the best years of her life, for that matter, as she often reflected in lonely moments—Miriam Challoner had been trying to prove to her own satisfaction that her husband was no worse than the majority of young men married to rich women, but she could never find the arguments whereby she might arrive at the desired conclusion. It is not to be wondered at, then, that eventually there came a day when the information was brought to her that even in the gay and ultra-fashionable world in which they moved people spoke of him as "that mad Challoner," and were saying that he was going a pace that was rapidly carrying him far beyond the horizon of anything like respectability —going to the dogs, in truth, as fast as her money could take him there.

Now Miriam Challoner was not one of those women who deceive themselves, if not their friends, when they say that if ever they hear of their husbands doing such-and-such-a-thing they know perfectly well what they will do. It is true that, like them, she did nothing; nevertheless, she could not be persuaded to discuss with any one the humiliating position in which her husband had placed her.

In a way, this attitude of hers was unfortunate, for

it was more or less responsible for the note of melan-
choly cadence which crept into her mind. And so it
was that before very long she was dimly conscious of
an emotion quite unlike anything that she had hitherto experienced: all the bitterness in her heart had
given way to a sickening sensation that she, as well as
as he, had been tried in the matrimonial furnace and
found wanting. Somehow, she had fallen grievously
in her own estimation!

And society's estimation? Illusions in that direction
were hardly possible; there, too, doubtless she would
incur the loss of a certain amount of consideration.
And even the non-possession of a highly imaginative
temperament did not prevent her from fancying the
expressive shrugs, and "Oh, of course his wife is to
blame," which, for the sake of an inference that is ob-
vious, would be voiced by more than one impeccable
dame of her acquaintance—as often as not superbly
gullible souls, whose eloquence increases in direct pro-
portion to the world's lack of belief in the fidelity of
their liege lords.

Nor were comments of that kind the worst that she
might expect! For, as a penalty for belonging to a
set which, to a greater degree, perhaps, than any
other, recognises the possibility of an up-to-date
couple having a mutually implied understanding that
neither shall object to the discreet—and more or less

temporary—faithlessness of the other—she knew that
it would be well-nigh miraculous if some kindly dis-
posed persons did not go still further for an explanation of his conduct, and point to her and her husband
as a conspicuous example of such a precious pair. But
though her whole being rebelled at the mere thought
that there could be people who would regard her in
such a light, she could not bring herself to take decisive action of any kind. There was nothing that
could be said, she told herself, nothing that could be
done—since a most conscientious and pitiless self-
analysis had failed to reveal any wifely shortcoming
—except to have faith that there were some of her sex
—not many, it is true, but still a few friends—who
would continue to believe her incapable of doing any
of the things that so many others did, for whom there
was far less excuse than there would be for her.

But whatever were the opinions of the women, there
was no disposition on the part of the men to hold her
in any way responsible for his behaviour. Far from it.
And in a favourite corner of an exclusive club, when
the names of fair ladies—mostly of the stage—were
bandied about as figuring in young Challoner's escapades, old cronies of his father, between sips of their
Scotch and sodas, were wont to boil over with con-
temptuous indignation and explosively give thanks to
the gods for willing that their lovable, old-time friend

should not live to see the confirmation of his fears.
And how well they recalled those fears!

For notwithstanding his very moderate circumstances, the elder Challoner had been that rarest of
mortals—a man blissfully content with his lot in life,
and, one who seldom missed an opportunity to
deplore the insatiable craze of the rich for more
riches, forever protesting that blatant commercialism,
haste and artificiality were the gods of the present
day; and no picture in their gallery of lasting im-
pressions stood out more vividly than the one in which,
surrounded by a group of young fellows, who had
"got him going," as they phrased it, he was declaim-
ing against—what was merely his pet hobby in another form—the egregious folly of poor young men
seeking riches through marriage.

" . . . and I, young gentlemen," he would con-
clude with great earnestness, "will always maintain
that such a union will make a man lose all incentive
to work out what the good Lord has put in him."

Little wonder, then, that on the announcement that
a marriage had been "arranged" between Challoner's
son and a daughter of a man whose name the world
over was significant of fiscal potency, the day bid fair
to be a memorable one at the club, his contempora-
ries preparing to make merry at the old fellow's
expense. But in a sense his "showing up" there had

been a disappointment; one look at the face, which showed symptoms of distress and a desire to be reassured, was sufficient to cause the banter to die in their hearts before it had reached their lips.

It soon came out that there had been a scene between father and son. These two, for many years, had been the only members of the family; and probably better than any one in the world the father had known the son's weaknesses: hypersensitive to new influences, vanity and inability to say no; and he had pointed out to him the many disadvantages—dangers to one of his temperament—which he could see in such an alliance. To the father's thinking, the boy would have no home—only establishments, yachts, racing-stables and motor-cars; and he had contended that there were far more desirable things in life than the possession of these—from which it can easily be surmised that J. Lawrence Challoner, senior, was a man little in sympathy with the ideas of modern fashionable society.

Now to appreciate the mental anguish of another organism—even if that organism is one's own parent —is never an easy matter; and of all men, the modern lover is apt to be the last to succumb to an argument that predicts a blighted future because of an intention to marry an heiress. And so it was only natural that Lawrence should have regarded his father as an old

fogy, have resented his warnings and have replied
that he was competent to look after his own affairs
and that, anyhow, the consent of the girl's parents
had been obtained and no interference was possible.
And with that the father's manner had completely
changed: he had wished the boy the best of luck; sent
him away happy. Obviously, all this was years ago;
parents on both sides had passed away; and yet
things had turned out pretty much as the old man had
dreaded. Indeed, matters had come to this pass: how
long this indulgent wife would continue to keep her
eyes shut to her husband making ducks and drakes
of her fortune, and why she did it, were questions
which interested all who knew this couple, but which
Challoner apparently thought wholly unnecessary to
ask himself.

An automobile—Mrs. Challoner's automobile—was
largely instrumental in bringing matters to a climax.
As trouble-makers the "machines" rank high; in fact,
there are moments when it would seem as if the arch-
fiend himself were in them; otherwise, how account
for the mysterious influence that makes people lose
command of themselves once they are in command of
them; that leads astray, as some one has said, the
great and the good as well as those of lesser clay; that
produces the extraordinary state of mind that rejoices
in riding rough-shod over the rights and feelings of

others; while one and all claim to recognise his handicraft in the ingenuity which the "machines" display in selecting the most inopportune times and least accessible places for an exhibition of their mechanical ailments.

But be that as it may, in this particular instance the devil was not lurking in, tampering with the improvements and refinements of detail in the big, red body of Mrs. Challoner's Mastodon model—no, it was not with the machine that he was concerned, but with the man himself, befuddling whatever brains he had left; and the devil it was and no other that incited Challoner to leave a certain establishment,—about which we shall have something to say later on,—take the wheel from the chauffeur and embark on a sensational, bacchic career up the Avenue at an hour when the view of that fashionable thoroughfare through the silken, shimmery curtains falling over a window in a corner house facing the Park was too alluring not to be irresistible.

And so it came about that the comments on the passing throng made by two women, indulging in afternoon tea in Mrs. Challoner's white and gold drawing-room, were interrupted in a manner that was as unexpected as it was embarrassing.

"Look, Miriam!" Shirley Bloodgood was saying to

her hostess, apropos of a woman passing by whom
they both knew, "did you ever see anything more atro-
cious than that gown?"

The other smiled her appreciation; and again the
voluble Miss Bloodgood went on:—

"And do look at the Heath girls in those huge hats
—what frights!"

But whatever were her thoughts on the subject, Miriam Challoner did not answer, for precisely at that
moment her attention was attracted by something
strangely familiar in an unusually insolent and insistent honking of a motor-horn, which was causing a
wave of apprehension to sweep down the long line of
vehicles. And a moment later they saw that chauf-
feurs were rudely interrupting the purring of automo-
biles lazing over their allotted miles; that drivers were
swerving their horses into closer relations with the
curb; that hardly had these attained a position of
comparative safety than there flashed by them and
fetched up in front of Mrs. Challoner's house a big
machine, which a distinguished though dissipated
looking man had been recklessly forcing with utter
disregard of the right of way, a performance which
called forth a volley of expletives not only from cab-
bies singularly unappreciative of his dexterity in ex-
ecuting perilously close shaves, but likewise from
angry pedestrians, who had halted on hearing the

groan with which the machinery protested his sudden braking.

For a moment that seemed minutes the atmosphere in the drawing-room was electric, the tension almost unbearable, for it was impossible for either of the women to doubt that the other saw what she had seen: the condition that the man was in who had leaped from the car and was now crossing the sidewalk apparently oblivious to the exclamations of wonder and lament that he had escaped authoritative vigilance.

Rising quickly, Shirley Bloodgood put out her hand. "Good-bye—thank you so much, Miriam!" There was an amazement of question in the eyes that involuntarily sought those of her friend; but her one thought was to escape what she wisely interpreted as an oncoming scene between husband and wife.

But though there was a mist before her eyes, a surging in her ears, not a muscle of Miriam Challoner's face moved; and she permitted the girl before her to perceive no emotion other than gentle surprise.

"Surely, my dear, you're not going?— What?— So soon?"

Conventional though they were, there could be no mistaking the tone of sincerity in Mrs. Challoner's words as she took the girl's hand in both of hers with an affectionate movement. Indeed, for the barest fraction of a second it almost succeeded in convincing

Shirley that the distressing incident of the motor had
entirely escaped her; at any rate, it augmented the
doubt whether the woman before her had even an ink-
ling of the stories in circulation concerning the doings
of her husband. Nor was such a conclusion at all il-
logical. Shirley Bloodgood could recall not a word
that Miriam Challoner had ever uttered during all
the years of her married life, nor a look that could be
construed as implying a knowledge of his dissipations; on the contrary, there had been times when the
girl had been so exasperated over the wife's outspoken
admiration for qualities in the man which Shirley
knew that he did not possess, that she had been sorely
tempted to enlighten her friend as to his escapades.
But gratifying as was the thought of the wife's possible ignorance, it by no means lessened the necessity
of a hasty departure on Shirley's part; and somewhat
confusedly but affectionately she kissed her hostess
good-bye.

"Oh, my dear Miriam, but I must—your tea is perfectly delicious though. If only I had time . . . "
Shirley stopped abruptly; her endeavour to conceal
her anxiety to be gone was making her uncertain of
her words.

"One's tea, like one's friends, my dear, should be of
the best," Miriam returned with a sweet smile. And
apparently thinking of nothing but her somewhat in-

sïpíd little compliment, she laughed pleasantly, passed
her arm lovingly round the girl's waist, and accompanied her to the door of the drawing-room.

Miriam's smile and manner touched Shirley deeply.
The inclination to offer words of comfort was strong
in this tall, rangy girl, whose every movement was as
graceful as it was impulsive. How sweet, how easy it
would be, she thought, if Miriam would only give a
hint that they would be welcome. But like many
another woman, Miriam Challoner had schooled herself to face the world with a smile; had learned that
to lay bare one's heart, even to one's friends, is to
court surprise, perhaps ridicule; and that to dissimu-
late though it kills is to play well one's part; and she
gave no sign.

On reaching the hall below, Shirley was able to see
through the open door Challoner ascending swiftly
but uncertainly the grey, stone steps. With a quick
movement she drew to one side while he sullenly pushed
by his wife's young butler, Stevens, and began to
stumble up the soft-carpeted, wide stairway; then, un-
noticed and with a sigh of relief, she fled out into the
street.

Left rather abruptly alone, Mrs. Challoner went
back into the drawing-room, and resting her arms on
the mantel, bowed her head upon them and gave way
to the misery of her reflections. It was not the first

time, to be sure, that Lawrence had returned in this condition, but heretofore he had been gracious enough to have had it occur at night; and she had cherished the belief that she was his only witness. Now, there was an element connected with his home-coming that was still harder to bear: the sympathy which pleaded for recognition on the face of her friend, and which told more plainly than words that she had seen all, understood all. Presently, lifting her head, she crossed the room and seated herself; then raising her hands she let them drop despairingly along the arms of the chair while the unbidden tears overflowed. In this position she remained until the sound of footsteps warned her of her husband's approach; then a moment of struggle for self-control; a brushing away of tears, and finally, rising, she left her seat for one behind the tea-table. And it was in this unquestioned point of vantage, apparently cool and collected, in the act of pouring herself out a cup of tea, that Challoner's gaze first rested upon his wife as, lurching in his walk but his eyes holding a purpose, he came into her presence.

"Well, Miriam, here I am . . . I've come home, you see!" he blurted out in a don't-care-what-happens sort of manner, and without waiting for an answer slumped into a chair and added sneeringly: "You're not over-demonstrative, my dear!"

Mrs. Challoner winced. During the long days and nights of suspense and wonder as to his whereabouts, she had solaced herself with inventing plausible excuses for his absence; how useless they were, his looks, manner, and more than anything else the intonation of his voice now showed; she dared not trust herself to speak lest she should give way to foolish invective.

Challoner came to the point at once.

"Miriam, I must have some money!" It was not a request; it was a command.

Up to this time the young wife had not lifted her eyes from the tea-cup in her hand. She was a woman with brown eyes and very attractive brown hair, but upon the face that still should have held the freshness of youth deep lines were beginning to appear. Pretty she was, in a way, though she had never been beautiful; and yet there was something that spelt beauty in the brown eyes which she now fixed upon him.

"For three days you have been away—where have you been?" The necessity for saying something alone was responsible for the question. Many days afterward in reviewing the painful scene, she was positive that she had not inquired nor had he volunteered the information.

"I don't know," he answered dully, half-truthfully. "All I know is that I landed at Cradlebaugh's." And after a moment, noting the look of mystification on her face, he snapped out: "Cradlebaugh's gambling rooms—gambling rooms, there—now you know."

With the last words he rose excitedly, stalked over to a table and smote it with his clenched hand.

"I tell you I must have some money!"

Miriam Challoner would not have been human if again bitter words had not risen to her lips. But one quick glance at the puffy face, the red-rimmed eyes was sufficient to warn her of the danger of exciting his anger while in his present condition; and instead she merely inclined her head—an action which instantly caused hope to surge into the eyes of Challoner.

"I want—I must have a thousand dollars." Here again, the attitude was not that of a suppliant; in the demand was more of the highwayman than of the beggar.

Mrs. Challoner's dark eyes met those of the man, held them steady; then she said firmly, decisively:—

"Lawrence, much as it hurts me to refuse you, I feel that I must. It is for your own good." The soft gown that clung to her figure seemed to take more rigid lines as she drew herself up and went on with: "I can give you nothing more—this sort of thing has gone quite far enough."

For an instant Challoner was stunned. His wife had never looked at him like that; there was something in the catch of her breath, too, as she ended, that meant denial, he was certain. But he took courage and renewed his attack; and meeting with no success, he turned to imploring, begging for the money. Did she not know that he would not ask her if he did not *have* to have it? Women never could understand why men had to have money—she didn't understand. If she would only let him have the money, he would pledge himself to mend his ways, anything—but he must have money. When men had to have money, they *had* to have it—that was all there was to it. And then a violent irresistible impulse to be perfectly truthful, to lay bare his mind before her, took hold of him; and that mind was so warped, his need so desperate, that he came perilously near to blurting out the real reason why he needed the money. For an instant he actually thought that his wife would see, understand, appreciate the reason as some of his male friends doubtless would.

"I'll tell you how it is, Miriam . . . " he had begun, and then suddenly stopped.

What was he about to do! Was there not something queer, something not exactly right, in his telling Miriam about the other woman? After all, that was the one thing in his life that he had never told her. She was welcome to the rest, but that—she mustn't know that; and he ended by pleading:—

"Surely, Miriam, you're not going to refuse me— come . . . "

"I am sorry, Lawrence, but I must." There was a sob in the refusal as she turned away.

And still like a spoiled child the husband would not abandon his plea. Besides, he had detected the sob. Once more his attitude underwent a change: he moved toward her, holding out his arms as though to gather her into them. It was a charm that always worked with Miriam; it would now, he told himself.

But Challoner was doomed to disappointment. It was the last touch needed to complete her humiliation; and waving him back, she cried:—

"Laurie, Laurie, anything but that!" There was a flood of tears behind her look of pain.

"But I must . . . . Cradlebaugh . . . " he came to a helpless pause.

Mrs. Challoner slowly repeated the name:—

"Cradlebaugh! I wish you had never seen that man —that class of men! Your money—my money very likely has been going to them! Well, if you want money you will have to . . . " The tension snapped and she drew her hand across her eyes, then broke down completely.

"A sign of weakening," Challoner said to himself, and promptly started toward her.

"No, no,—go!" she cried, drawing her hands up to

her face as if to shut out the sight of him from her gaze.

A moment later Challoner was seated in the motor-car. As the chauffeur threw in the clutch some instinct told Challoner to look back. He had a fleeting impression that he had seen a woman's face in the doorway. "Surely that's Miriam," he thought, and lifted his hat; but when he looked again there was no one there. Yet if his senses had been perfectly normal, he would have known that it was her face that he had seen. But the fates had no intention of letting him know that with his departure his wife's resolution had gone, and that she had come to the door to beseech him to come back; for even then they were cunningly spinning the web which was to encompass him about.

II

CRADLEBAUGH'S,—Cradlebaugh's house of a thousand chances,—rearing its four stories of brown stone, spreading itself out liberally on the north side of one of the side streets which is fast being given over to fashionable clubs and restaurants, is a thoroughly up-to-date establishment. Here, the *jeunesse dore* of the city are made welcome—once the critical eye of the sentinel behind the triple steel doors at the top of the brown stone steps has recognised in them the essential qualifications. In appointments, the house is luxurious and gorgeous, and is so closely shuttered that not a ray of light from outside is permitted to penetrate it: Cradlebaugh's day and night, night and day, is lit within by the glow of artificial lights; the sunlight has no chance in Cradlebaugh's. In addition to the main hall of play, there are accommodations for parties wishing to indulge in quiet games among themselves. Meals are served at all hours,— supper being the specialty of the house,—and notwithstanding that no charge whatever is made for them, the cuisine and service are beyond reproach. It can truly be said of Cradlebaugh's, that it has all the cheerfulness of the hearth, the quiet of the sanctuary, mingled with the glare of irresistible recklessness.

It was to this establishment, then, that Challoner directed a cabby to take him after hours of unsuccessful attempts to borrow money from his friends—unsuccessful, because they had come to know his irresponsibility, and to realise that his obligations were not the obligations of his wife. The consequence was that man after man invented an excuse or refused him emphatically. And finally, in desperation, he had offered to sell the Mastodon. But the dealers knew who owned the car—one of the handsomest cars in town—and on Challoner disgustedly ordering his chauffeur home, a dealer more daring than the others had said to him with aggressive familiarity:—

"Get your wife's bill of sale, Challoner we'll buy it then, all right."

A spark of anger immediately lit up Challoner's eyes, resentment was deep down in his inmost soul; but his brain had been absinthiated for days, his sensibilities blunted, and indignities fell from him like the proverbial water from a duck's back. Nor was it solely with his mentalities that the dissipations of the last five years had played havoc: his face, his body, were unnaturally thin, and his glance had become fixed and strained. Nevertheless, over-indulgence had not grossened him, he was still good-looking, and there was an air about him that few men had. In all his recklessness, whenever he wanted money he had

not forgotten that fact. It had always counted with
Miriam—until now. It counted still with Miss Letty
Love of the Frivolity!

There had been moments, it is true, when rushing
madly about town for funds, that he had felt it would
surely have been better for him if he had never gone to
Cradlebaugh's; but then like a flash would come the
thought that if he had not gone to Cradlebaugh's he
would never have known Letty Love! And by no
means had he arrived at the state where he could have
wished that . . .

With the thought of Letty Love there came another
indissolubly connected with it: Was Colonel Hargraves slowly undermining, ousting him out of her
affections? Not without reason he argued that
Colonel Hargraves had plenty of money, and the man
with money was going to win out in the graces of the
Frivolity actress! Challoner could see it, could feel
it, and now in this crisis he could not raise a paltry
thousand or two . . .

Suddenly a voice from overhead broke in upon his
thoughts with :—

"Front entrance, sir?"

Challoner started. The query was pertinent, frequently important, sometimes vital. But in all the
times that Challoner had driven to Cradlebaugh's,
never until now had this question been put to him.

The entrance on the street above, he was quite well aware, was for those whose livelihood supplied sufficient reason for preferring the more secret way, while the man-about-town,—such as he flattered himself that he still was,—the credential-bearing stranger, even those whose reputation might suffer, found that the arrangement of the main entrance furnished them with ample protection. Nevertheless, far from feazing him, Challoner felt that in some subtle way the question fitted in with his scheme of things. For a shadowy purpose was slowly forming in his mind— a purpose that required thought. His answer was of paramount importance, he must make no mistake . . .

"The rear—no," he quickly corrected, "the front entrance."

Before the main street door the driver pulled up his horse, and Challoner hurriedly walked—as one whose nose was straight and who followed his nose—into the whited sepulchre called Cradlebaugh's.

No one greeted Challoner as he passed into the main hall: it happened there was no one present at the table that he knew. In the old days it had been the custom of Cradlebaugh, the human spider, frankly to exhibit himself in the middle of his net, his grim smile and dry hand extended to each guest who came or went. But of late years—since he had shuffled off this mortal coil —there had been no one to make these obsequious

greetings; for, though Cradlebaugh's still was Cradlebaugh's, its ownership remained a mystery. And
whether it was a syndicate, an association, a reincar-
nated spirit, or a man, no one could tell. Of one
thing, however, its patrons were certain: there was
but one Cradlebaugh's!

For fully half an hour Challoner stood at the buffet,
every now and then unsteadily tilting the decanter.
And while this course of refreshment may have dulled
his wits, it certainly strengthened his courage, for
presently he said to himself:—

"I'll try him, yes, why not?"

And a moment later, still optimistic, he called a servant and asked:—

"Where is Pemmican?"

"Faro, sir."

Challoner ascended swiftly to the second floor, and
paused at one room whose door was open.

"How long?" he inquired, thrusting in his head, by
way of greeting to the group at the table.

Four of the men there did not glance up from their
cards; hollow-eyed, cigars between their teeth, they
were alive only to the hundredth chance that still
eluded them. The fifth man, a railroad president,
coatless, alone nodded to Challoner, and said senten-
tiously:—

"Forty hours—for me."

Half way down the corridor Challoner met Pemmican, head card-dealer of Cradlebaugh's, a man with a
pasty face, a low brow and shifty eyes—a man who
knew his business. This Pemmican seemed the all-
and-all of Cradlebaugh's, apparently general factotum; but though he simulated the appearance of an
owner, in reality he was a servile servant stamped with
a dread of the pseudo-Cradlebaugh, of the man higher
up. Nevertheless, whoever controlled the destinies of
this gambling-house had chosen him wisely.

Challoner came at once to the point.

"Pemmican, I want some money—about—" and
broke off abruptly, for the other was eyeing him
coldly.

Instinctively Pemmican of the low brow knew that
the game was up with Challoner; moreover, he saw
that, although the man seemed sober, in reality he was
very drunk. He walked away quickly, dismissing him
with:—

"I'm sorry, sir, but it's against the rules. I
can't——"

"What rot!" interrupted Challoner.

But by this time Pemmican had reached the end of
the hall, leaving the other to gather what he could of
his mumbled excuses.

In anything but an amiable mood, Challoner resumed
his position at the buffet. Suddenly he was conscious

of a light touch on the arm. Turning slowly, he found himself face to face again with Pemmican.

"Why don't you try Colonel Hargraves?" whispered the latter.

"What?" came from the clogged brain of Challoner.

"Try Hargraves," the other went on. "He's been down to Gravesend for two days; and he's back . . . "

Pemmican's meaning was lost on Challoner, for he merely exclaimed:—

"Well?"

Before answering, Pemmican of the low brow shrugged his shoulders and spread out his palms, then he said pointedly:—

"Only that he pulled out ten thousand on Flora McQueen—that's all!"

"What?" Challoner began to understand.

Pemmican nodded.

"Sure thing—ten thousand dollars!"

Slowly and deliberately Challoner refilled his glass to the brim. For a moment there was silence, then Pemmican repeated tantalisingly:—

"Ten thousand dollars—not a cent less!"

Challoner thought for a moment.

"How did you come out?" he asked, much to the other's surprise.

Pemmican shook his head.

"I lost a cool thousand because I did not back the

mare. I played on Tigerskin. I've got to get that thousand back, somehow."

Challoner emptied his glass.

"Was Colonel Hargraves down there alone?" His voice was thick, hoarse.

"Where?" returned Pemmican, as if he had misunderstood.

"At Gravesend?"

Pemmican looked long and quizzically into Challoner's eyes.

"He was . . . not," was his simple but significant answer, and moved away.

But Challoner followed him up, and seizing his arm, said somewhat gruffly:—

"Look here, Pemmican, if Hargraves comes in—I want to see him—tell him to wait for me."

For the first time Pemmican's eyes lost their curious tiredness, an enigmatical smile played about the corners of his mouth.

"Yes," he said simply, and nodding, went his way.

Left alone, Challoner found himself a prey to all the black fiends of rage, jealousy and desire for revenge. For a time everything was blotted out from his vision except the face of Letty Love and the face of Colonel Hargraves. "This small world," he muttered to himself, "is much too small for me and Colonel Hargraves!" With that there loomed up out of the mists of his mind the brilliantly lighted and ornate entrance of a certain apartment-house a short distance away; and a few minutes later, obedient to his subconscious will, his feet carried him down the stairs to a door evidently leading to the outside. A few words of explanation from Challoner to the man on duty there were necessary before he would proceed to undo the complicated system of bolts; and then he passed out and was under the starry skies. Challoner was not the first man of social prominence in the community that could directly trace the beginning of his life as an outcast to passing through that door!

III

HIRAM EDGAR LOVE—so read a faded yellow card on
the door-panel of Suite 10 in the "Drelincourt," an
apartment hotel in a section of the city which has ever
been popular with a class that has been well termed
the "fringe of society." The name was not printed,
not engraved, but written in ancient India ink in cop-
per-plate perfection by the careful, cleanly, genteel
Englishman that Hiram Edgar Love had been—
Hiram Edgar Love, that long since had been laid to
rest in a quiet Surrey churchyard leagues distant,
though his name still did yeoman service, for it spelt
respectability; it covered a multitude of peccadilloes;
his soul went marching on! For was it not the shade
of Hiram Edgar Love that had rented the Love suite
in the "Drelincourt," his shade that paid the rent, his
pipe and his slippers that lay near the fireplace for
the world to see?—Hiram Edgar Love the myth, the
constantly expected but never-coming master of the
house!

Before the entrance of this suite Challoner came to a
halt.

"I wonder if she's alone?" he mused, as with something like the palpitating deference of a stranger he
pressed the button underneath the faded card and

waited to learn his fate at the hands of the one woman in all the world for him. Nor was it by any means the first time that he had asked himself that question; all the way through the streets it had been in his mind every moment, and so absorbed was he with the thought, that he failed to see the familiar nod with which the diminutive god of the "Drelincourt" lift acknowledged his advent as he proceeded to carry upward his human freight.

"Same, sir, I suppose?" asked the boy.

Challoner made no answer; but leaving the car at the desired landing, he had turned to the right and directed his steps to the extreme end of the corridor.

It was a new experience to Challoner to wait among the shadows of the dimly lighted hall; hitherto his custom had been to let himself in, *sans* ceremony; but the apparently successful campaign of the racing Colonel had changed that—put him on a different footing.

"If *he's* there," he assured himself as he pressed the button again impatiently, "I'll know what to do, all right . . . "

But if Hargraves were not there! That was the contingency that sent a chill over him. He could deal with a man—but the woman! A woman who had never cared and who, he was only too well aware,

would never even pretend to care for him unless he had
the wherewithal with which to lure her back.

"If it were not for Hargraves—" he broke off
abruptly, for the door had opened with such unexpected suddenness that it required not a little effort to
pull himself together, and demand of the trim, little
maid who stood there:—

"Your mistress—is she at home?"

"Miss Love is not at home, sir."

Challoner was not so sure about that; in a trice he
was past her, going through room after room until
he had covered the entire apartment; and she had
barely recovered from the shock that his strange behaviour had given her than he was back again in the
small, square hall, eyeing her suspiciously.

"I want to see your mistress."

"Miss Love is not in, sir," she told him, just as if
he did not already know it.

"But you know where she went?" he asked meaningly.

"Indeed, sir, I do not," she replied, not at all dis-
concerted by his manner; and her eyes as they fixed
their gaze on his were as steady as the lips that said:
"She should be with her father, sir."

Challoner raged inwardly; he thought he detected a
gleam of mockery in her eyes. Once more he plunged
through the apartment, seeking some incriminating

scrap of paper, some evidence that would betray his divinity's whereabouts. But after a few minutes he was back again, standing over the girl, menacingly.

"I want you to tell me where Letty is?" he said in a tone that told plainly that such lies were not for him; but it had little effect on the maid: long practice in fencing with Miss Love's admirers had made trickery her forte.

"You might try Atlantic City, sir," she suggested blandly; "it's quite possible that they went there."

At this, Challoner looked ugly, and seizing her roughly by the arm, he led her to her mistress' boudoir, where, pointing to a Verne-Martin cabinet that stood in a corner, he exclaimed:—

"Who put him there?"

For answer the girl shrugged her shoulders. She made no attempt to disengage herself from his grasp, merely watched Challoner as his gaze rested angrily on a plain gold frame in which was an unconventional half-length photograph—Colonel Richard Hargraves, his arms akimbo upon a table, his shoulders forward, his smug, full, self-satisfied face thrust into the face of the world—of Challoner.

Even on paper Hargraves's lazy eyes seemed to insult and tantalise him, and an insane desire to crush, batter and destroy this counterfeit presentment came over him. For an instant he had a vague sensation of suffocation, almost to choking, and releasing the girl, his hand sought his throat; it encountered a scarf-pin —a trifle that his wife had given him long ago. Tearing it quickly from his scarf, he extended it toward the maid.

"That may fetch the truth from her," he said to himself, and aloud: "Tell me where Letty is, and . . . no"—the girl was reaching for the jewel, but he held it from her—"no, tell me first," he added hoarsely, toying with the pin.

"Well, then, if you must know, sir," she stammered, "she went to Gravesend—the races, sir."

Challoner's mind received this information with a certain morbid exultation; and thrusting his face into hers and pointing with the pin to the portrait, he cried:—

"Then she *is* with him?"

The girl was silent; she was figuring the value of the pin. It was worth fifty dollars, she finally decided, and looking up at Challoner, admitted the truth with a nod.

The pin fell into her ready grasp.

When Challoner spoke again his voice was calm and steady.

"Sit down there." He motioned to a seat and he took the one opposite. "We'll wait until they come back —just wait."

For minutes that seemed hours they sat facing each other, Challoner dogged but quiescent, the girl with a growing unrest upon her—a cat with a cornered mouse.

At last a buzzer sounded.

"Stay where you are!" Challoner commanded, as the girl made a movement to go. "If it's somebody else," he added quickly, still looking at her, but with a changed eye, "we don't care about them; they can go away."

Again the buzzer sounded.

"Has she a key?" he whispered.

"Yes," she answered, matching his tone.

"Has he?" persisted Challoner.

The girl held up her hand for reply: the jingling of keys in the outer hall, followed by the clink of metal in the lock, had reached their ears; then came the closing of the door, the click of high heels, the swish of skirts, the odour of violets, and then Letty Love, in all her pink and white loveliness, tall, supreme, her face flushed, her lips parted, her eyes sparkling, stood framed in the doorway. At the sight of the man and the girl sitting there like two culprits, she burst into laughter—a long peal of laughter that was her stock in trade, and which ran the gamut of her deep, contralto voice. And still neither the man nor the girl spoke, but continued to look ill at ease. To Miss

Love the situation was amusing—too amusing for words.

"Inconstant!—Naughty Lawrence!" she exclaimed, leaving his name stranded in the air—a coquettish way she had in speaking—and pointing her tiny gloved finger at him: "Perhaps I interrupt?" And now turning to the girl: "Patricia, I didn't know you could be so interesting . . . "

The maid gasped with relief as she left the room in obedience to a dismissing wave of her mistress' hand.

"Well, why don't the rest of you come in?" Challoner growled, fastening his eyes on the woman.

Letty Love opened her blue eyes wide—eyes that could look the innocence of a child or the wisdom of the ages—and feigned not to understand. And then as if his meaning had dawned upon her, she said with a good-natured smile:—

"Oh—why, I'm alone!"

"It's a good thing you are," he told her pointedly.

At once a hardness crept into her voice, and she asked coldly:—

"For whom?" And for a moment she delayed pulling off her wraps.

"For the other man."

"Silly boy! How ridiculous you are!" she returned lightly, as she tossed her wraps over a chair and began to pull off her gloves.

Challoner went over to the photograph, picked it up and wheeling round said threateningly:—

"Did you put *him* in that frame?"

"I did," she answered sweetly. "I'm very domestic, you know," and she smiled one of her most bewildering smiles; "I always arrange these little things myself."

"And what did you do with mine?"

Letty looked dubious. She touched a button, and to the maid who entered asked with mock anxiety:—

"Patricia, what did you do with the half-tone of this gentleman that I gave you?"

The maid regarded first one and then the other somewhat curiously.

"It's in my room, Madam."

"With the other notables?" And Letty Love lifted her eyebrows. "Patricia's room is quite a picture-gallery," she went on gaily. "You may investigate it, if you like—no?" And dismissing the maid, went over to the piano and began to strum the refrain of a popular song.

Challoner's lips emitted:—

"You—" They closed on a gasp of rage, disappointment, despair and impotent admiration. Had he dared, he would have gone on his knees to her then and there, taken her in his arms and kissed her; but the woman's indifference

appalled him, and instead he gritted his teeth, dug his
nails into the palms of his hand. Then, for the first
time, it dawned on him that she had worn for Hargraves the gown that he, Challoner, had selected for
her—a gown white, immaculate, simple, which followed religiously the lines of the superb figure that
left nothing to be desired, of Letty Lane, full-
throated, full-bosomed, with her jet-black hair that
gave no sign of fastening, with her blue eyes and dark
eyebrows, with her milk-white flesh, which, artificial
though it were, concealed nothing, revealed nothing
but the loveliness of the woman.

The man's eyes shone with pride as he observed her
finished appearance; for was it not he who had
taught her to gown herself like that, showed her how
to live, lifted her into the high places?

"And this is how she repays me!" he muttered to
himself, and then aloud: "What's the matter with you,
Letty—is it because my money has given out . . . "

This startled the woman into earnestness, and rising
to her feet, she drew herself to her full height, and
pointing to the door declared with an injured air:—

"No man can talk to me of money in this house!"

Challoner's face was a study, but he did not move.

"Especially when it's all gone!" he sneered, searching her countenance. Never until now had he realised the monumental, stupendous power of money.

Now that he had none and the car of juggernaut was slowly crushing him, he could understand that he belonged in the ditch with the maimed, the lame, the dying. There was no necessity for a reply from Letty. The woman's face revealed the contempt with which she regarded him. What mattered it to her that the man had surrendered everything that was worth while in life, that he had sacrificed himself at her shrine! She was one who demanded the firstlings of the flock; he was nothing save carrion for daws to peck at. The fruit was devoured; of what value was the rind?

"You had better go," she said superciliously; "there is no need of coming any more."

In a sort of daze Challoner was shambling toward the door when the telephone-bell rang. Instantly it roused all the deviltry and cunning that had oozed from him the moment before. Seizing the receiver, he thrust it silently against his ear.

"Hello!" began the voice at the other end.

Challoner did not answer.

"Is that you, Letty?" the voice went on.

Still Challoner did not answer. Then, as the woman stepped forward, he handed the receiver to her, at the same time placing his left hand over the mouthpiece, and said:—

"It's Hargraves—tell him to come up, will you?"

She shook her head.

Again the voice at the other end of the wire sounded, but she could not answer, for the thickness of Challoner's hand lay between her and communication. The suspense was unbearable—getting on her nerves. There was nothing to do but to comply with his wish; and upon her eyes suddenly yielding to his, he released the mouthpiece, standing on guard the while she obeyed him. Then he drove her, literally drove her into a far corner of the room.

"Now, let him come! We'll see . . . " he exclaimed, holding a revolver in his right hand; and as he stood there watching her as a tiger does a tigress, it was with a certain sense of gratification that he noted written across her face the altogether new sensation of fear, terror, and therefore respect for him. And he rejoiced in the knowledge that the hand that could no longer count out banknotes to her or sign cheques was a hand that held life and death within its grasp. Letty Love realised this, too, as she stood there cowed, trembling, listening, watching the door. Suddenly there flashed through her mind a way out of the situation, and smiling, she said lightly:—

"Oh, pshaw, Lawrence, the heavy is not your line! Come—suppose we have something to drink."

And without waiting for him to answer, she crossed the room and pressed the button there. Somewhat sheepishly Challoner slipped the revolver back into his pocket and dropped into a chair, while she ordered the maid to fetch some Bengal—a cordial, a distilled delight that had come down to her from a period so remote that the memory of man runneth not to the contrary. In his lifetime Hiram Edgar Love had possessed gallons of it; it had come to him in the night from the mysterious East, in the teeth of the revenue guns. And Challoner knowing it for the thing it was, his face flushed with the pleasure of anticipation. Letty took her place beside a small table, and presently a silver-topped, cut-glass decanter was in her hand, which she held over a glass, saying:—

"Will you help yourself or shall I . . . "

Challoner nodded.

"Go ahead—fill it for me, Letty."

Challoner drank—drank. He forgot Hargraves, forgot everything but the face of Letty Love, a kiss that he wanted, but that somehow he could not get, an utterance in a thick voice, a momentary hand-to-hand struggle, not with Hargraves, but with her, then, somehow, she eluded him and he was left alone— alone in the darkness that the Bengal had cast upon him!

But in all this there was no Hargraves.

*   *   *   *   *

A few hours later when he awoke, he was still sitting

at the table, but he was alone. He rose hastily, even steadily, and scoured the other rooms; there was no one there. He looked for the Bengal; but that, too, had disappeared. All of a sudden the jewels that were on her dressing-table—jewels that he had given her—caught his attention, and for the moment the temptation was strong to take them for the money that was in them. But even his dull wits soon recognised the folly of such a proceeding, since it was for her that he needed the money, and somewhat reluctantly he put them back in their case, muttering to himself as he left the house:—

"Letty must believe in me—things are bound soon to come my way."

In a little while he was back again at Cradlebaugh's, wandering about the rooms looking for Pemmican. Finally he saw him coming out of one of the rooms and hailed him with:—

"Hargraves showed up yet?"

The unwholesome looking factotum shook his head; at the same time he noted that Challoner was in a different mood than when he had talked with him earlier in the evening. Pemmican wondered as he turned away; but then it was not given to him to know that Challoner's experience that night had served immeasurably to strengthen a desperate purpose. True, that the joy that had been Challoner's—"his by rights," as he told himself—had been wrested away from him, for he was satisfied that Hargraves's absence from Cradlebaugh's meant that he was with Letty Love. But little by little the agony of jealousy was becoming a pleasurable sensation—a passion that obsessed him. So that far from brooding, he felt as feels the man of destiny: Whatever was to happen would happen. He would wait days, weeks, months, if necessary, for Hargraves.

A day rolled round. Night again at Cradlebaugh's, and Challoner still at his post of observation, waiting. It was past midnight when Colonel Hargraves finally appeared. Challoner felt his presence even before he stepped up to the buffet; and summoning to his aid all the suavity of manner that he possessed, for he knew he must be careful, as the other, doubtless, would be on his guard, he called out:—

"Colonel Hargraves!"

Hargraves turned quickly, and seeing it was Challoner, a flicker of a self-congratulatory smile broke over his large, round face, as he answered:—

"Why, hello, Challoner!"

The momentary gleam of triumph did not escape the other, and it required a supreme effort to force back the blood that was rushing to his temple.

"I want a word with you, Colonel!" And with a wave of the hand: "Room A—will that suit you?"

Colonel Hargraves hesitated for a moment; he moved a bit to one side and stared hard; but the other bore his look of keen suspicion with perfect serenity. The Colonel shrugged his shoulders. Finally he said:—

"Oh, very well, Challoner—that suits me."

To Room A they went; Pemmican followed with decanters. Possibly he suspected, feared, realised that the air was charged with electricity. In any event Pemmican was in charge of Cradlebaugh's; it was for Pemmican to see and to know.

There was a table in Room A, with chairs about the table; and a stand against the wall. There were also two large, heavy leather lounging chairs with arms. Pemmican placed his burden upon the stand against the wall, lingered for an instant, and then went softly out. Neither of the men spoke until after he had left the room and closed the door. When each had seated himself at the table, Challoner got down to business.

"Hargraves," he began with sinister familiarity, "you have ten thousand dollars in your pocket, I believe?"

Colonel Hargraves repressed a movement of impatience with difficulty. He nodded, and unconsciously took the attitude of the counterfeit presentment in the apartment of Letty Love.

"Ten thousand dollars," repeated Challoner with provoking coolness, as he likewise planted both elbows on the table, and added somewhat ominously: "And I'm broke!"

There was a pause in which the men looked straight into each other's eyes; then Challoner rose, walked over to the table, half filled two glasses, and placing them on the table, leaned far over it, declaring:—

"And yet, Colonel Hargraves, you and I are going to sit in a ten thousand dollar game to-night!"

Challoner drained his glass; his example, however, was not followed by the Colonel. Instead, he put his arms akimbo, his fists resting on his hips, and tilting back his head, he said with an air of contempt:—

"Indeed! What with?"

"With your ten thousand!" It was well said. Challoner's cool, passionless voice gave to the declaration the character of infallibility.

"And you—" Hargraves muttered in a puzzled way.

"Not a dollar," admitted Challoner.

Colonel Hargraves rose; he threw into his glance all his knowledge of Challoner's past.

"You must take me for a fool!" he burst out, and started for the door.

But he had gone only a few steps when he felt Challoner's clutch; turning, he felt the power of Challoner's eyes; and presently under their compelling influence he found himself once more taking his seat. He made no attempt to analyse his sensations, but he realised that Challoner had made a new impression. In all the eventualities he had foreseen, he calculated on Challoner's being a weakling, a wreck. But to his astonishment he saw within those eyes nothing but success. Challoner had become a man not to be disregarded—a man of strength.

"My proposition is a perfectly fair one," went on Challoner. "You put up ten thousand cash——"

"And then—go on——"

Challoner lifted his arm and pointed silently in the direction of the "Drelincourt."

Incredulity shone in the eyes of Hargraves; his scorn found vent in an attempt at levity.

"Rather like putting up something that doesn't belong to you, eh, Challoner?"

Challoner was not feazed; it was the answer he expected.

"It looks that way, Hargraves," and suddenly thrusting himself forward, "but I can make it uncommonly disagreeable for the other claimant. You don't know me—I'm an uncertain quantity—and women are blamed queer. If I win, I keep the ten thousand—and my chances."

"And if you don't win?" a bit breathlessly.

"If you win," went on Challoner, "you keep your ten thousand, and—I'll quit without a murmur."

In the pause Hargraves thought hard—never in his life had he thought harder. The more he studied Challoner, the better he liked the proposition. The moment was fraught with something new and significant. In more ways than one he feared Challoner, for he was by no means certain of his own place in the woman's affections. And then in his mind there was one certainty—Hargraves knew that the game was already his; knew that Challoner, steady though he seemed, was unquestionably drunk. Never was victory more certain than at the present time.

"If I win," at last he said with great earnestness, "you will swear to leave me—you will leave *us* alone?" Challoner nodded.

Hargraves seized his glass and extended it to bind the bargain. Challoner seized his, but found it empty. He left his seat and came back with it filled.

"It's a go!" he said, and pressed a button.

With the same sense of responsibility upon him, Pemmican responded; and on Challoner's order he went out and returned with ten new packs of cards, tossing them on the table with their wrappers unbroken.

"Cold hands," announced Challoner, "five hundred a throw."

Hargraves pulled forth his roll of bills and placed it on the table; then, placing a hand on the arm of Challoner, he exclaimed vehemently, so that the other should not forget it:—

"It's understood now, Challoner, that if I win you're to leave us alone—sure?"

Pemmican left the room and closed the door behind him. Challoner smiled across the table, and a new, strange expression crossed his features that Hargraves did not, could not understand.

"Sure," repeated Challoner, placing the decanter upon the table. Then they started in to play.

*   *   *   *   *

Twenty minutes later Pemmican rushed pell-mell into Room A.

"There's a big row on," he said to himself; "a row over a lady and a game of cards."

And so it proved.

There was a row on between the men who occupied Room A, and but for the isolation of the room it was a row that might well have roused the house.

"You've lost, I tell you!" one of the men exclaimed; the other laughed boisterously, defiantly, victoriously.

"If I've lost, so have you!" he answered.

What followed happened in an instant and before Pemmican had been in Room A thirty seconds. For suddenly one of the men there had whipped from his

coat-pocket a weapon that glinted in the white light;
as suddenly he had taken aim, and then came a flash,
a report, a cloud of smoke.

Pemmican looked on, speechless.

Presently one of the men crossed the room and sank
into a chair in a dazed sort of fashion, his head lolling
across the upholstered arm; while the other glanced
about him for an instant, looked at Pemmican, looked
at the figure lying on the chair, and then started suddenly toward the door.

Three minutes later Pemmican switched off the lights
and plunged the room in darkness.

"A row over a lady," he murmured breathlessly, "a
row over a lady and a game of cards."

At two o'clock that morning, Officer Keogh of the
night squad, patrolling a dimly lighted thoroughfare in the rear of Cradlebaugh's, stumbled over an
object lying in deep shadow.

"Good Lord! It's a man!" said Keogh, stooping
down suddenly and as suddenly drawing back. He
drew himself together, bent down again, felt cautiously about, wiped his hands and shuddered, and
drew back once again, as he whispered to himself:—

"A dead man—shot to death!"

He rapped wildly with his night-stick—the wild, ir-
regular tattoo that makes the slumberer rise suddenly
in bed and tremble, and then crouch between the bed-

clothes shivering—and pending the arrival of as-
sistance he stooped once more and fumbled in the
pockets of the dead man.. Presently from the breast-
pocket of the coat he drew forth a yellow pigskin wallet, and upon its corner in glaring gold, that even in
the dim light glittered garishly, appeared the letters,
"R. H."

In this wise the body of Colonel Richard Hargraves,
man-about-town, was found lying in the gloom at two
o'clock that morning.

IV

OFFICER KEOGH, an hour later, under the white light
of the desk lamps over at the ———— Precinct, was telling his story to the desk-sergeant behind the rail. The
desk-sergeant listened disinterestedly until he heard
mentioned the name Cradlebaugh. At that juncture
he held up his hand, placed a warning finger on his
lips, nodded toward the drowsy doorman and toward
two of the reserve squad in the room, and looking
Keogh in the eyes, whispered:—

"Officer, speak low."

Keogh, taken aback for the moment, dropped his
voice as he went on with his story. Once more the
sergeant stopped him.

"The most important thing is just where the body
was found. Be exact now, if possible; it's important."

Keogh went on to give a minute description, and
wound up by saying:—

"The man was dragged, all right, after he was dead."

The desk-sergeant's eyes narrowed to pin points as
he demanded:—

"In which direction?"

"To the west."

The desk-sergeant shook his head portentously, and
observed:—

"Looks for sure like this was pulled off in Cradle-baugh's."

"*That's* what *I've* been telling everybody," returned Keogh, the pride of proper diagnosis resting cheer-fully upon him.

The desk-sergeant shot out his forefinger and ex-claimed:—

"The least you have to say about the matter the better. This is not a case for you or for me, but for the captain in the morning."

The captain appeared unusually early in the morning with some half-dozen papers in his hand. Slapping the morning editions, scareheads, up-permost in front of the sergeant, he blurted out:—

"What's this here?"

The sergeant glanced at the topmost sheet and skimmed rapidly over the details.

"Don't know where they got the facts, but it looks like they got 'em *right*."

The captain scratched his head, then for the next few minutes he looked out of the window and watched the passing throng; he was pondering deeply. Finally he inquired:—

"What did you do?"

The desk-sergeant grinned.

"Not a bloomin' thing," he answered.

The captain shot a glance of surprised approval at his inferior.

"For once, by gum," he conceded, "you hit the nail upon the head. This isn't a case for the police—not yet."

"Then for who?" The desk-sergeant looked dubious.

"For Peter Broderick," said the captain, nodding.

"What's Peter Broderick got to do with it?" inquired the desk-sergeant, still doubtful.

The captain seized the telephone, but paused to explain:—

"Peter Broderick has got everything to do with it, since the people put this blatherskite Murgatroyd into the prosecutor's office. You know as well as I do that there's been too many rumpuses in Cradlebaugh's —and Murgatroyd sent word from the court-house that the place would be closed up, cleaned out, if there was any more trouble there."

"And Broderick?" persisted the sergeant.

"Broderick gave me orders to be tipped off hard when anything happens to Cradlebaugh's—no matter what. And that," concluded the captain, "is enough for you and me; we've got to obey orders— see?"

He removed the receiver from its hook and was about to talk to Central, but changed his mind, hung

up the receiver, wheeled round on the sergeant and
asked:—

"Were you going home?"

The other stretched his arms and yawned.

"Yes. Why?"

The captain passed over two black cigars.

"Smoke 'em—they'll keep you awake. And say," he
went on, placing his hand soothingly upon the other's
arm, "you wouldn't mind looking up Chairman Peter
Broderick, would you? It isn' t everybody I can
trust."

He seized a pad and wrote hastily for a moment, and
finally handing the slip of paper to the sergeant,
added:—

"First, try these four addresses. If he's not at any
of these, then try his home; you'll be sure to find him
there. But see him—don't take no for an answer,
and after you have told him the whole story, get his
orders—see?"

It took an hour and a half to locate Chairman Peter
Broderick; the sergeant found him home—in his
rooms on the ground floor of the Iroquois Club. He
waited for some time before he could gain access to
that estimable gentleman, for Peter Broderick's hour
for rising was high noon. The boy who aroused him
awakened a slumbering lion; the Iroquois Club cowered when Broderick woke up; others cowered, too.

Broderick's word was law everywhere, and yet he wore no badge of authority, held no office—he did not even want one. He was higher than authority, stronger than civic force: he was power personified. He had attained that mystical position in the universe, known wherever men cast ballots as Chairman of the County Committee, which meant to owe no man a duty, but to demand servitude and fealty from every man. It meant more—it meant to hold the bag! It meant that whatever Peter Broderick wanted he got.

"Well!" roared Broderick to the sergeant; "what in thunder do you want?"

The desk-sergeant briefly set forth his credentials and authority, and then plunged boldly into the purpose of his presence.

"The captain wants to know what he's to do about this Hargraves murder?"

Broderick stared hard at him.

"Hargraves murder?" he repeated. "What Hargraves?"

The sergeant told him.

"Great Scott! So he's dead. Confound him! He bled me like thunder at draw the last time I met him!"

The sergeant went on to give him the facts; Broderick the while was thinking deeply. Finally he interrupted the other with the question:—

"Look here, sergeant, what was there to prevent

Hargraves being shot down by a highwayman or a
thug? Can you tell me that?"

"Officer Keogh says——"

"Hang Officer Keogh!" yelled Broderick. "Keogh
is going to say nothing but what he's told to say.
Look here—do you know who killed Hargraves?"

"No."

"Does anybody know?"

"Not yet."

"So far so good. Now, then, that's a dark street,
isn't it? And other houses as well as Cradlebaugh's
have an opening on that street, haven't they? I say
that this thing wasn't pulled off inside of Cradlebaugh's; it was the work of an unknown assassin—a
thug. Do you understand?" he declared emphatically.

"You want the captain to work it out on that theory!
Isn't that it?"

"I don't want the captain to work it out on any
theory!" yelled Broderick. "Let the captain sit still
—do nothin'!—say nothin'! I'm doin' this thing—
I'll work out all the necessary theories! Do you
hear?"

"The captain told me to remind you that Prosecutor
Murgatroyd——"

Broderick sprang to his feet and stood glowering
over the sergeant.

"Murgatroyd! Nobody has to remind me of Murgatroyd—confound him! I'm always being reminded of him. He's the only office-holder in this burgh that hasn't got the decency to know that what *I* say goes! Sergeant," he went on confidentially, "this is a blamed important thing, and before I do anything I'm going down-town to consult Mr. Graham Thorne. I'll bring him up to Cradlebaugh's; you tell your captain to meet us there in an hour and a half. That's all he's got to do—all you've got to do—I'll do the rest. Now go!"

Twenty minutes later Broderick waddled into the private office of Graham Thorne, Esquire, counsellor at law.

"Thorne," he exclaimed, lounging back comfortably in a chair, "have you seen about this thing? Do you know what happened *there* last night?"

Thorne smiled grimly and pointed to the pile of morning papers on his desk.

"I knew about it at six o'clock this morning. I've been waiting for you to turn up for the last four hours." There was a note of superiority in his voice, which, strange to say, Broderick in nowise resented.

Broderick ever since he had met Thorne, had felt an admiration for this tall, handsome, dignified young man, with the grey just commencing to creep in his hair. Thorne possessed all the qualities that go to

make up a clever, astute counsellor at law. Of his an-
tecedents, it is true, no one knew aught; he had merely
arrived a few short years before, opened his big law
office, stalked into the courts and out of them, into the
clubs and out of them. It cannot be denied that he
made his best impression upon laymen and not upon
the lawyers, although even the members of the Bar
conceded that Thorne had ability. That he earned a
great deal of money was quite manifest, for he spent
it with a free hand, if a trifle too ostentatiously. He
was not a politician in any sense of the word, and yet
unquestionably he had the air and the earmarks of the
man who some day might become a statesman. He hob-
nobbed with the best people, knew everybody worth
while, and everybody worth while knew him. Broderick felt that if fate could regenerate him he should
like to be Thorne.

"Well," blurted out the politician, "what are you
going to do about it?"

"What are *we* going to do about it?" asked the lawyer in turn.

"I can handle the police," Broderick affirmed.

"That goes without saying; but we're up against
something more than the police."

"If Tom Martin or Sam Apgar was the prosecutor
now," wailed Broderick, "we'd have no trouble. They
used to come to me regularly for instructions——"

Thorne rose slowly, paced the entire length of his long private office, treading noiselessly the thick, green carpet like a cat.

"But," he protested, "Martin isn't prosecutor, neither is Apgar. Murgatroyd is prosecutor, and——"

"Confound the man!" interrupted Broderick. "He's so straight that he leans over backwards. It was he who said six weeks ago that the Tweedale suicide was the last straw; that if another fracas occurred inside of Cradlebaugh's it would be good-bye to Cradlebaugh's. And now there's this blamed murder!"

Thorne looked Broderick in the eye for a moment and asked:—

"Do you know that this murder happened inside of Cradlebaugh's?"

"No; but I'm satisfied it did."

"Have you talked to Pemmican?"

Broderick stared in surprise.

"No; but haven't you?"

Thorne shook his head.

"You forget that I waited here for you. Now that you're here, my idea is to see Pemmican and get the facts."

"The captain of the —— Precinct will be there," explained Broderick. "He understands that you're counsel for Cradlebaugh's—see?"

"Come on," repeated Thorne; "we'll go and see Pemmican."

Broderick remained seated. Presently he said hesitatingly:—

"Just a second, counsellor—I wish you'd draw a cheque for five for me."

"Dollars?"

"No."

"Hundreds?"

"No."

"Five thousand!" Thorne whistled. "Coming it just a bit strong, Broderick."

Broderick vigorously shook his head.

"Now, look here, Thorne, I've got no complaint to make of you, and you've got no complaint to make of me. You've paid me well, but you've had blamed good returns for it, haven't you? Come now!"

"Yes," admitted Thorne. "But——"

"No buts," interrupted Broderick. "This is a crisis."

Thorne drew down the corners of his mouth.

"Do you think that I don't know it's a crisis?" He went back to his desk, drew forth a cheque-book and wrote a cheque. Before passing it over to Broderick, he looked him squarely in the eye, and added:—

"Peter, I've always paid you by cheque and taken your receipt."

"Sure!" returned Broderick. "I'm no office-holder. You could publish it in the newspapers; nobody could find fault."

"The point is," continued Thorne, referring to a memorandum, "that I've passed over to you a sight of money."

"And you got a sight of influence in return," retorted Broderick.

Thorne passed over the five thousand dollar cheque, seized Broderick by the arm, marched him out, then he began to relieve his mind.

"Broderick, I want more influence. I've got a pet scheme, a great ambition that is overweening, overwhelming. It won't down; it owns me body and soul." He paused a moment before finally coming to the point. "I want some day to sit in the Senate of the United States."

"Phew!" whistled Broderick. "Nothing stingy about you!"

"I shall want every iota of your influence," Thorne went on; "I shall need it. And, Peter, I want to know whether I'm going to have it. I want to know that *now.*"

Broderick stopped him in the middle of the sidewalk and shook him by the hand.

"Thorne," he exclaimed, "there isn't a man I'd rather send to the United States Senate than you! I mean it;

there's my hand on it." And pushing Thorne into the
waiting taxicab he commanded the driver to take them
to Cradlebaugh's back entrance.

"Quick as you can!" he added, as they drove off.

Once in Cradlebaugh's, the domineering influence of
Broderick again asserted itself.

"Where's Pemmican?" he inquired gruffly; and without waiting for an answer: "send him along right
away!"

The liveried man who did his bidding bowed a bit
familiarly to him, but very deferentially to Thorne.
The latter he knew as a patron of the place, but one
who did not play.

Almost instantly Pemmican came. His face was
haggard, pale, his eyes heavy with sleeplessness, and
upon him generally was the air of a man who had
passed through some nightmare that with the dawn
had turned out to be hideously true. He took them at
once to the private room where the captain of police
was waiting.

"Captain," said Broderick, "this is my counsel. He's
a rattler for advice when a man's in a tight hole, and
I thought I'd just fetch him along. Captain Whally
—Counsellor Thorne." And turning at once upon
Pemmican, Broderick proceeded to interrogate
him.

"Now just where did this thing happen?"

Pemmican looked at the captain, at Broderick and then at Thorne before answering. Then he said:—

"Room A."

"Then it *was* pulled off in here?"

"Yes."

"And how did he get out there on the street?"

Pemmican rubbed his hands together, looking first to Thorne and then to the captain for approval.

"I dragged him out."

"Good work!" was Broderick's brief comment.

"Who did this thing?" asked Thorne.

Pemmican gulped. After a second he answered:—

"Challoner."

"Laurie Challoner? You don't say!" ejaculated Broderick. That was all the surprise manifested. Challoner's proclivities were too well known to everybody in the room; besides, Cradlebaugh's was always expecting the unexpected to happen.

"Challoner," exclaimed Thorne with a show of satisfaction, "is a client of mine!"

Broderick's eyes brightened.

"Great! That simplifies matters. You'll defend him?"

"I shall," admitted Thorne, "if he be apprehended."

"But we must fix it so that he won't be," remarked Broderick.

"Or, if apprehended," continued Thorne, "so that he

won't be brought to trial." And turning again to
Pemmican: "Where is Challoner?"

Pemmican spread his hands apart, shrugged his
shoulders and finally answered:—

"Gone—nobody knows where."

Just then the telephone bell rang. Pemmican answered it, listened for an instant and then resigned the
receiver as he called:—

"Captain, it's for you."

The captain with some trepidation seized the instru-
ment, and talked in low tones while the rest remained
silent. Finally he hung up the receiver and announced:—

"It's my office. Murgatroyd is there now." The captain looked worried as he declared: "He wants to talk
to me."

"Let him wait!" Broderick blustered out. Nevertheless a shadowy gloom settled down upon them all.
Thorne was the first to break the silence.

"If Murgatroyd drags Cradlebaugh's into this murder case there'll be the devil to pay."

"He's got to keep it out," insisted Broderick. "Confound it! If he drags Cradlebaugh's into it, he'll drag
into it his own organisation! He doesn't know the
men who are behind it—its party affiliations, its patrons. If he makes this case a handle for his confounded investigations—well——"

"He will!" interrupted the captain of police. "See if he don't . . . ."

"What if he does?" protested Broderick. "There isn't a grand jury ever been picked that would indict Cradlebaugh's! And there you are!"

"So long as public opinion don't get to work," ventured the captain.

Broderick started.

"You've hit the nail upon the head, captain," he assented, as he smote the table with his clenched fist. "That's why I'm worried. If public opinion gets to work, why say, it will——"

"Keep cool now, keep cool," counselled Thorne. "I'll see Murgatroyd," he went on; "this is the time of all times that he's got to do what we tell him to do; and if he don't—we'll break him on the wheel!"

Thorne smiled and jerked his head toward Pemmican.

"We even have the sole witness to this tragedy in the hollow of our hands."

There was a gentle tap on the door. Pemmican opened it and held a whispered conversation with one of the attendants of the house. Then he came back into the room and looking at the captain, he said:—

"They say downstairs that two of the prosecutor's men were seen leaving the 'Elevated' a few minutes ago, and that they were working their way over to the West."

"Jumpin' Jerusalem!" exclaimed the captain, leaping to his feet. "They're coming here. That ends me—I'm off!" He caught up his cap and disappeared.

Pemmican once more locked the door; then Broderick resumed the conversation.

"By George, that's so!" he said to Thorne. "Pemmican is *the* witness; we can keep him muzzled."

Pemmican edged forward from his position near the wall. Advancing to the table he placed both hands upon it and looked at the two men belligerently.

"But you won't keep me muzzled!" he exclaimed.

Broderick gasped:

"W—what?"

Pemmican drew himself together. Hitherto his attitude had been one of fearful deference toward Thorne; now he was defiant.

"You can't keep me muzzled!" he repeated.

Broderick took a long breath and rose as though to throttle Pemmican. Thorne waved him to his seat.

"Pemmican," said Thorne, "you need some sleep."

"I don't need sleep nor coaching either," retorted Pemmican. "I'm going to tell the truth about this murder."

"Well," said Broderick soothingly; "you've told it— to us."

Thorne fastened Pemmican with his cold, penetrating

glance of displeasure. Pemmican shivered, but was game.

"This murder," Pemmican maintained desperately, "was committed by Challoner in Room A of this gambling house! I don't care if the house does pay me my salary, I don't care if I am in charge here, the house can't make me lie!" He paused for a moment and then went on:—

"This killing followed a row over a game of cards. I heard the row; I saw the shooting; and it's up to me to lay my cards down on the table. I'll give up what I know!"

"You'll do nothing of the sort!" said Thorne threateningly.

"I'll do nothing else!" retorted Pemmican hotly.

"If Murgatroyd comes here," suggested Broderick, "or sends for you, you keep mum—do you understand? That's your game! We'll take care of you the same as we are going to take care of the captain. He's true blue; and you've got to be true blue." And pointing toward Thorne, he added:—

"There's Thorne—he's your counsel, too. You do as he says, and he'll take care of you."

"I can take care of myself," returned Pemmican, doggedly, "and I'm going to do it. I'm going to tell the truth about this thing to Murgatroyd!"

There was another knock upon the door—a short,

sharp, curt, commanding knock. Pemmican sprang to the door, unlocked it and threw it open.

Three men entered: One was Mixley; another McGrath—both detectives in the employ of the prosecutor's office in the court-house; and the third man was William Murgatroyd, the newly elected prosecutor of the pleas.

V

THE yellow light of the early June afternoon grew softer as it sank into, and was absorbed by, the deepening dusk; but to Miriam Challoner, propped up with red silk cushions in a strange attitude of expectancy, these things had ceased to matter; for out of her life a living presence had gone, leaving a void more harsh than death. For weeks now she had patiently waited, her ear strained at every sound, trying to associate it somehow with her husband's return; the servants seemed to tread on tiptoe, as they went about their duties; the house was curiously hushed as though listening, always listening.

The room that she was in was beautifully proportioned and panelled in dull red; there were numerous divans well furnished with cushions and upholstered in the same hue as the walls; and as her eyes wandered over its rare pictures, bronzes and costly knick-knacks, she was reminded of the early days of her married life, when it had been her purpose to make this—Lawrence's room—as attractive and pleasing to him as money could make it. Fate, indeed, had played havoc with their lives; nothing was left but the memory of the happiness that once had been hers.

"Oh, why doesn't he come!" she cried, an agony of

despair in her voice, and began to pace the room in nervous agitation.

At that moment a man noiselessly entered the room. She did not hear him until, suddenly looking round, she saw Stevens, the butler, advancing respectfully toward her. For an instant it startled her; disappointment and embarrassment struggled within her; finally she asked somewhat fretfully :—

"What are you doing here, Stevens—I did not ring —I——"

Stevens held the silver salver before her, on which were several letters. Taking them apathetically from him, she sank back limp among the cushions, her nerves on edge as she proceeded to scan each in turn. There were nine in all—the last of which she quickly tore open as the sole missive fraught with possibility. But she was doomed to disappointment; and handing them back to him, she told him to put them on the desk.

The man complied, and then stood quietly at attention.

"And, Stevens," she added falteringly, "send Foster to me at once."

Stevens turned on the instant and found Foster in a passage-way, shuddering.

"What's the matter with you?" he whispered, at the same time placing his arm about her.

"What are you doing?" exclaimed Foster with indignation, but made no attempt to release herself from his embrace. "Don't you hear the newsboys? What are they saying?" she went on, nestling closer to him. "Listen!"

They did not have long to wait, for just then the hoarse, raucous voices of the newsboys calling early specials reached their ears; but such words as were at first distinguishable seemed of no importance to them. Then like a bolt from the blue rang out the words:

CHALLONER

CAUGHT IN CHICAGO!

"They've caught him!" the maid almost shrieked, pushing Stevens violently away from her; and starting in obedience to her mistress' commands, she added sympathetically:—

"I hope she hasn't heard——"

And as fortune would have it Mrs. Challoner had not heard, but went on to inform the maid that she was going to her room to lie down for a while, ending with:—

"There are some things which I wish you to attend to first, Foster."

On reaching her room, however, Mrs. Challoner abandoned her intention to lie down; apparently calm and collected, she took a seat near the light and started mentally to place her house once more in order. Item after item she checked off from her memorandum upon her household pad until at last, with her finger upon one hasty entry, she looked up and said:—

"Foster, ask Stevens if the stone masons have finished patching up the cellar wall; and then you may fetch me those letters I left on Mr. Challoner's desk."

Meanwhile, the French window looking on the rear porch in Challoner's room slowly opened, and a man quickly but stealthily entered, directed his steps to the table-desk, switched on the green-shaded light there, picked up several letters and proceeded to scan each carefully in turn—just as Mrs. Challoner had done a few moments previous. Suddenly the sound of footsteps reached his ears, and with the same movement that characterised his entrance he retreated to the balcony and disappeared, leaving the French window open behind him. The night was cool, there was a strong breeze from the east, and the chill, spring air poured into the room.

When Foster came into the room a little while later, she saw at once that the green-shaded light on the table-desk had been switched on, and that the letters that her mistress sent for were not there. Then all of a sudden she noticed that the window was open and there was a general air of mystery about the room. She fled into the hall and called:—

"Stevens! Stevens!"

Stevens, who dogged the maid's footsteps and who was generally to be found in her vicinity, was soon on the scene.

"See! The window's open!" she whispered tremblingly.

Stevens shook his head.

"I locked it myself," he said, going over to it to examine the lock.

"It has been forced," he informed her, and beckoned to her to come and look at it.

With the gloom which the newsboys' cry had cast over them, the sight of the broken fastening filled them with horror.

"Who did it?" wailed Foster.

Stevens stepped out upon the porch; there was no one there. He glanced into the restricted space below; he saw nothing, heard nothing. So he stepped back into the room and closed the window, and looked at Foster with significance. Finally he answered:—

"One of those stone masons must have done it. He looked queer, acted queer; that is, to me."

Foster caught him by the arm.

"Could he have anything to do—with the case?" she gulped.

Stevens pointed hastily about the room at various objects of value easily appropriated.

"Just like as not," he answered. "If it was a thief, he'd have taken that an' that an' that——"

"Isn't it terrible!" gasped Foster; "and isn't it shivery and cold!" She seized a match, crossed over to the fireplace and lit the fire.

"What's that?" she started suddenly.

There was an almost unheard tinkle of an altogether unseen bell; and before its sound died away Stevens had stolen from the room and plunged almost headlong down the stairs. Foster quickly followed him to the door, where she encountered Mrs. Challoner coming down the hall.

"I thought I heard the door-bell just now?" she asked; for while oblivious to the noises of the street, there was little that occurred indoors these days that escaped her notice.

"Yes, ma'am," Foster stammered; "Stevens is answering it."

One glance at the maid's face, however, had sufficed to convince her mistress that something had happened; and for a moment it took all the courage she could summon to her aid to keep her from breaking down completely.

"What is it? Speak!" she exclaimed in a tremulous voice; and then without waiting for an answer, for the sound of voices in the hall below reached her ears: "If that's somebody to see me, I don't want to see them——

I don't want to see anybody—I can't see anybody—
I won't! . ., ,. " she ended almost hysterically;
and gathering her trailing skirts in her hands, she
fled to her room.

But no sooner had she reached the door than Shirley
Bloodgood followed on her heels.

"It's I, Miriam," she began; "and how are you,
dear?" And without further ceremony she pulled off
her gloves, tossed off her hat and planted herself in a
chair.

"I just simply couldn't stay away from you any
longer," she declared. "I know you don't want me
here, but I can't leave you."

Miriam Challoner sank weakly at a table and covered
her face with her hands. Alone with the servants, she
had borne up, but in the presence of the strong, sym-
pathetic girl, Mrs. Challoner's courage vanished. Finally she leaned toward her visitor, and asked, a world
of pathos in the question:—

"Is—is there any news outside?"

Shirley glanced at the fire sputtering in the grate;
she hesitated imperceptibly, then she answered:—

"None—I—I haven't seen the papers—no, there's
nothing new."

Mrs. Challoner rose, staggered across the room to
the girl and threw her arms about her.

"Shirley, Shirley, I'd have gone mad, I think, if you

hadn't come!" she cried, and fell to sobbing; but after a moment she straightened up again. There was a defiant look in her face now, a tremor in the voice that said: "I don't care what he's done—I want Laurie to come back, do you understand? I want him back—I want him . . . "

Shirley Bloodgood bit her lips.

"I know, I know, Miriam—I do understand——"

"Oh, but you can't understand," she persisted; "you haven't a husband and you don't know . . . "

"Yes, yes, Miriam, I know," were the only words that rose to the girl's lips to comfort her, for at that moment the faint sound of the insistent door-bell broke in upon them.

Mrs. Challoner's slight frame shook with sudden agitation as she exclaimed:—

"That door-bell will drive me crazy!" And almost instantly recovering her composure she gasped:—

"If it should be Laurie!"

The girl glanced at the smouldering fire in the grate, where to her excited fancy in all their hideousness rose before her the headlines she had read in the evening papers: "Challoner Caught In Chicago!"

"It isn't Laurie," Miriam went on; "no, of course not; but whoever it is, Shirley, you must see them for me—unless it should be —" she faltered. "Then come back, but don't leave me to-night—you'll stay, won't you?"

"Yes," the girl assured her. "But you must promise me that you'll rest for a little while—there—on that sofa. Then we'll have a bite together, and——"

Without a word Miriam Challoner went over to the sofa, and soon gave way to the first sleep she had had in many days.

"How are we ever going to break the news to her," sighed Shirley, as she noiselessly crept from the room. Just ouside of the door she encountered Stevens, and quickly placing her finger on her lips, she motioned him to be silent. When they were well out of hearing he announced in a confidential tone :—

"Mr. Murgatroyd, Miss Bloodgood."

"Mr. Murgatroyd! William Murgatroyd? What does he want, Stevens?" She was plainly excited.

"Sh-h-h!" warned Stevens gently; "he's the prosecutor of the pleas."

"Oh, then it *is* Mr. William Murgatroyd. But what does he want?"

Stevens shook his head, for they were now well in hearing. The next moment Shirley Bloodgood had entered the drawing-room and stood gazing into the face of William Murgatroyd.

For an instant the man started back; he could not believe his own eyes.

"Shirley Bloodgood!" The name fell incredulously from his lips. "You here?"

Shirley held out her hand.

"And you—what are you doing here?" she asked quickly. "I didn't know that you were a friend of the family?"

Tall, well-built, with a smooth-shaven face, a square chin and a nose that stood well out into the air, Murgatroyd was a man who appeared to be without enthusiasm; but although sharp and business-like, his manner was easy. Turning to Shirley, he came to the point at once.

"I want to see Mrs. Challoner," he announced. "But I'm glad you're here, for I don't know her very well, and——"

"You can't very well see her now," Shirley interrupted, shaking her head. "She's frightfully unstrung—she's ill. You know it's almost three weeks now since Laurie first went away, and——"

"I know," he broke in just a bit impatiently.

"What?" Shirley gasped, the truth at last dawning upon her; "you don't mean to say that you're here in —in your official capacity?"

Murgatroyd smiled grimly.

"It's the only capacity in which I'm likely to be here, Shirley," he reminded her.

"But," she protested, "I thought they left these things to——"

"The police," he finished; and again smiled grimly. "They do, but there are reasons—— You see," he went on to explain, "since I was appointed prosecutor of the pleas, I've turned up a thing or two in the Police Department, and, well, the Police Department and I are somewhat out of tune. This case they have put up to me and my men——"

"Surely you can't mean to imply that you have to do this kind of thing yourself?" The girl looked askance.

Murgatroyd raised his eyebrows.

"Yes, it's up to me . . . ."

Shirley shifted her position. She didn't like Murgatroyd in this new rôle, and yet there was something in the grim determination of the man that pleased her.

"I am sorry to remind you," he went on, the full responsibility of his office upon him, "that I am here to see Mrs. Challoner; to find out where Challoner is; to persuade her to persuade him to come back." Murgatroyd chopped out the sentences as though he were a machine.

"Then he wasn't caught in Chicago!" Shirley exclaimed almost jubilantly; and then touching him on the arm a bit familiarly, she added:—

"Billy, you don't really believe that Laurie murdered Colonel Hargraves?"

Murgatroyd laughed a short laugh.

"If I didn't know you, Shirley, I should imagine you were sparring for time . . . If I didn't know you I wouldn't answer your questions. As it is, I must answer them in the same way that I would do anything you asked of me—short of crime."

"If you put it that way," returned Shirley, drawing away from him, her tone growing cold, "you needn't answer me at all."

Murgatroyd did not heed her.

"I don't know," he went on evasively, "whether Challoner murdered Hargraves or not."

"You don't know . . . "

· "No," returned the prosecutor; "so far the evidence is purely circumstantial."

Shirley Bloodgood had been hanging on his words. She drew a long breath and echoed excitedly: "Circumstantial—" There was a flicker of a smile on her face as she added:—

"Then the newspapers were wrong when they said it was a certainty!" . . .

Murgatroyd held up his hand and went on to explain:—

"What I tell you is confidential—you understand?"

"Yes, yes," she said impatiently; "but tell me about it—the real facts—that is, if you can."

"There's no reason why I shouldn't, I suppose," said the prosecutor of the pleas. "The real facts as we have them . . . as we have them, mind, are simple. Challoner quarrelled with Colonel Hargraves——"

"What about?" asked Shirley impulsively.

Murgatroyd flushed.

"That makes no difference," he answered with some confusion; "the point is that they were enemies. It was a quarrel in which the passions of each were roused to the utmost. To make a long story short, Colonel Hargraves won ten thousand dollars at Gravesend—the men met in Cradlebaugh's—another quarrel followed——"

"And then?"

"Then," went on the prosecutor, "they parted. That was all—save at two o'clock next morning Hargraves was found in the street back of Cradlebaugh's with a bullet through his heart."

Shirley was quivering with suppressed excitement; nevertheless, she managed to ask:—

"What does that prove?"

"Nothing—only a man named Pemmican of Cradlebaugh's witnessed both quarrels—and Challoner has run away. Looks bad for Challoner, I should say."

"But," persisted Shirley, "surely that evidence is not conclusive . . . "

"One moment, please," went on the prosecutor calmly; "Hargraves had the ten thousand dollars in cash with him, and——"

"That is conclusive," she commented. "Surely you don't think Lawrence would steal?"

Prosecutor Murgatroyd paused for an instant and placed finger-tip against finger-tip, then he answered slowly:—

"Frankly speaking, I do. I believe," he went on, speaking as though with conviction, "that Challoner would do anything."

Shirley shook her head.

"It's impossible! Why, the Challoners have any amount of money!"

Murgatroyd shrugged his shoulders.

"Challoner's wife has, but——"

"It's the same thing," Shirley protested; "and she just adores him—you do not know how much she adores him, Billy!"

Again Murgatroyd shrugged his shoulders.

"But how about him?"

The girl shook her head and answered somewhat sadly:—

"I know, I know, she's blind to everything, Miriam is . . . "

Once more she placed her hand on Murgatroyd's arm, unconsciously, impersonally but impulsively.

"Oh, it's perfectly dreadful, the whole thing!"

Unwittingly, Murgatroyd changed his mood to meet hers.

"Yes," he said, "to have ruined himself like this! It's a tragedy to see a man like Challoner go down hill. In the old days he was such a decent chap."

"You were a friend of his, weren't you?"

"Yes, before he married, when he was poor and decent like the rest of us—yes, I was a friend of his."

Shirley Bloodgood drew her brows together.

"Indeed! You must have been a good friend to let him take his downward course."

For an instant this imputation seemed to rest heavily on Murgatroyd's shoulders; but he cast it from him quickly with a sigh, and answered:—

"A man's best friends are like a man's good wife; they do not desert him, whatever happens; he deserts them. And so it was with Challoner."

"And so at the last he has no friends?"

"Evidently not, save a flock of vampires that feed upon his purse and will continue to feed so long as he has a purse." He pulled out his watch. "But," he protested, "I am wasting time—I— Oh, pardon me," he quickly corrected, flushing with embarrassment, "I did not mean my time, exactly; but frankly, I must see Mrs. Challoner."

Shirley shook her head.

"Miriam Challoner is ill, much too ill to see any one. She gave orders——"

"Excuse me, but Mrs. Challoner is not too ill," persisted Murgatroyd, "to walk from room to room. My men have seen her through the windows. I wish you would say to her, please, that I must see her."

Seeing the futility of resisting further, Shirley made a movement to go.

"Oh, I can't tell her!" she cried. "I'll ring for Stevens." She rang. "Stevens," she said, as he came into the room, "will you tell your mistress— Oh, I can't—I can't," she faltered.

Murgatroyd stepped into the breach.

"I am the prosecutor of the pleas," he said to Stevens, "tell her that, and that I'm sorry to disturb her, but I must see her."

The servant left the room. Shirley sank into a chair and half covered her face with her hands.

"I don't believe—I never will believe that Lawrence did these things!"

There was a pause. After a moment Murgatroyd remarked half aloud:—

"There is but one way to reform a man like that——"

The prosecutor did not finish, for standing in the doorway was Miriam Challoner, pale as a ghost, a look of interrogation in her eyes. Shirley ran quickly to her.

"Miriam, dear, I didn't send for you!" she cried, placing an arm around her. "It was Mr. Murgatroyd . . . "

Mrs. Challoner bowed and smiled faintly.

"I believe I have met Mr. Murgatroyd before," she said with a grace peculiarly her own.

Murgatroyd returned her greeting with:—

"I need not assure you, Mrs. Challoner, that this is a very painful duty."

Mrs. Challoner moistened her lips and held herself together with great effort.

"Please don't apologise," she said gently, "I understand. It may be easier for me to have some one whom I've met."

Murgatroyd bowed; and placing a chair for Mrs. Challoner, begged her to be seated.

"If you don't mind, Miriam," spoke up Shirley, "I'll leave you now, but if you need me—call me."

Miriam clutched the girl by the shoulder, and cried excitedly :—

"No, Shirley, stay where you are—I want you here with me !"

Murgatroyd placed a chair for the girl beside that of Mrs. Challoner; he took a seat opposite.

"Mrs. Challoner," he began in a voice that was even more gentle than at any time before, "believe me that I've no desire to give you trouble unnecessarily."

"Please don't apologise," Mrs. Challoner repeated holding fast to Shirley, as though she pinned her faith to that young woman.

"I shall begin at the beginning, Mrs. Challoner," he said. "I suppose, of course, that you have had the report that your husband has been found in Chicago?"

"What! Found?" To the great surprise of the prosecutor no emotions other than joy and relief were visible on the woman's face.

"Laurie has been found!" she went on. "Thank heaven! I'm so glad—now he must come back home."

"I had thought," said the prosecutor, in even, business-like tones, "that the news of his arrest would—would have been an unpleasant shock to you . . . I find that the shock is yet to come."

Quick as a flash Miriam Challoner read the truth in the man's face.

"You don't mean—you can't mean that——"

Murgatroyd bowed.

"I have already told Miss Bloodgood that the report was a mistake. Your husband was not arrested in Chicago."

At that Mrs. Challoner really broke down. She sobbed silently on the shoulder of the girl beside her. "Oh, Laurie, Laurie, then you're not coming home!" she cried. "Most three weeks, Shirley, he's been away!"

Murgatroyd waited patiently until she had recovered, never once forgetting that he was the servant of the people. His was a double duty. He must apprehend the guilty, and so do it as to save the community great expense. Of late murders had been expensive luxuries. Murgatroyd knew that in this case he would be hampered by lack of funds.

"Mrs. Challoner," he said with simple directness, "the whole substance of the matter is this: I believe—we believe that Mr. Challoner has not left the East, and that he may still be here in town—in this house even." He had reseated himself, but suddenly rose again.

"In this house!" Miriam returned with a faint smile. "I wish he were, indeed I do wish he were——"

"Mrs. Challoner," the prosecutor went on, ignoring her words, "it is necessary that my men, now while I am here, while you are here, should search these premises—this house——"

Shirley Bloodgood shook herself from the grasp of Miriam; she stood erect, her slender form tense.

"This is an imposition; it is preposterous, Mr. Murgatroyd, that you should doubt her word!"

Murgatroyd was unmoved.

"It is necessary for my men to search this house,"
he repeated; and not unwisely, for he well knew that
there is something that brings men—good, bad and
indifferent men—back to their homes.

But Shirley was adamant.

"No, I won't allow it!" she exclaimed indignantly.

Mrs. Challoner placed a restraining hand on the girl,
for Miriam Challoner once more held a strong grip
upon herself.

"Search the house if you wish, Mr. Murgatroyd,"
she consented; "if you find my husband, no one will
be more pleased than I."

Murgatroyd left the room and returned almost instantly followed by two men—Mixley and McGrath.
It was one of these men a short while before who had
stolen in through the French window and tampered
with the letters on the desk.

"You will search here first," he ordered; and turning
to the women: "Would you prefer to go or stay?"

"We'll go, of course," Shirley flung at him as she
drew Miriam toward the door.

"Of course not, we shall stay," said Miriam, freeing
herself from the girl.

The men passed in unceremoniously and proceeded to
search the room—places that even Miriam had forgotten about; they overlooked nothing, but silently,

quietly in their business-like way turned everything
topsy-turvy, replacing things, in the end, as they
found them. Presently they turned to their chief, and
said:—

"It's all right, Prosecutor."

"Cover the rest of the house," again ordered Murgatroyd.

They grinned sheepishly.

"That's all done," they answered.

"What?"

McGrath nodded.

"Yes, while you were talking in here," he said, "we
showed our shields and they showed us through." He
drew near and whispered: "We thought it best to take
'em by surprise; they hadn't no time to fix things,
don't you see?"

"Nothing found?" asked Murgatroyd.

Simultaneously they shook their heads, and answered:—

"Nothing."

Murgatroyd waved his hand and commanded them to
wait for him at the door, ending with:—

"I won't be a minute." And turning to Mrs. Challoner, he said a trifle apologetically: "My men tell
me that your husband is not in the house. One thing
more, however; if you know where Mr. Challoner
is——"

"She doesn't!" snapped Shirley.

"If you know where he is," Murgatroyd repeated, ignoring the interruption, "if you have any means of communicating with him——"

"She hasn't!" once more interposed the girl sharply.

"I want you to use your influence with him to make him come back. His flight amounts to a moral confession of crime. He has nothing to gain, you see," he went on to explain, "by staying away. He is bound to be caught; he cannot escape!"

"I want him to come back," stammered Mrs. Challoner. "Yes, yes, he must come back and face this charge. You—you don't think him guilty, Mr. Murgatroyd?"

Murgatroyd walked toward the door. If he had spoken his mind he would have answered in the affirmative; but instead, he compromised with:—

"I don't know;" and abruptly left the house.

VI

"BRUTES every one of them—and Billy Murgatroyd
the worst of all!" The exclamation fell from Shirley
Bloodgood's lips.

Miriam Challoner had been resting her head forlornly on her arms as she sat at a table, but on hearing the young woman's bitter remark she raised her
head and smiled a wan smile.

"Mr. Murgatroyd?" The tone was one of surprise.
"Why, I thought you liked him, Shirley?"

The girl hunched her shoulders expressively.

"You have things badly twisted, Miriam—*he* likes
me." And suddenly rising to her feet, she clapped
her hands impulsively. "Oh, Miriam, I almost forgot
—I've good news—good news for you!" Then she
ran swiftly toward Mrs. Challoner and swiftly back
again to the window. "No, they're out of sight—almost . . . "

"Good news? What good news?" Miriam asked incredulously.

Shirley placed a hand upon her lips.

"Prosecutor Murgatroyd," she began, "told me in
confidence——"

"In confidence!" Miriam repeated; "then you had
better not——"

Shirley shook her head belligerently.

"Oh, no!" she laughed. "It's all right! Billy Murgatroyd likes to tell things to me. He told me once that he believed that to be one of the controlling motives that led to matrimony . . . That a man should have somebody to tell things to."

Mrs. Challoner's curiosity got the better of her.

"And he told you—" she inquired eagerly.

"He told me the facts—gave away his evidence to me." Shirley tossed her head.

"But—" again protested Miriam.

Once more Shirley silenced her.

"No—I shall tell you—this may be a matter of life and death; besides, you are entitled to know the truth."

"Yes, yes," assented Miriam, "tell me—I must know —but first, wait a moment." She pushed a button and Stevens entered.

"Stevens," she said in a low, strained voice, "don't let any one in the house. Do you understand? I simply cannot stand it—to see another person."

When Stevens had left the room the girl resumed:—

"Murgatroyd told me, Miriam, the greatest cock-and-bull story you ever heard." Miriam looked as if her brain would snap. "It seems that the papers have distorted, exaggerated everything. The fact is, Miriam, dear, the case is the flimsiest . . . . "

Miriam drew a deep breath.

"How? Explain yourself!"

Then Shirley went on to tell that nobody had seen
Hargraves killed, nobody had seen the shot fired; that
they had only got some disreputable gambler or other
who claimed to have witnessed a quarrel between them.

"And, oh, yes," she added a moment later, "the man
that killed Hargraves robbed him of ten thousand dollars—and of course Lawrence Challoner wouldn't rob
a man, much less kill one—so don't you see, there's
nothing in the story at all."

"I don't know," answered Miriam slowly, "whether
he would or not."

"What!" gasped the girl.

"Don't misunderstand me," pleaded the woman.
"There are two Lawrence Challoners—one is the man
I love—that loves me; the other is the Lawrence Challoner who—well—I don't care," she added fiercely,
"what he's done, I want him back." She sobbed for
an instant. "You didn't know, Shirley, that we had a
quarrel—I treated him badly, shamefully; he hasn't
come back since."

"You quarrelled—you, Miriam!" The girl opened
her eyes wide. "What about?"

"Money," admitted the conscience-stricken woman—
"money. He wanted me to give him some—a perfectly natural request, wasn't it?—Men have got to
have money," she went on, repeating his words, "and

I wouldn't give him any. It was brutal in me—I can never forgive myself!"

A look of astonishment crossed Shirley's face.

"You wouldn't give him any money? And he didn't have any when he went away?"

Miriam wept. After a moment she answered:—

"No. My poor Laurie—think of him starving, freezing, perhaps dying!"

Shirley Bloodgood drew a long breath.

"And Colonel Hargraves was robbed," she murmured to herself.

"I don't think you understand," Miriam went on, breaking in upon her thoughts. "Of course I don't believe that Laurie is guilty of the things they charge him with; but he must come back and stand trial and be acquitted—and I must stand by his side through it all." She broke down completely.

"On the evidence they have," Shirley returned, trying to comfort her, "they'll——"

"What's that?" inquired Mrs. Challoner, starting up nervously, in alarm. "It's that horrible bell ringing again," she went on breathlessly. "Don't you hear voices below? Listen—I thought I heard . . . "

Shirley stole to the door and listened. Presently she called back:—

"Don't worry—whoever it is, Stevens is sending them away!"

"I hope so," sighed Miriam, "for I can't see any one —I won't see any one, unless— Oh, Laurie, Laurie," she cried out, "why don't you come home!"

Suddenly Shirley fell back from the door; it was being stealthily pushed open.

"Oh," she gasped, "it's only Stevens! How you frightened me!"

Stevens stood in the door at attention, looking neither to the right nor to the left, but straight over the heads of the women. He drew a long intake of breath, then he spoke the name:—

"*Mr. Challoner.*"

And hardly were the words out of his mouth than he was thrust aside, and there stood in his place a spare, gaunt, tottering figure—a man dishevelled, soiled, exhausted—James Lawrence Challoner had come home!

At the sound of the name the young wife's face turned pale, and for a moment words failed her. Then all of a sudden she sprang to her feet and rushed to him, crying in an ecstasy of joy:—

"Laurie, Laurie, you've come home to me at last!" And throwing her arms around his neck, she kissed him many times, laughing hysterically and crying the while: "You've come back to me!" And once more the freshness of youth, joy and hope were in her voice.

But Challoner, still standing just within the entrance

of the room, did not heed her; he cast her off with a
frantic sweep of the arm.

"Keep away—keep away from me!" he cried. "I'm
tired, dog-tired—I've got to sleep, sleep."

Painful as was the scene, Shirley was keenly alive to
what his presence there might mean.

"Stevens," she called, pointing to a window, "pull
that curtain down. I pulled it up after *they* went;
pull it down."

Challoner now turned upon her.

"Leave the curtain alone, I tell you," he said, "I
don't care if it is up. I don't care about you either
—nor you," looking at his wife. "I don't know you.
I must have sleep—sleep—sleep."

Deep down in her soul Shirley knew that she should
not hear all this, and she would have fled if she had
not promised Miriam not to leave her. Suddenly she
wheeled upon Stevens as if she and not Miriam were
the mistress of the house, exclaiming peremptorily:—

"Stevens, leave the room!"

Stevens obeyed her as he would his mistress, and left
the room post haste.

Miriam now went over to the girl.

"You're not going to leave me!" she exclaimed,
clinging to her. "You and Laurie are the only
friends I have—you must stay here with Laurie and
me."

Shirley saw the agony in her face and patted her affectionately as she promised:—

"There, there, Miriam, dear, of course I shall stay." And Miriam, at once reassured, darted back to her husband, and cried:—

"Laurie, dear," kissing him and pushing the hair back from his forehead, "so tired—so tired."

But Challoner, a wolf now and not a man, jerked away from her, and answered:—

"I came home, didn't I? Well, then, I must have sleep, sleep, I tell you, sleep." And tottering over to a dainty silken covered sofa, he threw himself upon it with a deep sigh, saying as though to himself: "Sleep —I must have sleep."

Spellbound, Miriam watched him for a moment, then following him to the sofa, she went down on her knees and drew him to her in a close embrace.

"Everything's all right now that you've come back," she told him in soothing tones. "And, dear, you'll forgive me for quarrelling with you—I'm so sorry, yes, I am, Laurie," kissing him on the lips, the face, the forehead. "Say you'll forgive me, Laurie, dear?"

His answer was a snore. Challoner lay supinely where he had thrown himself, sleeping as does the beast that has crept back to his lair after days of hunting by the man pack.

"Miriam," the whispered name came from Shirley,

"you and I, dear, must now think of things. We must not forget that Murgatroyd and his men have only just left. We must not let him lie here; it was lucky they searched the house when they did . . . "

Miriam waved the other back.

"No," she objected strenuously, "he must sleep; we must let him alone."

"No, no, Miriam," persisted Shirley, putting great emphasis on the words, "we ought to tell him what kind of evidence is against him. He ought to know that. If we didn't warn him in time, he'd never forgive us—he'd never forgive you. He's a man . . . "

"Perhaps you're right, Shirley—you seem to be always right. Yes, I suppose he ought to know." Gently Miriam shook him, rocked him to and fro upon the sofa, as some fond mother might wake a drowsy, growing boy on a lazy summer morn.

"Lawrence," she cried softly in his ear, "wake up! Wake up, dear, wake up!"

For an instant Challoner stirred. Presently there came in guttural tones:—

"Yes, yes, that's all right . . . " But he slept, and kept on sleeping.

"I can hardly realise that Laurie is back," murmured Miriam, happily. Unconscious of the other's words, she remained kneeling at the side of the dainty sofa with its far from dainty burden, her arm still about the neck of the man who slept upon it.

"Yes, yes," returned the girl, "but don't you think we had better warn him?   He must not be found——"

The other laughed joyously, trying lovingly to smooth out his tangled hair.   After a moment she answered absently:—

"They'll find him now, I suppose; but I don't care— I've got him back."   She turned and kissed him once again.   "My Laurie," she murmured in his ear.   Somehow she thought he heard and was glad to hear.

The girl stooped down and caught her by the shoulder.

"But, Miriam," she expostulated, "we must take no chances—we ought to wake him."

Miriam looked up at the girl helplessly.

"You must not stop, Miriam," insisted Shirley, "we must wake him——"

At that instant as they stood clustered about the sleeping thing, the bell once more broke out in feeble clamour.   They clung to each other in abject fear.

"The bell!" chorused the women, and stood frozen, silent.   They heard Stevens toiling up the stairs; waited; watched the door; finally they saw him enter. Neither of the women spoke, but gazed at him questioningly.

Stevens met their gaze with frightened eyes. At last he found his voice.

"It's the prosecutor's men again, Madam. They've come to——"

"Stevens," interrupted Shirley, "surely you didn't tell them that——"

"Not one word, Miss Bloodgood. But they said they saw him——"

Shirley groaned and pointed to the sofa; Mrs. Challoner rose to her feet and stood before it as if to hide the man upon it.

"You left them outside, Stevens?" Miriam was calm and apparently in full control of herself now.

"One of them—the other forced his way in and sent after the prosecutor."

There was a tap at the door, and the maid, quivering with fear, excitement and indignation, entered, bursting forth with:—

"There's a man coming upstairs, Madam—but I stopped him. He said he'd wait out there on the landing to see you—said he knew Mr. Challoner was in the house and he was going to arrest him."

Challoner continued to sleep noisily.

"Oh, dear, there's nothing to be done, I suppose, but to let the man in." Mrs. Challoner was speaking to Shirley now; and then without waiting for a reply she ordered Foster to show the man up, adding: "I hope he'll wait until Laurie wakes."

Instantly Miriam crossed to the sofa and once more rested her soft, warm face on his, hoping that he could feel the love that she bore for him, then she shook him somewhat roughly.

"Laurie, dear, you must wake up." And then like a flash the thought of resistance crossed her mind. She sprang up with a cry, rushed past Shirley, past Stevens, reached the door, closed it, fumbled for an instant, and finding the key locked it tight.

"No, no," she muttered, "they shan't take him—I won't let them—he belongs to me!"

In a frenzy she piled up the light chairs and tables, and pushed them against the door to form a barricade, crying the while to Stevens: "Help me, quick! We've got to keep them out! We must not let them in, must not . . . "

Shirley went over to her and caught her in her arms, whispering while she affectionately rested her head on Miriam's shoulder:—

"Don't, dear, don't! We can't help it, don't you see? There's no other way out of it but to let the men come in."

"Of course we can't help it," after a moment Miriam said resignedly, and proceeded to pull the chairs and tables away that she had so vigorously piled up. "Yes, yes, let them in," and wearily fell into a chair.

Stevens unlocked the door, and Mixley entered the room, McGrath following soon after.

"There's no help for it, ma'am," they spoke as one man.

At the sight of them Miriam rushed back to her husband and shook him slightly, speaking his name softly. Then she turned plaintively to the men:—

"If you would only let him sleep—just a little while longer," she said falteringly.

"You must leave him to us, ma'am," spoke up Mixley; and pointing to the far corner of the room, added: "Will you take that chair, there, please? Don't be afraid, ladies," he went on, glancing at Shirley; we won't hurt the gentleman, see if we do."

And suddenly, together, the men bodily lifted Challoner from the sofa and as suddenly dropped him back again.

At this use of physical force Miriam covered her face with her hands and cried:—

"Don't do that—please don't . . . "

They desisted, but for quite another reason.

"There's a hump here that we'd best attend to," said Mixley to the other detective, meaningly, running his hand over the outline of Challoner's clothing. "He may not be so sound asleep as he seems to be."

At this juncture Shirley motioned to Stevens to leave the room; the next instant revealed a revolver which they took from Challoner's hip-pocket.

"Is the thing loaded?" queried McGrath. Together

they examined it; then simultaneously they glanced in the direction of the women.

"Ma'am—ladies," said Mixley, crossing the room, "we're fair people, and Prosecutor Murgatroyd is fair. You seen us take this here firearm from Mr. Challoner just now, didn't you?"

Miriam and Shirley nodded in acknowledgment. Challoner dropped back into his former position and continued to snore.

Mixley came closer to them and requested that they take a good look at it.

"Don't give it to me," cried Shirley, eluding the outstretched hand and its contents.

"Give it to me," said Miriam, unhesitatingly.

McGrath crowded up.

"You see that there's five chambers loaded, don't you, Mrs. Challoner?"

Mrs. Challoner turned the revolver upside down and looked at it helplessly.

"Five chambers loaded?" she asked innocently, unsuspectingly.

"Here," broke in Mixley, "let me show you." And he counted slowly: "One, two, three, four, five—all full, see?"

"Yes, five chambers," Mrs. Challoner agreed.

There was a pause in which Mixley looked meaningly at McGrath; then he said:—

"And one chamber empty?"

"Oh, yes," she acknowledged almost eagerly, as he placed his finger on it, "there's surely one chamber empty—I see it now."

McGrath hesitated, but Mixley went on:—

"Will you smell it please—just the end of it—the muzzle. What do you smell?"

Mrs. Challoner smiled faintly.

"A Fourth of July smell," she ventured; "gunpowder, of course."

"Burnt powder, exactly, ma'am," they said, and smiled, too. But McGrath had still another card to play.

"Look at this here figure on this here gun, will you, ma'am? Here—there it is. I want you to tell me what it is."

"What is it, Shirley?" asked Miriam, bringing it closer to the light.

Shirley shook her head.

"I'd rather not."

"Please," asked Mrs. Challoner.

Shirley peered at it. Finally she declared:—

"It's '.38,' " touching the gun lightly; "the figures are '.38.' "

Mixley fell back admiringly.

"There now—no one can say we ain't been fair. You saw us take it from him; you examined it; and you told us what you saw. That's fair. You're fair and we're fair—see?"

"Yes. But what of it?" asked Shirley and Miriam in one breath.

McGrath opened his eyes in mock wonder.

"Why bless me, didn't you know? This here Colonel Hargraves was shot by a bullet that came out of a thirty-eight calibre revolver. That's all. We wanted to be fair."

Shirley rubbed vigorously the hand with which she had touched the gun.

"Fair!" she cried bitterly. "And Mr. Murgatroyd sanctions such methods—will use us for evidence—make a case by us?"

But even then Miriam did not understand. She was watching Mixley, who had returned to Challoner; watching Mixley and McGrath, who were lifting Challoner up and dropping him—watching them draw him up to a standing posture and then throw him back again on the sofa, calling the while:—

"Wake up! Wake up!"

"I've got to sleep," was all they could get out of Challoner.

At last, however, a lift and a drop a trifle more vigorous than the preceding ones caused Challoner to open his eyes and look about him. Then he closed them again.

"Are you James Lawrence Challoner?" asked Mixley loudly, peremptorily.

"I am," Challoner answered; "now leave me alone."

And now again the bell; and a moment later Murgatroyd, the prosecutor, stood in the doorway. The heat of much haste was on his brow; he looked neither at Mrs. Challoner nor at Shirley; it was toward Challoner and his men that he directed his gaze.

"Has he talked?" Murgatroyd asked, standing over Challoner.

"No," answered the men, "he ain't awake yet."

"Lift him to his feet," ordered the prosecutor.

The men did so.

And then it was that the women heard him say in a tone that cut into their souls:—

"Challoner, wake up! This is Murgatroyd, prosecutor of the pleas." It was a summons; Challoner obeyed it. He opened his eyes, closed them, yawned stupidly, and then, awake, stood squarely on his feet without any help.

"Hello, Murgatroyd!" he said.

"Challoner," said Murgatroyd severely, "remember that I am not here as your friend—I am the prosecutor, do you hear?"

"I understand," said Challoner.

"Very well then," went on Murgatroyd, "you know

why I am here. You are charged—I charge you now, Challoner, with the murder of Colonel Richard Hargraves. Do you understand me?"

"Perfectly," was Challoner's reply. "You want to take me into custody? All right—only let me sleep when I get there, will you? I——"

"Wait a minute, Challoner," persisted Murgatroyd. "It's my duty to inform you that anything you say will be used against you. You must not forget that I am the prosecutor."

Miriam came forward quickly.

"Oh, Laurie, dear, don't say anything, just yet," she cried in alarm.

Shirley seconded her warning, saying quickly:—

"Don't say a word to Mr. Murgatroyd until you have seen a lawyer."

Challoner, still sullen, looked over his shoulder at his wife.

"Who's saying all this? Only a lot of women—what do they know?" And turning back to Murgatroyd: "See here, Murgatroyd, let's get this straight, shall we?" And he looked him full in the eye. "You're the prosecutor—and anything I say will be used against me. Is that right? Well, this little matter is just as simple as A, B, C." And suddenly drawing himself up to his full height, he went on in a loud, clear voice:—

"I waited for Richard Hargraves with——"

"I warned you," cried Murgatroyd, stretching forth a hand.

Challoner scornfully refused to listen.

" . . . and when I found him——" he glanced about him defiantly and gave an imitation of a man taking aim and shooting. "There, now, you know the facts."

Murgatroyd turned to his two men.

"It's a case of wilful, deliberate, premeditated murder—murder in the first degree. Take him away!"

Shirley was on her feet in an instant.

"Oh, Mr. Challoner," she cried, springing forward, "why did you tell him?"

"Come on!" Challoner called out gruffly to the men. "Take me away!" He did not even glance at his wife, who clung to the girl, and sobbed on her breast.

The prosecutor nodded to his subordinates, and immediately they seized Challoner by the arm and started toward the door.

"No, no," cried Miriam, tearing herself from Shirley's hold, "don't take him away!" And again and again with all the force left in her: "No! No! No!— Oh, Laurie!——"

The doors closed behind the men. Then Miriam sank down upon the soiled sofa where he had lain, and sobbed as though her heart would break.

VII

On the morning after Challoner's arrest the prosecutor of the pleas was sitting at his desk in his private office in the court-house when Mixley and McGrath entered.

"You've done as I instructed? You've got Challoner outside?" the prosecutor asked.

The men replied in the affirmative.

"Bring him in," commanded Murgatroyd.

In a few minutes they returned with the prisoner. Challoner looked better than he had the night before. In a thoroughly impersonal way, curtly but not unpleasantly, Murgatroyd addressed him.

"Good-morning! How do you feel?"

The prisoner, still half man, growled:—

"Better. I got some sleep, but I'm still tired as thunder."

"I sent for you this morning," went on the prosecutor, "because of what you said last night. I am not sure that you meant all you said—indeed whether you remember it?"

This interrogation evidently struck Challoner as amusingly superfluous, for he laughed aloud; but the laughter had a note of aching bravado.

"Of course, I remember it," he said presently, and

pointing with a steady forefinger to a weapon on the prosecutor's desk, "I shot him with that gun there."

Murgatroyd could not restrain a movement of surprise at Challoner's *Sang Froid;* neither could those trained witnesses, Mixley and McGrath, leaning well forward lest they should miss a word.

"Most decidedly, then," continued the prosecutor, "you do not recall that I told you that anything you might say would——"

"I heard all you said," the prisoner broke in, shrugging his shoulders, "but what's the use—it had to come—I knew it. I was getting tired of hiding in out-of-the-way places, and never having a wink of sleep. Besides, I knew that Pemmican—Cradlebaugh's man—saw the whole affair. There was no sense in trying to escape."

Murgatroyd's face adequately expressed his approval of the prisoner's point of view. His voice, however, was distinctly non-committal in tone when he observed easily:—

"Pemmican saw it all," then?"

"Certainly he did," Challoner volunteered.

There was a short pause, in which the prosecutor turned over some papers lying on his desk; when he spoke again he did so without looking up from the documents he was scanning.

"I haven't examined Pemmican—my men have, though," he said. "I've got him under lock and key; he's in the house of detention; and he'll have to stay there until——"

Challoner moistened his lips.

"Until my trial, I suppose," he interposed. "Poor devil! That's hard lines!"

The prosecutor ignored the comment, but he reminded the prisoner again that he must be careful not to say anything that could be used against him, concluding with:—

"You came here from the jail quite willingly this morning?"

"Don't you think we can cut all that sort of thing out, Mr. Prosecutor?" a little scornfully.

Before answering, Murgatroyd shot a glance at his men as if to sharpen their attention.

"Very well, then," he said finally, "if you're quite willing I should like to know the exact details. As I understand it, both Hargraves and you were fatally infatuated with an actress at the Frivolity—quarrelled over her—is that right?"

Challoner reddened. For an instant a wild look came into his eyes.

"Surely there is no necessity of bringing any other names into this," he answered hotly; and then little by little calming down he recounted graphically all the

incidents leading to and of that memorable night, saying in conclusion:—

" . . . And then Room A at Cradlebaugh's
and——"

A most unusual performance on the part of the
prosecutor cut him short. All the time Challoner had
been laying bare the facts as he remembered them,
Murgatroyd had been toying silently with a pigskin
wallet on which appeared in gold the initials: "R. H.";
and just when his prisoner was on the point of ending
his story, he tossed it over to him.

Challoner caught it "on the fly."

"Do you recognise that?" Murgatroyd demanded.
The prosecutor desired, if possible, to add robbery to
the motive in the case.

Challoner never winked an eyelash.

"Know it? he replied glibly, "I should think I did!
It was Hargraves's. When I saw it last there was ten
thousand dollars in it." And turning it almost inside
out, he asked in an offhand manner:—

"Where's the money gone?"

Murgatroyd's eyes searched the face of the man before him as if he would read his very soul.

"You took it," he asserted coldly.

Challoner passed his hand across his face, striving to
clear away his muddled recollections.

"I took it? Decidedly not!" he exclaimed indignantly. But the man's dipsomaniacal doubts and fears tinged the tone of his voice and lessened the impressiveness of his denial, though he added: "Why, your witness, Pemmican, can tell you that—he saw the whole thing."

Mixley and McGrath had something to say now. In chorus they wanted particularly to know whether Challoner was positive that Pemmican saw "the whole thing." This joint interrogation seemed to have an irritating effect on the prisoner; and when Murgatroyd silenced them by inquiring of Challoner whether it was not a fact that he had tried to borrow money all over town, the "Yes" he elicited was muttered angrily.

"But I didn't touch that," Challoner resumed, the beads of perspiration standing out on his brow. "In any event, it is not one of the main facts in my memory. If I did take the money, what in the world have I done with it—tell me that? But look here, Murgatroyd, let's get down to business and have this over with. I'm tired of the whole affair. I told you that I waited for Hargraves for two nights. We had a game in Room A—there was a compact—Hargraves won out! Hang him, he always won out! We had a row then and there . . . I pulled that gun and fired at him point blank!"

"And then?"

"I killed him; and I would do it over again, I assure you. I don't remember any more—but Pemmican was there—you've got his story—he knows all about it."

"His story," observed Murgatroyd, laying a forefinger on the edge of the desk," amounts to just what you said last night—that drunk and sober, you watched your chance, and when you got it, you made good—or bad, whichever way you please."

"You've got it," returned Challoner, "now take me back."

There was a loud rap on the door. Mixley answered it, and left the room, holding a conversation in somewhat strenuous tones on the other side. He returned in an instant.

"It's Counsellor Thorne," he announced to the prosecutor. "He wants to see you."

Murgatroyd shook his head impatiently. He and Thorne did not pull well together.

"Tell him to wait," he said brusquely.

"He won't wait," persisted Mixley. "He insists . . ."

"You tell him that he's got to wait," returned Murgatroyd.

But Thorne did not wait. No sooner had Mixley left the room than Thorne entered and strode up to the prosecutor's desk. Mixley followed him.

Resting one hand on the table Thorne waved the other toward Challoner.

"Murgatroyd," he cried fiercely, with an injured air, "what's this? You call yourself a reputable member of the bar; you call yourself a reform prosecutor of the pleas; this is a most unfair advantage."

Murgatroyd sighed wearily.

"What now, Thorne, what now?"

"Most unfair," repeated the other counsellor-at-law. "You've got my client here—my client!"

Murgatroyd looked at Mixley and then at McGrath.

"Your client! Where is your client?"

"There he is," pointing, "James Lawrence Challoner!"

Murgatroyd rose and said suavely:—

"I beg your pardon, Mr. Thorne. Are you retained? I didn't know. Challoner said nothing of it. Why didn't you tell me, Mr. Challoner?"

"I didn't know it," Challoner told him shortly. "But it's all right—I supppose Mrs. Challoner retained him."

"Yes, she did," Thorne informed him.

"Well, I'm sorry, Thorne," said Murgatroyd. "If I had known you were in the case——"

"Sorry!" echoed Thorne. "This is outrageous! I went up to the jail this morning and my client was not there." He waved his arm as if addressing a jury.

"And when they told me that you—you had the effrontery to have him brought down here—for the third degree— This is a matter for the *Morning Mail*."

Murgatroyd lolled back in his chair and lit a fresh cigar. Presently he said:—

"Thorne, my duty is to the people as well as to your client; so far I've done my duty to both. Go to the *Morning Mail* if you want to."

"And leave my client here alone!" said Thorne, doggedly. He shook his head to let Challoner see what a determined man he was.

Murgatroyd leaned back over his desk and for a moment busied himself with his papers. Then he announced:—

"Mr. Thorne, your client is going back to jail at once;" and added jokingly: "If you wish to ride with him in the van, you may do so." And with that he ordered Challoner taken away.

Before going, Challoner stretched out his hand and said half genially:—

"I've no fault to find with you, Mr. Prosecutor; it had to come to this."

"But I won't forget this—not for a moment, Prosecutor Murgatroyd," said Thorne grandiloquently, as he stalked out of the door, followed by the prisoner and his guards.

After the men had left Murgatroyd paced the floor for a while in deep meditation. Something in the prisoner's attitude had moved him, puzzled him. "There's a discrepancy somewhere," he told himself; "and yet where the deuce is it?—Challoner killed this man as sure as fate. The motive, the opportunity, were there . . . . And then there's his confession . . . But—" He pushed a button; and when McGrath answered the call he was ordered to have Pemmican sent down from the house of detention, his order ending with: "I wish to see him at once."

"Yes, sir." The officer then placed a card upon the prosecutor's desk and added: "That's a party who wants to see you, sir."

Murgatroyd picked up the card negligently and glanced at it out of the corner of his eye. Instantly a dull flush mounted to his face, and rising to his feet, he said:—

"Tell the lady to come in, please."

VIII

THERE was a flush on the face of Shirley Bloodgood as she entered the prosecutor's office, which was fully as deep as that on the face of the man eagerly awaiting her. Jauntily she held out a gloved hand and said with a breeziness that was perhaps a trifle forced:—

"You must excuse me, Mr. Prosecutor; I'm quite alone—" and she drew attention to her unconventional act by placing her finger on her lips, which were pursed into a big O— "I have no chaperone."

"Won't I answer?" suggested the prosecutor lightly, as he took her hand; and placing a chair close to his desk, "Sit here, please."

"The fact that I'm alone," went on Shirley, taking the seat indicated, but moving it a little farther away from him, "should prove conclusively that I'm not afraid to beard the lion in his den."

"Did it require so very—much courage?" he asked with mock seriousness.

Shirley made a little moue.

"After last night, seems to me you're a bear."

Murgatroyd seated himself; it was thoroughly characteristic that he should waste little time on a preliminary skirmish with any one.

"Then it *is* about this Challoner affair that you have come to see me?" he asked tactlessly. "I warn you, Shirley—don't! Hands off!——"

At once Shirley assumed an aggressive, business-like attitude; close to his desk she drew her chair, and then leaning on both elbows looked Murgatroyd squarely in the face and said with great earnestness:—

"Billy Murgatroyd, you've got to help these people out!"

Murgatroyd flushed and answered with a smile:—

"If such a thing were possible, Shirley, you're the one person to make me do it."

His compliment found her unresponsive; she was too preoccupied with her own thoughts.

"You must do it," she persisted, and looked at him appealingly. "Of course the man could not have been himself."

"Probably not," he said coldly. "But of one thing you may be sure, Challoner had a purpose in all this."

Shirley frowned; the man changed the tone of his voice with a versatility that she declared to herself was little short of scandalous; he went on:—

"That purpose was to kill Hargraves. Last night you heard his confession to that effect; this morning he substantiated it in detail."

Shirley wrapped one hand over the other and sat looking at Murgatroyd with white drawn face.

"I suppose you realise that this thing is going to kill Miriam Challoner?"

The man shook his head vigorously.

"Bosh! If grief could kill the woman, living with Challoner would have accomplished that long ago."

"How unfeeling! How like a man! You understand women so well!" she declared, looking up at him with a mocking smile; and then went on to plead: "You must do something—you must get him free! Surely it remains for his friend to do this much for him! You will—won't you?" There was a suspicion of moisture in the girl's eyes.

Shaking his head, Murgatroyd rose and began to pace the floor, not because he wanted to think, but merely to give the girl time to regain her composure. At last he stopped directly in front of her.

"Shirley"—it was surprising how gentle his voice could be at times—"I want you to realise the circumstances of this case, which you seem to have forgotten. In the presence of several people, including yourself, this man has deliberately confessed to a premeditated murder; a man in my custody is a witness to the facts; at least five men know of the motive—his quarrel with Colonel Hargraves. No," he concluded severely, "if Challoner were my brother or my father, more than that, if you were in Challoner's place to-day, I should

have to try you—convict you.   There would be no
escape."

"But the condition that made him do this thing was
abnormal," she persisted; "bad companions and bad
habits had warped his mind."

"Like other men of his kind," returned Murgatroyd,
"Challoner's decent at times—conducts himself like a
man; but generally speaking, he's irretrievably
bad."

"But can't you delay the trial—get him off in some
way—some time?   There are ways—the thing is done
every day, and you know it."

Murgatroyd smiled grimly.

"My dear girl, if I would do this thing, I couldn't.
I shall go a step farther.   If I could do it, I wouldn't.
I couldn't look you in the face, guilty as I should be
of gross malfeasance in my office."   He waved his
hand in finality.   "Not another word on the subject,
please."

"You're immovable!   You're cruel!" she cried, rising
to her feet.   "I ought not to have come!   However, I
have done what I could for a friend," she flung back
at him, looking him straight in the eye, and started
toward the door.

Murgatroyd blocked her way.

"No," he said good-humouredly, not the least dis-
concerted by her parting shot, "it's my turn now.

You have attempted to corrupt me, swerve me from
my duty and——"

"And wasted your time, I suppose, as you were good
enough to remind me on a previous occasion," she returned, looking up saucily at him under her lashes.

Murgatroyd was quick to detect her change of mood
and took his courage in both hands, saying:—

"Won't you for the moment forget the Challoners,
Shirley? Be kind—you give me little opportunity
to see you alone these days. Think only of yourself
and me——"

"If you're going to make love to me in that awfully
serious way of yours or, for that matter, in any other
way, I'll go."

"Aren't you going to marry me, Shirley?" he demanded with characteristic directness.

"Same old story," laughed the girl.

"Yes, this is the sixth time now that I've asked you.
Again, will you marry me?"

"Don't be silly! This is hardly the place, Billy . . . "

"I quite agree with you. But one has to make the
most of opportunity. As I said before, the occasions
are all too rare when I find myself alone with you.
And unless you want me to keep asking you, speak the
word now, Shirley—make me happy. You may as
well say it first as last, for I'm determined to win you
—I'm going to have you!" he wound up energetically.

"'Sure of that, Billy?" she asked coquettishly.

"'Positive." And there was a world of determination in the way he said it.

"'Then why bother about my consent?" A flicker of a smile hovered around her lips.

"Why do you persist in refusing me?"

Shirley flushed. She seemed amused and serious, in turn. Finally she looked up at him quizzically for a moment, then asked:—

"Do you really want to know?"

He did not answer the question, but ventured:—

"Is it because of Thorne? Is he my successful rival?"

Shirley looked perturbed. She was struggling for expression.

"No, it's not because of Thorne. I wish it were . . . " And after a moment: "Do you still want to know?"

"Yes. I've got to know, Shirley." And he waited for her words as though his life hinged upon them.

"Will you be very quiet and stay right where you are if I tell you?"

"I promise," raising his right hand half playfully.

"Well, then, it's because—I love you," she said easily.

Murgatroyd sprang toward her, the colour rising in his face, fire flashing from his eye.

"Shirley !"

The girl quickly waved him back.

"It's because I love you or believe that I do that I shall never marry you. I mean it," she hastened to add, for the faintest shade of doubt had appeared on his face.

"But why?" he faltered, turning his eyes inquisitively on her.

Shirley sighed unconsciously.

"It is time that I made myself plain, understood to you. Not because you're entitled to an explanation, but because, well, because I like you just a bit——"

Again Murgatroyd took a step forward; but with laughter still lingering in her eyes, the girl made a pretty little movement of her wrist and motioned toward his chair. Instantly he stopped, catching his breath in sheer admiration of her beauty. He was dimly conscious of putting his hands behind his back; it seemed the only means of preventing them from touching her. But now as he gazed upon her, he saw that there was something behind those laughing eyes. A serious look was on her face. She seemed suddenly to have changed. The thousand and one little mannerisms that were so large a part of the girl's attractiveness were all there, but the voice was no longer the mirthful voice of the Shirley that he knew and loved. She spoke as though in a trance :—

"Can you understand me when I say that I have got to have something more than love? I am too practical, Billy, to fool myself—or you! Perhaps I'm cursed with the instincts of my kind—of the American girl. Oh, let me tell you how it is!" she exclaimed impulsively. "All my life I've been surrounded by men who were failures. My grandfather was a failure; my father was a failure; and my brothers are failures. They have tainted my happiness—don't misunderstand me—I love them, but I can't look up to them."

Murgatroyd nodded appreciatively. He believed that he should feel the same way about these men.

"But—you don't want money?" he protested. "You're too much the right sort of an American girl for that."

"No, not exactly money; but the man who appeals to me is one who can surmount all obstacles," she answered with grave tenderness; "who has success running in his veins." Not a shade of her former gravity now showed on the speaker's face; it lighted as if a flame of enthusiasm had escaped from the temple of her soul. She paused for a moment and lifted her head, and in the transporting gaze that seemed to pass beyond him and was lost into space, for the first time the man read and understood the girl's nature.

"Have you ever lain awake at night, Billy, ever curled up on a window-seat in the daytime and

planned your future?" She did not wait for an answer, but kept on: "I have; and in these dreams of
mine I would always take my place by the side of my
great knight errant, helping him to become greater
—the damsel riding on the pillion of my lord's war-
horse as he goes to war. At times he has been a diplo-
matist, a jurist, a law-maker; and I have always lent
him strength. When I marry, Billy, my husband's
work will be my work; his struggles, my struggles;
but the man must have greatness running through his
veins."

Murgatroyd smiled sheepishly. He had his full pro-
portion of conceit, and he did not quite relish this.

"Then I haven't figured often in the limelight of
your dreams?"

"If only you had, Billy, but you haven't, much as
I have tried my best to fit my knight's armour on you
and place you on his war-horse. Now can't you see
what it would mean if we tried the experiment of marriage? Marriage would not make me happy; it would ·
be misery——"

"Misery?" he snatched the word from her lips.

"Yes, misery for you," she finished. "Can the girl
who must have money make a poor man happy, much
as she may love him? Can the butterfly make a book-
worm happy, much as she may love him? A woman
with social ambitions loves a man with none; can she

make him happy? No! And while I am none of these, yet, somehow, I've got to fulfil my destiny; and I'm not going to chafe, anger and everlastingly offend the man who doesn't belong—doesn't fit in with my ideas!"

"But I do fit in, as you phrase it," Murgatroyd maintained. "Haven't I ambition? And am I not a fighter?—You'd think so if you knew the devil of a fight I am having right now with my own organisation—with Cradlebaugh's; and I'm going to win!"

Shirley smiled faintly at his almost boyish earnestness, but she shook her head.

"You are too much of a reformer, too much of a crank—no, I'm sorry to tell you so, but in my inmost soul I believe you will fail. You're built that way! I don't know why, but men of influence have weighed you in the balance and found you wanting. William Murgatroyd, politically you're dead—that's what they tell me. There's no future for you; you have ruthlessly antagonised every valuable interest needlessly. That's not success!"

Murgatroyd's face paled; his hand trembled as he raised it in protest.

"But the people—the people believe in me?"

Shirley smiled again in spite of herself.

"You haven't an ounce of diplomacy in your whole body!"

"Not if you call obeying orders from Peter Broderick, diplomacy."

Still the girl was merciless.

"You hit from the shoulder wildly; it lands on and hurts your opponent, but it kills you. You're only honest, Billy, nothing else."

Murgatroyd swung about nervously and glanced out of the window as he cried:—

"Only honest! Doesn't that count with you—doesn't it signify?"

"It's easy enough to be honest, but it is great to make your honesty save and not destroy you. To get these men behind you instead of opposed to you; to make your organisation do what you want it to do; to rise upon its shoulders because you make it lift you up— Ah! . . . "

"But, Shirley," interposed Murgatroyd, "can't you see that the man who stands up for a principle cannot fail?"

"What have you done so far?" she kept on persistently. "You're prosecutor of the pleas, your first, last and only office. Am I right?"

"I'm afraid you are," he answered dully. "In a way what you say is the truth. Politically I shall die—" Murgatroyd shuddered as he spoke—"unless I can force this issue to a finish while my office lasts."

"And then?" Her manner in putting the question nettled him.

"Well, then I suppose I shall live and die poor. But at least I shall die honest," he added.

Shirley shifted her mode of attack.

"Look at Mr. Thorne!"

"Ah, it *is* Thorne, then."

"A while ago I told you it was not Mr. Thorne." She paused a moment and then, as if speaking to herself, said: "But some day I shall meet the man I'm looking for—some day——"

"When you do, Shirley Bloodgood," he was quick to remind her, "it's an even chance that he won't care for you."

Shirley lost no time in retorting:—

"It's a chance I'm going to take! I can love," she went on wistfully, "yes," and then blushing, added very tenderly: "I am laying my soul bare to you, William Murgatroyd, because I believe somehow that you have a right to see it. Again I repeat: Look at Mr. Thorne!—a prospective United States senator!"

"You admire him?"

"He succeeds."

"Do you know why it may be possible for him to get the nomination for senator? Have you any idea, young woman, what it costs in this State to be chosen senator?"

"Does it cost anything?" was her naïve rejoinder.

"Just about three-quarters of a million to swing the thing! Thorne has money and backing and——"

"And you have neither," she finished for him.

"Precisely."

"Why not emulate Mr. Thorne and get both? To be a United States senator is one of the few great real successes possible of achievement in this country."

"His methods are not mine," pleaded the prosecutor, falling back upon his platform.

"Exactly. He secures support; you, opposition."

"Would you have me adopt his methods?"

"I would have you secure his results," she declared firmly.

There was a hungry look in the man's eyes as he spoke:—

"And if I do? . . ."

"Oh, if you only would!" her young voice rang out clearly, hopefully.

"And I'll find you waiting for me?"

"At the top of the hill, Billy!" She held out her hand. "Think over what I've said— Good-bye!"

IX

'AFTER seeing Miss Bloodgood to her carriage Murgatroyd's thoughts were in a maze of bewildering com-
plexity. As a matter of fact, his peace of mind was
wholly gone; and it was with a far different feeling
than any he had heretofore experienced that he sought
his down-town club for luncheon. It chanced to be at
a time when stocks were buoyant, and in consequence
the atmosphere of the dining-room was charged with
cheerfulness. But Murgatroyd was in no mood to
join any of the various groups lunching together; on
the contrary, he took particular pains to seat himself
at a small table apart from the others, where he gave
himself up at once to a mental rehearsal of the scene
in his office a half hour ago.

Success at any cost! Yes, that was the way she had
put it. Well, and why not? Was not that the modern idea—the spirit of the age? And should he hold
a mere slip of a girl responsible for putting into words
what every woman thinks? Ridiculous! . . . And
the United States Senate was her conception of greatness! Ah, that was for Thorne! The organisation,
the brewers, the railroads, would send him there—buy
him the job! Yes, her friend Thorne would be a success, achieve greatness; while he, William Murga-

troyd, would be likely at the expiration of his present
term of office to find himself dead politically, become
a cipher professionally as well.

Presently the waiter brought his luncheon. None of
the dishes suited him; the servant was taken to task;
the head-waiter was summoned; the dishes were
changed, and still they did not taste right. Finally
muttering to himself comments derogatory to the
club's cuisine, Murgatroyd pushed away his plate, lit
a cigar and hastened out of the building.

Lost in an abyss of depression he sank wearily into
the seat at his desk. It was thus that McGrath found
him when he entered to announce that he had brought
down Pemmican.

Murgatroyd stared at him dully.

"Pemmican?" he repeated. "Who the deuce is Pemmican?"

"Thunderation!" burst from the lips of McGrath.
"Why, your star witness in the Challoner case!"

This brought Murgatroyd to earth.

"Well, don't bring him in," he said impatiently;
"I'll ring when I want you."

McGrath was dumbfounded. In fact, his astonishment at his superior's evident disinclination to proceed immediately with the examination of Pemmican
was such that it came very near to making him forget
that there was another reason for his presence there.

"Another lady to see you, counsellor," said McGrath half-apologetically. "It's Mrs. Challoner this time." Murgatroyd looked up quickly.

"Mrs. Challoner! Why didn't you say so before? Show her in at once!" And as that person came through the door Murgatroyd rose and went forward to meet her, saying:—

"How do you do, Mrs. Challoner? If you had let me know that you wished to see me, I should have been glad to call on you. What can I do for you?"

For a moment Mrs. Challoner did not answer, but looked suspiciously about to see whether any one else was present.

"Mr. Murgatroyd, I do not wish it to be known that I have come here," she began, as she dropped into a chair. She looked haggard, pale and worn. Her manner, the tone of her voice, at once indicated to the prosecutor that she was labouring under some suppressed excitement. It was a situation not at all to his liking, and he watched her narrowly while she proceeded:—

"I have come to see what can be done for my husband."

"Miss Bloodgood was here a short time ago on the same errand," he observed, to put her at ease.

"Miss Bloodgood!" Amazement leaped into the young wife's tired, brown eyes. "She did not tell me

she was coming—but that's just like her—she never
tells half the good things she does. She's a friend—
indeed, Shirley's a good friend."

There was an embarrassing pause in which both were
silent. Apparently she was nerving herself to go on.
Presently courage came, and she said:—

"Will you tell me, please, what my husband's chances
are?"

"Every man is supposed to be innocent until he is
proven guilty . . . But first as last, I may as well
inform you, Mrs. Challoner, that I can do nothing, absolutely nothing for you. Your husband must stand
trial!"

"Yes, yes, I know. But you don't quite understand.
The man was not himself. Surely you must know
that! Let him live, Mr. Murgatroyd; he's worth sav-
ing. Give him time—a chance. He'll be good—I
shall make him good. I have tried, and I shall continue to try all the harder . . . "

Murgatroyd sat motionless. His profile was toward
Mrs. Challoner. It was a clean-cut profile, and upon
its contour there was no sign of yielding. After a
while he looked up and said:—

"I am very sorry for you, Mrs. Challoner, and I dis-
like intensely to hurt your feelings. But do you realise that your husband . . . shot this man in a
quarrel over——"

Mrs. Challoner quickly cut him short.

"That woman! What do I care for that! You don't know what my husband is to me! I love him no matter what he has done. Besides, it was all my fault. Let me tell you how it was. Laurie wanted money— his money was gone—he had spent it all, and——"

Murgatroyd held up his hand.

"I cannot let you speak this way. You are simply supplying me with evidence against him."

"And I refused him," continued the woman, too excited to hear what the prosecutor was saying. "I hardened my heart against him—drove him from home, and then—this dreadful thing happened."

"It would be dastardly in me to listen further. You are making your husband's guilt more evident with every word. When Hargraves was found he had been robbed of ten thousand dollars!" And with that Murgatroyd rose as if to indicate that the interview was at an end. "There is nothing I can do, Madam," he declared flatly; and then added: "There never was but one way to cure a man like Challoner; it's too late now."

Minutes passed . . . . Murgatroyd watched her intently; but she did not move: she sat rigid as if preparing herself for some ordeal yet to come. All of a sudden her attitude changed. Mistrustfully she peered about her once more, then leaning far over toward Murgatroyd, she whispered:—

"We are alone?"

The lawyer regarded her with pardonable curiosity before he answered:—

"Yes. Why do you ask?"

Mrs. Challoner wrung her hands; she seemed uncertain how to proceed. In the end she said:—

"I am going to do a terrible thing. It frightens me almost to death. I don't know how to begin, but my love for Laurie is my excuse for what I have to say. I hope you won't misunderstand me. Supposing Shirley was in Laurie's place—if she were accused of crime, what wouldn't you do for her?"

"The cases are hardly parallel," he answered indifferently.

"They are precisely parallel," she maintained. "You love Shirley as I love Laurie—I know you do. Don't say no—women have a way of knowing those things." Her eyes sought his for confirmation. "Am I not right?"

"I would do anything to win her," he spoke up quickly; evidently she took the rest for granted, for she continued to persevere:—

"I know that you have great ambitions; and with such a girl at your side there is no reason why you should not become a great man."

This sudden interest on her part in matters concerning his future, for the moment rattled him. Nevertheless, he was conscious of a decided sensation of relief that the conversation had taken its present course; and her words: "With such a girl at your side" found a welcome in his heart. On her part, Mrs. Challoner was becoming more and more composed. And now in a voice that seemed to him ringing with conviction, she went on:—

"You will have up-hill work, I know. Your party is against you and all that sort of thing; but if only for Shirley's sake, I want you—you must succeed!"

For some reason which he did not attempt to explain Murgatroyd found himself actually confessing to this woman that he thought he deserved to win out.

"It's only money that you lack, I know," she ventured now. "With money they couldn't keep you down. With money of your own—" she stopped abruptly; the tension was getting too much for her. Presently she cried out: "Oh, Mr. Murgatroyd, don't you see what I mean, and won't you help me?"

But he failed to understand her meaning, and was obliged to ask her to explain herself. He was staring hard at her now.

And then at last it came out.

"Only this, Mr. Murgatroyd," she said, meeting his

gaze. "I will give you one hundred thousand dollars
to set my husband free!"

Murgatroyd instantly sprang to his feet.

"You mean to bribe me!"

Miriam Challoner cowered before him. She had not
put the matter to him in quite the way she had in-
tended. She was desperately afraid that she had de-
stroyed all hope of success by blurting it out like this.
"Please don't be hard on me—condemn me," she
begged as one before the judgment seat. "I know it's
awful!"

For a full half minute Murgatroyd fastened his gaze
on her face. Then he walked to the door, stepped inside the vault and satisfied himself that there was no
one there, looked into every corner of the room and
underneath the table; and when at last he was convinced that he had taken every precaution, he came
back and stood directly in front of the woman and
told her to repeat what she had said.

In fear and trembling she reiterated her words:—

"I will give you one hundred thousand dollars to set
my husband free!"

"Mrs. Challoner," the prosecutor asked, falling into
his habit of putting finger-tip to finger-tip, "how
much money have you?"

"In all?"

Murgatroyd nodded.

"In just a minute . . . "

With a hard look on his face Murgatroyd watched her pull a little book from a bag, watched her take out the stub of a pencil, waited while she busied herself in adding figures, waited until at the end of a short calculation she looked up at him and made known the result.

"In all, I have about eight hundred and sixty thousand dollars left."

"What?" exclaimed the prosecutor, unable to conceal his astonishment. For since he had begun his investigations it had come to him that Mrs. Challoner's affairs were in a bad way. A moment later he said: "And that eight hundred thousand dollars or so is——"

"All in negotiable securities," she promptly assured him, "payable to bearer. I get six and seven per cent. on some of them—the old ones."

"Where are these securities?"

"In the Fidelity Safe Deposit vaults."

"In addition to these," went on Murgatroyd, "you have your house on the Avenue?"

"Yes. There's a small equity in it."

He raised his eyebrows.

"It is subject to mortgage, then?"

"Of course," she answered glibly. "I get six per cent. on most of my securities, and have to pay only four and a half on my mortgage. It would have been foolish to pay it off."

Murgatroyd smiled a cold smile.

"You're quite a business woman, Mrs. Challoner."

"I have to be," she acknowledged with a smile that was intensely pathetic.

"And that's all you have?" he asked a moment later.

"Absolutely."

"Your house," mused Murgatroyd, half to himself, "will take care of Thorne's fee."

"How much will that be?"

Murgatroyd jerked his head nervously.

"Thorne?—Oh, he'll take all he can get!" There was a short silence which Murgatroyd suddenly broke. "Mrs. Challoner, your attempt to bribe is no longer an attempt. You have succeeded. I shall set your husband free!"

Mrs. Challoner smiled while the tears trickled down her cheeks.

"I shall get you the hundred thousand dollars right away," she said, as if it were a mere bagatelle.

"Just one moment, please," continued Murgatroyd, waving her back into her seat, for she had risen. "I shall set your husband free for *eight hundred and sixty thousand dollars!*"

Miriam Challoner leaned back in her chair. She seemed to hesitate.

"For everything I have!" she muttered half aloud. Murgatroyd reached over and touched her on the arm, and repeated in the same tone:—

"Everything you have!" And added: "Surely you did not think that I would sell myself for less?"

"No, no, of course not," she faltered. "I wish I had millions to give you. You are a good man—you are doing a good act."

Murgatroyd shook his head and said somewhat impatiently:—

"Mrs. Challoner, this is a business transaction; let us close it. You can get those securities to-day, I suppose?"

"Yes," she replied in the next breath, the flush of joy still on her face.

"Then do so, please." His voice was hoarse now. "And bring them to me here wrapped up in brown paper. You understand that nobody must know about this. You know what it would mean to me, to you, to Challoner . . . "

"Yes, yes," she cried eagerly, and held out her hand. "It's an agreement."

But Murgatroyd purposely ignored her hand and abruptly turned away, saying:—

"This matter must be closed at once."

And with a confident "I'll be back in half an hour,"

Mrs. Challoner passed out of the door, which Murgatroyd had softly and noiselessly unlocked.

*   *   *   *   *

The man who presently was brought out of the
barred anteroom and taken before the prosecutor
might have been anything from a floor-walker of a big
department store to a manager of a renowned raths-
keller. It was evident from the manner in which he
bore himself while under the constant surveillance of
the minions of the law, that he was perfectly at home
in the presence of strangers, and that unusual situa-
tions did not feaze him. In the matter of general
adornment of the person, however, Pemmican of the
low brow was an exception to his class: no diamond
blazed from his shirt-front or fingers; moreover, he
was dressed in the most sombre of blacks, and under his
soft felt hat of the same colour the hair was brushed
forward with scrupulous care. The long, thin,
smooth-shaven face, the little, deep-set eyes, the ab-
normally low brow, which was accentuated by this odd
arrangement of his hair, the pasty complexion, all
gave one the impression of dignified sleekness. In
other words, one could easily have pictured the man as
performing in a most impressive manner the last offices needed by man here below. To sum up, the attitude of the man now waiting for the prosecutor to
address him—Pemmican of the low brow always

knew his place—produced the effect of distressed meekness.

"Pemmican," said Murgatroyd, all geniality and good-fellowship now, "how are they treating you?" And then, with a chuckle: "You look peaked, my man!"

It was second nature to Pemmican to swallow his indignation and simulate cheerfulness, but he answered peevishly:—

"No wonder I'm all to the bad. But why am I kept locked up in this house of detention?"

McGrath grinned and spoke for the prosecutor.

"Witnesses is wary game and scarce; it ain't always the open season, so we got to keep 'em in cold storage, see?"

Pemmican ignored this remark, but turned to the prosecutor, and there was a whine in the voice that said:—

"You made my bail so infernally large that my friends would not put it up for me."

"I did it purposely," Murgatroyd declared, still smiling. "This is an important case; you are the only witness; and I've got to keep you where your friends cannot reach you—" here a faint flush spread over the prosecutor's countenance—"cannot corrupt you, Pemmican."

Suddenly Murgatroyd rose from his revolving chair. He nodded a dismissal to McGrath; and then going

over to a table in the centre of the room, he drew to
him a sheet of foolscap from a pile lying there, and
said:—

"Come over here, Pemmican!" There was an article
of some kind in the hand that rested on the table.
"Just sketch me here—on this paper—a little plan
showing the position of the men in Room A that
night."

"Sure," volunteered Pemmican, taking the proffered
pencil; "now, here was Colonel Hargraves, here
was——"

He stopped abruptly. For he had seen that the
article in Murgatroyd's hand was a wallet marked
"R. H."

"Go on!" said Murgatroyd.

"And here was—" Pemmican stopped again.

"What are you looking at?" Murgatroyd asked.

"Oh, that? he said casually, and passed the wallet to
Pemmican.

Pemmican started and backed away.

"I don't want it. It ain't mine. I don't know what it
is—what is it, anyhow?" he gulped. "No, counsellor," he added; "and besides, I wasn't looking at
it."

Murgatroyd patted the wallet.

"It was Colonel Hargraves's pocketbook," he said.
"I thought you recognised it."

"Never saw it before, counsellor," he repeated sulkily; "never saw it before."

"You must have seen it," persisted Murgatroyd; "it's pretty well worn, and he must have carried it a long time. He was one of your patrons. The fact is, Pemmican," he went on, "this wallet was the occasion of my sending for you just now. I am informed that when Hargraves last carried it the wallet was full of bills; and when he was found in the street it was quite empty. It is a mere detail, but I should like to know whether Challoner robbed this man as well as killed him."

Pemmican slowly shook his head.

"Can't help you out," he answered, "for I never saw the wallet. I don't know . . . "

Murgatroyd went off on another tack.

"Very well, then; but there's another thing that you may clear up . . . By the way, Pemmican, perhaps you don't know that Challoner has confessed?"

Pemmican's physiognomy lost its doleful appearance. And he cried joyfully:—

"Confessed? Gee, that's good—great! Confessed? Well, say, counsellor, it just had to come to that!"

"Yes," conceded Murgatroyd; "but there's another thing which bothers me, though I don't know that it complicates matters exactly. It's a mere detail again. Challoner says he shot his man in Room A in Cradlebaugh's; you say the quarrel took place there, that Hargraves went out first, and that Challoner followed him. Hargraves, as we know, was found dead in the street above. That's right—isn't it?"

"Sure," returned Pemmican, positively. "I didn't see him fire the shot; nobody saw that. It's a good thing, though, because between you and me, Prosecutor, notwithstanding my testimony I thought that you'd have some trouble in making out a case. Circumstances is something, but they ain't everything, you know."

Murgatroyd agreed to this, and added:—

"We've got certainty now, because he's confessed—but he's mixed as to the place of the shooting. He thinks it was in your place—that you were present, that's all."

Murgatroyd seemed satisfied. He sat down at his desk and from a drawer he drew a box of cigars. Now he leaned toward Pemmican and said confidentially:—

"Pemmican, I want your testimony in this case—I want it *right*. Have a cigar?"

Pemmican accepted, and finding a ready match in his pocket, struck it on the heel of his boot and lighted the cigar before the slow-moving Murgatroyd could pass him his matchbox.

"Thank you, counsellor, I have one," he said, and blew a cloud of smoke to the ceiling. "You can depend on me; I'll tell the truth—the whole truth and nothing but the truth, so help me—" His gaze returned again to the pigskin wallet on the desk. "But say, I never saw that thing before."

Murgatroyd picked it up and spoke in a still lower tone now.

"Pemmican, suppose I were to fill this with, well, say ten thousand dollars and give it to you; how would you testify in this case, eh?"

"But," protested Pemmican, "I never saw ten thousand dollars in it— No . . . "

"No," repeated Murgatroyd; "but if you should right now have it filled with ten thousand dollars, how would you testify for me?"

Pemmican stolidly shook his head and answered:

"To the truth, counsellor—I'm an honest man."

Murgatroyd still persisted.

"How much would you take, Pemmican," he went on, "to swear that Challoner did not commit this crime?"

Pemmican started back in alarm, and once more shook his head.

"Counsellor, I'm an honest man," he answered doggedly.

Murgatroyd gave it up as a bad job.

"You're honest, all right, Pemmican," he said. "You can go back now; but I'll have you down again before the trial, and together we'll go over the testimony carefully." He placed his hand upon the other's arm. "You see, I'm most particular about this case." The next moment Mixley and McGrath entered and took Pemmican away.

*   *   *   *   *

Fifteen minutes later Mrs. Challoner arrived. She was accompanied by Stevens, the butler, carrying a large parcel, which he deposited on the prosecutor's table as directed. He was then dismissed; and when the door had closed on him, the man and the woman stood for a few minutes listening in silence to his retreating footsteps. Then in low, rapid tones Mrs. Challoner assured the prosecutor that she had accomplished her purpose without arousing the suspicions of any one—not even the servant. Murgatroyd noiselessly locked the door, and putting his hand upon the parcel on the table, looked at her interrogatively.

"Yes—the securities—they're all there," she hastened to assure him.

"Shall I——"

Mrs. Challoner's hand waved her permission. The big, heavy parcel had been clumsily tied up with brown paper. This, Murgatroyd tore off, and there stood revealed two long, sheet-iron boxes, old and somewhat battered. They were heavily sealed, and across each on a pasted piece of paper appeared in big letters the name "Miriam Challoner."

"I brought them just as they were," she went on to explain. "You may break the seals, scratch off my name, and then they will be yours to do with as you please."

"For the present," Murgatroyd told himself, as his eyes fell on the vault door, "that will be their resting place." And turning to her, he said aloud:—

"The deal is closed. You understand the terms? Everything is left to me—I am to free your husband —I am to keep your money?"

"Yes," she breathed, as if some heavy burden had rolled from her young shoulders.

And now for the first time Murgatroyd looked Miriam Challoner full in the face, and said solemnly :—

"One thing more: absolutely no one must know of this. Not Challoner, nor Thorne, and above all, not Miss Bloodgood. Everything depends on your silence —your silence is the essence of this contract. You agree?"

Mrs. Challoner bowed.

"I do." And she might have been taking an oath from the way she said it.

"Remember you will say nothing to Miss Bloodgood . . . "

"Shirley will never know of it."

"Most decidedly not Shirley." But the prosecutor remarked this to himself when once more he was alone.

X

THE trial of James Lawrence Challoner had progressed with uncommon haste, the fourth day finding
all the witnesses heard and the case ready to sum up
to the jury. The court-room was crowded: the newspapers were there; the people were there; public
opinion was there. Brief and to the point had been
the State's case—made up out of Pemmican's evidence
and the confession of the prisoner. But in the prosecutor's presentment of his evidence there had been an
undercurrent as unusual as it was unexpected: every
question that he hurled at Pemmican had a hidden
meaning; every interrogation point had a sting hidden in its tail. Not that he made any attempt to
switch the issue or to side-track the facts, but it was
clearly apparent that from start to finish he was making a supreme effort to include within his facts, to
embrace within the issue and to place on trial, together
with the prisoner, one other culprit in this celebrated
case—Cradlebaugh's.

However, if such were the prosecutor's chief purpose,
it failed. Thorne, the counsel for the defence—who
represented more than one client in this case—met him
at every turn, parried his every thrust.

"Objection sustained," the Court had ruled wearily

many times during the trial, "the prosecutor will proceed."

And upon such occasions Graham Thorne, from the
counsel's table in the front, had flashed a triumphant
glance at Peter Broderick; and Peter Broderick, in
turn, from his seat in the rear of the court-room,
would return the gaze with a smile, the brilliancy of
which was outshone only by the big diamond that
blazed from where it rested comfortably on his highly
coloured shirt-front. To these two—not in the least
interested in the outcome of the trial, so far as Challoner was concerned—the case was highly satisfactory.
There was no crevice in the mystery of Cradlebaugh's
in which Murgatroyd could insert the thin edge of a
wedge; its foundation still remained unshaken after
the impact of his battering ram; the Challoner case
was to be the Challoner case, and nothing more.

. . . "That's all, Mr. Pemmican," were the words
with which the prosecutor had concluded the examination of his principal witness.

On Pemmican of the low brow leaving the witness
stand, he had glanced expectantly toward the counsel
for the defence. Throughout the trial there was in
his manner a peculiar deference toward Thorne which
had been there from the first day. Under Murgatroyd's sharp interrogation he had seemed quite at
ease; but his attitude toward Thorne had always ap-

peared to be that of a man whose hand was constantly kept raised to ward off blows. However, notwithstanding that he had been recalled at least five times, Pemmican, on the whole, apparently was well satisfied with his performance. Unquestionably he had been loyal and wary, and had confined his testimony as to motive to the woman in the case—a row over a lady— keeping that portentous game of cards well into the background—out of sight.

"Surely you're not going to detain me any longer?" whispered Pemmican to the officers who had placed themselves on either side of him. "What! You're not going to let me go?"

"Not on your life!" remarked one of them genially; and showing to the prisoner a slip of paper which he drew from his pocket: "There's a warrant for your arrest."

Pemmican for a moment looked bewildered and murmured incredulously:—

" . . . my arrest?"

"Sure," replied the officer. "The chief's begun his raid on Cradlebaugh's, and you're one of the main guys . . . "

Pemmican wiped his forehead and stammered sulkily:—

"And—and the prosecutor's goin' to lock me up after all I've done for him?"

"That's what!" replied the officer, and a moment later added complacently: "Unless you can get bail."

"Confound 'em!" exclaimed Pemmican.   "They won't go my bail!"

The detective placed his ear quite close to Pemmican.

"*Who* won't go your bail?" he queried interestedly. Pemmican smiled.

"They," he returned, not for an instant off his guard.

"If Prosecutor Murgatroyd only knew who *they* are," went on the detective, "if he knew who backed you up, there'd be some interesting goings on 'round here."

"He won't find out from me," replied Pemmican, doggedly.   "I play a straight game with the men who hand out my bread and butter.   You can lay your bets on that!"

"Sh-h-h-! The prosecutor's talkin' over there," whispered the detective, raising his hand, and he hustled the prisoner out of the room, as Murgatroyd, rising once more, bowed toward the bench and announced:—

"The State rests, if the Court please."

And then Thorne at his end of the table also rose to his feet and declared:—

"The defence rests."

Presently he began to address the Jury. During the

trial his line of defence had been insanity—the defence of the defenceless, the forlorn hope of the hopeless. The Bench had frowned at it; the Jury had shaken its head as one man: insanity to juries in the metropolis had become as a red rag to a bull. But the crowd in the court-room had leaned forward with huge expectation,—waiting for the hidden places to be revealed with much the same anticipation and interest one experiences in waiting for the dénouement of a stage drama.

Before turning to the jury, however, for his last effort, Thorne stooped down for an instant and whispered to Mrs. Challoner:—

"I'm sorry, Mrs. Challoner, that we couldn't do better with our facts. It seems to me to be the weakest defence I have ever seen put up in any case. Indeed, it seems to me we have no defence at all."

But somewhat to his astonishment this remark was received by Miriam Challoner with that same degree of confidence that had characterised her attitude all through the trial. On her face was a certain unexplainable something which not only he had noted but which the people had noted, the men at the press-table had noted, and commented upon freely in their copy—a glow that had never faded from the eyes of the woman, a flush upon her cheek that had never paled, and which said more plainly than words that she was certain of the acquittal of her husband.

"Devilish fine actress!" Thorne thought to himself, for such optimism in a case like this was wholly beyond his comprehension; and it was with a certain feeling of admiration that he heard her whisper with a reassuring smile:—

"You're making a glorious fight, Mr. Thorne; you're bound to succeed."

And indeed, such was her marvellous hopefulness, that it succeeded in enheartening him, and was reflected in his illustrations to the jury when dwelling at some length on the many fine points in the character of the accused. He was particularly happy in impressing upon his hearers that Challoner was a man with a most peculiar temperament and mental bias; that if Challoner had taken the life of Colonel Hargraves, it was only after the man's soul and mind had eaten poison from the hands of his enemy—Colonel Hargraves.

Of the life and character of that gentleman, he had little to add to what was already known, and was seemingly content to dismiss him with:—

"The least said of him the better, now that he is gone."

Thorne paused.

Suddenly he assumed a dramatic pose, and now turn-

ing toward a beautiful and fashionably gowned
young woman with a bar of sunlight streaming down
her face, who occupied a seat underneath the third
high window in the court-room, he riveted his gaze on
her, all eyes following in that direction.

"There," he said, his voice sinking to a whisper, but
a whisper that could be heard all over the court-room,
"is the woman in the case—the real culprit! A temp-
tress! A vampire! A Circe! A woman who has made
a mess of the lives of two men, and only God knows
how many others! A woman who played the game
to her own selfish ends! . . . And here you have
the result!"

For a full minute Letty Love unblushingly returned the lawyer's probing glances; plainly she rejoiced in the stares which she felt were focussed upon
her,—for no one knew better than she that her beauty
was infecting all present,—and it was not until she had
drunk her fill of the cup of publicity that she turned
her head away and looked out upon the sunlit street.

From where he sat Challoner, too, was able for a
brief moment to see the face of the woman who was responsible for his misfortunes. That same second, however, brought his wife also into his line of vision, making it possible for him to contrast the two counte-
nances; and he was surprised to find himself not only
admiring the wealth of colouring and glow upon Mir-

iam's face, but actually loathing himself for ever having admired the ugly lines which he now saw on the sunlit face of Letty Love; and his whole nature revolted against her.

"If only I had left her to Colonel Hargraves," he muttered to himself; and immersed in similar bitter reflections, he lost all but his counsel's concluding words:—

" . . . and all that I want, all that I ask of you, gentlemen of the jury, is that you give us what we have not had so far—a fair, square deal!"

Thorne sat down, satisfied that he had made an impression. At all events, he had done the best he could —under the circumstances. Out of his material he had hewn the inevitable result—debauchery; out of this debauchery he fashioned the conclusion—insanity; out of a victim he had made a murderer; out of a murderer he had made a hero whose irresponsible emotions cried out to a jury of his peers for justice, even for retribution against the murdered man. Base metal though it were, it seemed pure gold to his listeners. Even the jurors drew long breaths and looked each other questioningly in the eye; the crowd murmured its sympathy; and Thorne, glancing at the little coterie behind the prisoner, was pleased to see that even in the eyes of Shirley Bloodgood he had raised a new hope for Challoner.

In the interim that followed Shirley and Miriam leaned over and shook hands with Thorne.

"We can't lose," whispered Miriam; and again there returned to her face that mysterious expression of confidence which was decidedly inexplicable to her lawyer. And so it was that a little while later he turned to Shirley and said:—

"Does she understand that we must lose?"

Miss Bloodgood shook her head.

"Oh, no! No one can tell her that." And bestowing on him a rare smile, she added: "And now, Mr. Thorne, after what you have said no one can tell *me* that either."

Well pleased with her flattery, Thorne returned the smile, but he warned her that when those twelve men got into the jury room they would get down to facts.

And it so happened that the twelve men got down to the facts before they even started for the jury room, for already the prosecutor had begun his speech and was stripping the case of everything save the truth.

"This, gentlemen," he now told the jury, quietly, "is not an unusual case; it's an every-day story growing out of jealousy and hatred; one bad man shot another bad man—that's all."

At this the temperature of the crowd dropped from the fever-heat of frenzied sympathy down to the freezing-point of common-sense. Challoner stirred uneasily; Shirley Bloodgood shivered; only Miriam Challoner sat with the same placid look on her face.

Murgatroyd now left his jury, walked to the table where the prisoner sat, and without taking his eyes from the face of the accused, he continued:—

" . . . This man Challoner is a wilful, deliberate murderer! This is not his first offence—he began to murder years ago . . . "

At this point the prosecutor went back to the time when Challoner married a beautiful young girl, emphasising the fact that he had married this mere slip of a girl for her money.

"Her money! And he has never earned a dollar since!" he told his listeners with great scorn. "And his life! What has he made of it? Ah! You men know the things that are done in this city between midnight and morning, and the up-hill fight that is being made to clean it of corruption and vice! Well, this degenerate, this profligate, did these things of the under-world. They appealed to him; he was no mere youth to be led astray!"

Challoner winced; not that he quailed before the menacing posture that the prosecutor had assumed, but because of a guilty consciousness that the accusing lips meant every word that they uttered. The audience shifted uneasily in their seats; Shirley Bloodgood held her breath as she placed a protecting arm about Miriam, which Miriam gently shook off; for what need had she for sympathy?

Murgatroyd returned to his place in front of the jury rail, and briefly reviewed the evidence.

Then with great emotion in his voice he went on:—

"And what part, gentlemen, did the wife have in all this? His wife, who sat through the weary hours of the night waiting for the thing she loved, while her husband not only lavished his affections but her money on others—his friends. His friends! Had he friends? If so, where are they? No, long ago he turned his back on his real friends; they were in the light; he sought the darkness."

As the prosecutor went on with his merciless flaying, Challoner grew hot and cold by turns.

" . . . Gentlemen, behold the result of riotous living!" he declared, pointing his finger at the prisoner. "The pace that kills! . . .

"And so, in view of these facts, in view of the prisoner's private history, I tell you that the defence here is absurd, ridiculous. Gentlemen, on behalf of the people, in the name of justice, I ask you to convict this man."

For an instant he stood eyeing the twelve jurors. Then, raising his right hand solemnly he brought it down with full sudden force upon the railing between himself and them.

"And let me warn you, gentlemen of the jury," he continued ominously, "that the honour, the integrity of this metropolis hangs in the balance. If you acquit this defendant and set him free, the people of this State, the people of the country, will say henceforth that all that a murderer need have to secure an acquittal—his freedom, is money, money, money."

As the prosecutor seated himself, there was a gasp of relief from the people in the court-room. Broderick ventured inside of the railed space set aside for counsel and shook hands with Thorne.

"Counsellor," he said, "you certainly handled that trial like a veteran. You saw your duty and you did it."

Thorne nodded his thanks, and answered:—

"I held Murgatroyd down to the woman in the case, all right. He had to stick to that one motive. This verdict will let everybody out——"

"But Challoner," added Broderick.

"Everybody but Challoner," agreed Thorne; "and the incident will be closed."

Broderick, with a certain self-satisfied air, went on:—

"When you were talking, I put up ten dollars with a chap back there in the court-room that Challoner 'd go free."

"Not in a thousand years!" declared Thorne, flatly.

"I'm afraid you're right," said Broderick, and added with a twinkle in his eye: "I hate to lose that ten. Still if I do lose it, it'll be tougher for Challoner and her—" he jerked his head toward Mrs. Challoner at the other end of the table—"than it will be for me. Oh, well, such is life! The world is full of the wives of criminals, and they all marry again and have children and live happily ever after."

Once more, he glanced in the direction of Miriam Challoner, and presently commented in a low voice:—

"There's a plucky little woman, Thorne; nothin' can feaze her. I've been watchin' her; and she's just as sure of that jury as I am of my own assembly district after it has gone through my trousers pockets the night before election." And clapping Thorne on the shoulder familiarly, he took his departure, saying:—

"I'll be back to hear the verdict."

*   *   *   *   *

It was nearly two o'clock. The Court had charged the jury; the jury had filed out; they were still locked up in the jury-room. The crowd had left the court-room, Challoner had been taken down-stairs, Pemmican had been housed in jail under the gambling warrants; only Thorne, Miriam and Shirley remained.

"Wasn't that a terrible arraignment of Prosecutor Murgatroyd!" exclaimed Shirley. "When he faced Laurie and told him what he thought of him—it was

simply awful!" and the girl covered her face with her
hands as if to shut out the sight of it all.

"Why, Shirley," said Miriam quietly, "it's a prosecutor's business to say these things about a prisoner.
It's all in a day's work, isn't it, Mr. Thorne?" And
she smiled faintly.

Thorne was about to speak when a uniformed at-
tendant suddenly entered at one door and swung
across the court-room to another. In passing, he
called to Thorne:—

"The jury has agreed!" He disappeared in the direction of the prosecutor's private office.

A moment later another court-officer strode toward
the judge's private chambers, and likewise announced
in passing:—

"The jury 's coming in!"

Thorne looked cheerful, by way of encouragement
to the women. Shirley blanched, her lips whitened, she
trembled from head to foot; but Thorne noted that
Miriam's eyes only grew brighter; she concealed her
agitation well.

"It will all be over in a minute now," Miriam exclaimed joyfully, "and he'll be free, free!"

Without, within, everywhere was bustle, expectation.
The crowd filed back into the court-room; Murgatroyd came in from his private office; the Court took
its seat upon the bench; and then just as Broderick

waddled in, the barred door in the far corner opened, and Challoner, as though in a daze, walked down the aisle, an officer in front and one behind him. The clerk glanced about him to see that all was in readiness, and then nodding to an officer, he said:—

"Bring 'em in!"

A minute that seemed minutes elapsed, and then the jury filed in—a jury whose faces, whose demeanour told nothing, gave no sign. Then there was an interval of silence, and in that interval a cutting pang seized upon the soul of every human present—the agony of suspense, the travail that precedes the birth of a verdict.

"Gentlemen of the jury," said the clerk rapidly, "have you agreed upon your verdict?"

"We have," came in chorus.

"Who do you say shall answer for you?"

The eleven men pointed toward their foreman.

"Gentlemen of the jury," said the clerk, "look upon the prisoner; prisoner, look upon the jury. Gentlemen of the jury, how do you say you find— guilty or not guilty?"

The foreman glanced upon the piece of paper which he held in his left hand and gripped the rail before him with his right.

"Guilty," he replied.

"What's that?" exclaimed Graham Thorne in affected astonishment.

"What?" came from Miriam Challoner shrilly; and
the next moment all the colour had left her face; she
was pale as death.

"Guilty, your Honour," repeated the foreman in a
louder tone.

"Guilty of what?" queried the Court impatiently.

"Of murder in the first degree," answered the jury
as one man.

"Gentlemen of the jury, your verdict is guilty of
murder in the first degree, and so say all of you?"
reeled off the clerk, looking at his minutes.

They nodded.

"You are discharged, gentlemen, with the thanks of
the Court," announced the Court with approval. "Be-
here to-morrow morning at ten o'clock."

Meanwhile Challoner sat sullen, desperate, his chin
resting on his hand, glaring into space. Around him
was confusion, expostulation. The spectators were
pressing forward toward the rail to get another look
at the accused, while the jury was passing out. All
of a sudden the sound of buzzing whispers died down
and was followed in a moment by an intenser silence.
There was a stir among those in the front seats, and
the judge, looking up, was surprised to see that it was
caused by the defendant's wife, who had moved from

her place and was making her way to the prosecutor's
desk, determination standing out on her countenance.
Immediately all eyes were fixed on her, as she placed
her hand upon Murgatroyd's arm, and looking him
full in the face, exclaimed hysterically:—

"They found him guilty—guilty, do you understand? What have you got to say?"

Murgatroyd looked at her, but he did not answer.
Her grasp became a clutch as she repeated:—

"What have you got to say to me? Speak!"

Murgatroyd was imperturbable.

Miriam, aghast at his coolness, stared at him; then
she began again:—

"You—you—" Her voice failed her, and relaxing
her grasp, she clung to the table for support. Shirley
ran to her, held her, saying gently:—

"Miriam, dear, you are beside yourself—come, come
away!"

But Miriam braced herself and resolutely shook herself free from her friend.

"No," she replied evenly, "I am not going!" and
her voice rose as she went on: "Don't let anybody go!
What I have to say I want all of you to hear!" And
tottering over toward the bench as the spectators
pressed tumultuously forward, Peter Broderick among
the rest, she exclaimed:—

"Your Honour! Your Honour!"

"What is it, Madam?" asked the justice. And considering that the Court believed that it had to deal with a case of hysteria, the voice was surprisingly little tinged with irritability; but then the learned judge felt that he must make some concession to a woman of Mrs. Challoner's high social standing; and therefore he added politely: "You must be brief."

"I shall be brief," answered Mrs. Challoner, sending an accusing glance toward the prosecutor. "I desire to make a charge against Mr. Murgatroyd, the prosecutor of the pleas!" She was well contained, but her tone was harsh, cutting.

The Court glanced sympathetically at her, and then smiled gently, indulgently in the direction of the prosecutor.

"I accuse him of bribery!" she went on. "He promised to set my husband free!"

Shirley Bloodgood clutched her once more, pleading with her to stop.

"Miriam, what are you saying? You must stop this . . . "

"Bribery?" asked the justice, somewhat startled. "Bribery?"

For an instant there was a subdued uproar. Graham Thorne pressed forward toward the Court; Broderick from the crowd behind pushed his way into the enclosure; reporters thrust their pads and pencils into the scene; spectators stirred, became noisy; but Murgatroyd never moved.

"Let Mrs. Challoner go on," demanded Thorne.

The Court rapped loudly with his gavel; the crowd slumped into silence.

"Clear this court-room!" ordered the justice, standing up until his command was obeyed.

The process took five minutes. At the end of that period none was left within the room except the officers and those within the rail, which included Broderick. No court-officer who valued his position dared to disturb Broderick.

"Now close the doors!" ordered the justice.

That took an instant more. At last, the Court said:—

"Now, Mrs. Challoner . . . "

Miriam's Challoner's eyes flashed fire.

"I want everybody here," she cried, "to know and understand what this man has done! He arrested my husband," she went on, her face still turned toward Murgatroyd, her eyes holding his glance; "I begged of him to set him free—he refused. He told me he could do nothing for me—could do nothing but his duty. I couldn't move him; he wouldn't budge an inch until finally I offered him money."

She paused. Peter Broderick moved a few steps nearer, gnawing his finger-nails; Thorne watched

Murgatroyd closely; but Murgatroyd was unmoved. He returned Miriam's glance with interest; he gave no sign.

" . . . until I offered money," she repeated. "I offered him one hundred thousand dollars; he refused to take it."

"Naturally," interposed the Court.

"He refused to take it," went on Miriam, irritated by the interruption, "because he knew there was more. He demanded eight hundred and sixty thousand dollars— all I had,—to set my husband free! He took it and agreed to set him free. And now," she concluded, advancing toward Murgatroyd as though with a threat upon her tongue, "see how he has kept his word!"

"It can't be true," Shirley Bloodgood was heard to say, half aloud.

Broderick crept up close to Thorne and nudged him. The latter interpreted correctly the action.

"Let Mrs. Challoner go on," suggested Thorne; and the Court ordered Mrs. Challoner to proceed.

"That's all," said Miriam, quite close to the prosecutor now, "except what I have to say to Mr. Murgatroyd."

And now as she stood before him, her eyes glistening, her breast heaving, remembering only that she was a woman robbed of her mate, she cried:—

"I am going to make you suffer for this as you made

him suffer in this court-room," and she waved her hand
toward Challoner. "I'll invoke every law against
you," she went on, "and if the law can't help me, I'll
spend my life to make you pay for this. You made
an agreement with me and you must keep it, or I will
. . . " Suddenly she sank exhausted into the chair
next to Challoner and buried her face upon the prisoner's shoulder.

"Laurie, Laurie," she sobbed in her despair. For the
first time Challoner showed some feeling; he found her
hand and patted it with affection for a moment.

The justice shook his head. Presently he said incredulously :—

"Mrs. Challoner, this is a terrible charge to make."

She sprang up but immediately sank back again.

"It's true, it's true," she wailed.

Shirley turned to Thorne and said feelingly :—

"The trial has been too much for her. She's overwrought."

Broderick, who overheard the remark, grinned sar-
donically. Turning to Thorne, he remarked :—

"I'm an expert in these matters. It's got all the earmarks of the real thing. Murgatroyd did well." And
then, as one who enjoyed all the privileges of the
court-room, he advanced close to the bench, and shad-
ing his mouth, while he spoke, suggested genially :—

"Your Honour, get out the Penal Code."

But the Court merely beckoned to Thorne and suggested that he take charge of his client; that the strain had been too much for her.   And much as Thorne wanted to believe her story, he felt as the Court felt: that the tale was little short of preposterous.

"But—it's true," Miriam persisted to her counsel, "incredible as it may seem."

Thorne eyed her steadily for a few moments.   At last, he said:—

"At any rate, it may have some effect upon the verdict."   And then addressing himself to the bench, he exclaimed: "Your Honour, Mrs. Challoner assures me that this charge is absolutely true."   And finally turning to Murgatroyd: "I should like to hear from Prosecutor Murgatroyd as to the truth or falsity of this?"

As the two men faced each other, Shirley once more touched Miriam's arm, and said affectionately:—

"Miriam, do you realise all that you are saying?— Look into my eyes, dear, and tell me candidly is it true? . . . "

"Before God, I swear it."   And a moment later she added: "And he never kept his word."

"Well, Mr. Prosecutor, what have you got to say?" asked the Court, a trifle apologetically.

During the pause that immediately ensued, Miriam Challoner wondered what Murgatroyd would say;

what he could say; what was left for him to say. The prosecutor stood in the centre of an open space, and looking first at Miriam, then at Thorne, and finally at the Court, he answered gravely:—

"Your Honour, I have heard the charge. I don't see that it behooves me to answer it at this time, nor indeed," bowing toward the Court, "before this tribunal. If it be a charge made in earnest—as it seems to be —then the only question that can possibly interest this Court, is whether I have done my duty toward the people of the State. The charge assumes the proportions of a bribe to free a guilty man. My answer is, I have convicted Challoner. If there was a bribe, it was a bribe that didn't work."

The Court stared with the rest. Peter Broderick gazed at Murgatroyd in open-mouthed admiration; even Miriam felt baffled unaccountably.

"Mr. Thorne," said the Court, "if this charge be made in good faith, and even assuming it to be literally true, isn't the prosecutor right? It cannot be that this charge is true; but if Mrs. Challoner claims it to be true, if you believe it to be true, her remedy, then, is to go to the Grand Jury and indict, to the legislature and impeach." He paused judicially, and added: "The fullest refutation, after all, is that the prosecutor did convict."

Thorne considered for an instant.

"I agree entirely with your Honour," he assented, bowing.

"The incident is closed," went on the Court, rising. "You have your remedy— Good afternoon!" And he left the court-room.

And still Murgatroyd stood his ground while the others stood aloof. Presently two officers seized Challoner and disappeared with him through the barred door. Graham Thorne then approached the prosecutor and exclaimed:—

"Prosecutor, we have wondered all along just what your price might be. Now we know."

"The last dollar that a woman has," sneered Peter Broderick.

And still Murgatroyd gave no sign. It was only when Shirley Bloodgood approached him and he heard the tremor in her voice that the man trembled imperceptibly.

"Mr. Murgatroyd," she declared, "I am forced to believe all that Miriam has said. Oh, Billy, Billy, it is inconceivable that you are the man that I have respected all these years! You have lost the one thing I admired most in you." Her voice broke, and turning to Miriam, she cried: "Come, Miriam, dear, we're going home."

Mrs. Challoner touched Thorne upon the arm, and said with a final look at Murgatroyd:—

"I want you to take every legal measure to indict, to impeach this man, and I want you to begin at once."

After all had gone, Murgatroyd remained for some time where they had left him, imperturbable, inscrutable, gazing doggedly into space.

XI

"I came here again, thinking perhaps you might wish to explain your action." The words came from Mrs. Challoner, who, unattended, had found her way into the prosecutor's office.

Murgatroyd quickly laid down his cigar. Doubtless he was annoyed, but in spite of himself he could not help admiring the pluck which she showed in coming directly to him; and as he came forward to meet her, he saw that it was with difficulty that she kept on her feet. For a moment they faced each other in silence, yet in the eyes of each there was a look of fearful misunderstanding. Again the woman spoke.

"What have you to say to me?"

Murgatroyd frowned, his bearing slipped off some of its deference when he retorted in a voice full of emotion:—

"What have *you* to say to *me?* . . . "

The prosecutor's perfect self-possession and earnestness unnerved her for an instant.

"I—" she faltered and stopped before his scornful glance.

"Yes, you, Mrs. Challoner. Do you recall our compact? Your silence was the essence of it. Why did you break it?"

Miriam Challoner checked a wild desire to laugh hysterically.

"But you broke it first!"

Murgatroyd smiled.

"How?"

The woman looked steadily at him.

"By this conviction!"

"What was our compact?" he asked sternly.

Miriam's courage was returning; it was with an indignant tone that she replied:—

"That you should set my husband free!"

Murgatroyd tapped the table with his hand.

"And have I failed as yet?"

"Yes," she answered fiercely. "You have convicted him."

Murgatroyd drew his head slightly to one side; pursed up his lips; drew his brows together; and narrowed his eyes before he spoke:—

"Did you assume for an instant, Mrs. Challoner, that I was such a bungler as to release your husband at the first trial—for all the world to know—to suspect? When I said to you that I would set your husband free, did I say—*when?*"

Of the scene that followed Miriam Challoner never retained a very clear impression. She remembered that at first, as if in a trance, she kept repeating his last word, while by degrees its meaning stole in upon her;

then of a sensation of being about to faint through
mere excess of joy. Suddenly the thought of her
temerity flashed through her brain—the enormity of
the thing she had done; and she would have gone on
her knees at his feet had he not caught her in time.
Quickly recovering, she looked up at him. Somehow
his face seemed to hold little resentment now—too little, in fact, to suit her surprising desire to humble herself in his sight.

"After all, she's rather a fool of a woman," his expression had plainly said to her overwrought senses,
"and I will spare her." And yet she craved so to hear
words of pardon from his lips, that she broke out almost breathlessly :—

"You will forgive me—you must . . . I have
done you an unutterable injury, I know." She
stopped, and then with a sudden lapse to her old air
of fear: "Oh, but what will happen now—what will
happen to Laurie? I have failed you; you have the
right to . . . "

Once more cold and indifferent, Murgatroyd looked
out of the window, though he interrupted her last
words by saying frigidly :—

"When I make agreements, Mrs. Challoner, I keep
them. You may be sure that I shall keep this
one."

Still awed in a measure by his masterful personality,

but with joy in her heart, Miriam Challoner started to leave the office.

With a gesture Murgatroyd checked her quickly.

"Mrs. Challoner," he said with reproof still lingering in his voice, "there is no necessity henceforth for personal interviews. In the future if you have anything to say to me, kindly let it come through your counsel, Mr. Thorne. It is much better so—much safer. I prefer to deal with him only."

Miriam bowed acquiescence.

Directly on leaving him Miriam Challoner went to Thorne's office. It was in accordance with her promise to aid him in formulating the charges which he was preparing against the prosecutor on her behalf. These charges were for the legislature and the Grand Jury: on the one hand, impeachment; on the other, indictment. Now whether the accusation had been true or false mattered little to Thorne. On the whole, perhaps, he was inclined to disbelief; but Broderick, his colleague in the organisation, was by no means of that opinion. In any event, since it came from such an authoritative source—the lips of Mrs. Challoner—it was a charge that possessed merit, inasmuch as it would injure Murgatroyd—and Thorne was not slow to recognise that. In consequence, then, there was, unmistakably, a note of gratification in the words with which he greeted Mrs. Challoner that afternoon in his office.

"Here it is—in the form of an affidavit—just what you told me, Mrs. Challoner. Please read it."

Trembling slightly while searching her mind for some clever way in which she might express her change of plan, Miriam Challoner slowly read the document. Nothing was left out, nothing exaggerated, and without a word she returned it.

"Will you sign here, please?"

There was no time to arrange any idea she may have had for new tactics: it was Thorne's voice that was insisting; it was Thorne who was holding a pen for her and indicating the correct place for her signature. And with a violent effort, Mrs. Challoner braced herself for the first lie in her life.

"It's not true. I cannot sign it."

Thorne started back. Instantly he was spluttering his annoyance at what he considered merely a woman's whim.

"Not true! Why only a short time ago you declared it was true."

"So it was—but only in a way," she said laboriously. Her face burned and paled. "I tried to bribe him, but——"

"Bribe him! How? . . . "

"With the money—the money I had left," she replied cautiously.

"What have you left?" he ventured.

Curiously enough, Mrs. Challoner found herself taking a certain amount of satisfaction in telling her lawyer what now was unquestionably true.

"My home—only."

"But that's mortgaged, I understand?" There was more than idle curiosity in the speaker's eyes.

"Yes. But there's an equity of about twenty or twenty-five thousand," she explained.

"And you tried to bribe Murgatroyd with twenty thousand dollars?"

There was no answer; and interpreting her silence as assent, he went on persistently:—

"And he refused?"

Miriam was very white now.

"He did."

"I should think so," returned Thorne. "Two hundred and fifty would be more like Murgatroyd's price —if he can be bought."

"No, he cannot be bought," Miriam ventured with perhaps a trifle more confidence in her tone than Mr. Thorne liked; and then she added, in a changed voice: "I want you, please, to retract this story. I want to take it all back. I was unstrung, I——"

"I will retract nothing," he cut in rudely. "Not a

thing. Leave it as it is. If you begin to retract you'll get yourself in trouble. If Murgatroyd desires to make a move, let him . . . "

And with a promise to that effect, a hurried acknowledgment with an inclination of the head that she accepted his words as ending her interview, she left the office, leaving him far from certain that Peter Broderick's appraisement of Murgatroyd's character was not a correct one.

That night when the papers came out, people read them in anger and dismay; by the next morning they merely laughed; likewise the Court.

"If he were bribed," said public comment, "it was a bribe that didn't work."

And Murgatroyd, submitting to interview after interview, reiterated over and over again to the reporters:—

"I point with pride, gentlemen, to the conviction of Lawrence Challoner. That's all I have to say."

The fiasco had helped Murgatroyd infinitely more than it had hurt him, Thorne felt in his inmost soul. For once the masses refused to believe what on its face appeared to be true.

*   *   *   *   *

One evening a few weeks later, while Murgatroyd was dressing to dine at his club, as was his custom nearly every night, his servant handed him a note

which the bearer had said was to be delivered immediately. It was but seldom that a square white envelope
came at this time, and with a pardonable look of surprise and curiosity on his face Murgatroyd opened it
and read:

"I must see you. Will you come to the house to-
night?

                                    "S. H. B."

An hour more, and he was in Mrs. Bloodgood's
drawing-room, waiting more nervously than he would
have cared to acknowledge to himself for the daughter
of the house to appear. It was the first time that she
had ever sent for him to go to her, and he was conscious of some degree of anxiety as to her motive.
Clever lawyer though he was, he dreaded her cate-
chising, particularly so, because he knew that whether
she acknowledged it to herself or not, that it was at
her instigation that he had adopted the rôle which,
with or without her approval, he was now determined
to play through to the end. The sound of a light step
on the threshold of the room checked his disturbing
speculations, and he looked up to see Shirley Bloodgood entering the room. As usual she did not permit
him to open the conversation after the preliminary
courtesies of greeting between them.

"Something very urgent made me send for you, Mr.

Murgatroyd," she began, but her lips trembled so that she stopped abruptly after adding: "I want to talk with you."

An instinct told Murgatroyd that it would be a grievous mistake not to accept without a protesting word the note of aloofness, the desire to avoid any suggestion of former intimacy that was in her tone. Rightly he told himself that the slightest advances on his part would result in adding to her distress; that however much he would like to break down the barrier that had arisen between them, he must bide his time and trust to her emotional nature to accomplish that. And he was not mistaken, for presently an impulse to speak her mind at any cost took possession of her, and she burst forth:—

"Billy, why did you take this money? Why? . . . "

Carried away by the tender accents with which she pronounced his name, Murgatroyd essayed to speak, but she interrupted him.

"Don't"—covering her ears with her hands—"don't tell me! I know you did it—because I—I—oh, why did you listen to me! I thought I knew what I was talking about," she went on, while he sought control of himself by looking away from her; "but I knew nothing of conditions; of men. I thought that a man —that you could accomplish anything you really wanted to do. But you were right. There are impos-

sibilities. I understand now—now that it's too late.
I have had my lesson. Only a few months ago you were
honest, and now you are corrupt, and I alone am responsible!"

By the time she had finished speaking Murgatroyd
had become as imperturbable as he had been at the
trial, and there was only a hint of tenderness in the
reassuring words that he now uttered.

"You must not blame yourself—" he was neither ad-
mitting nor denying the impeachment—"for anything
I may have done."

"But I do, I do," she cried bitterly. "And you must
blame me. I always thought Adam was a coward to
cast the blame on Eve. But now my sympathies are
with him—the woman was to blame then—I am to
blame now. I gave you of the apple, and you— Oh,
there would have been no apple—nothing but Eden if
I had only listened to you and you had closed your
ears to me."

"Eden," he said wistfully. "Yes, but hardly the
Eden you cared for."

Abruptly her mood changed. She lost all semblance
of calm, and her voice rang with a scorn that, before
she ceased, seemed to include him as well as herself.

"What do I care for success or failure! I could cut
my tongue out for telling you that my father was a
failure. A failure! Why, I know that not only was

he not a failure, but that he was really great! A man in the highest sense of the word—and that's all I want you to be. I don't care an iota that you should be a senator—I don't want you to be a senator. I have sent for you to-night to tell you so—to stop for good and all the thing I set in motion." She was silent for an instant; and then suddenly with a quick return to gentleness, and with appeal in her eyes, she murmured: "I want you to come back—come back."

In turn he murmured words that sounded to her like "to you."

Shirley shook her head as though that were a thing out of the question.

' "No, to your honest self," she said earnestly but kindly. "To the Billy Murgatroyd that was."

For a moment they looked steadily into each other's eyes. From the time of Miriam's exposure of him in the court-room there had never been any admission, any concession on Murgatroyd's part. Nor was there any now; but unknown to himself, there was an air of appeal, not wholly free from anxiety even, for her face was again showing signs of hardness as he spoke:—

"I can hardly do that. I cannot stop. And if I should—where is the inducement? You have no apple to offer me; you are beyond my reach."

And as if to disprove his own words, an impulse of

adoration, too powerful to be checked, seized him, and he caught her hand and pressed it.

A brief moment only Shirley allowed it to rest in his, then slowly withdrew it; and her action told him plainer than words that there was to be nothing further between them—she was through with him—she must despise him. As an evangelist, as the good friend she had sent for him, but as lovers—no, that was all over. And yet, had she faltered once, had she but opened her arms to him, if only for the last time, Murgatroyd could not tell what he would have done. In all probability he would have suffered exile—sack-cloth and ashes for his huge misdeed.

And the girl! Shirley felt, knew that there could be no compromise. Murgatroyd must purge himself, even though it involved a lifetime of shame. And after he had yielded up his shameless gains, what then? Shirley did not know—she could not tell. But it was not given to Murgatroyd to know that he was the subject of her perplexities; nor could he read, as he should have, any hope in the words which she now spoke:—

"And if I am out of your reach—it's your own fault. If you had been half the man I thought, you would never have listened to me. But you never cared for me, even though you said so," Shirley said, casting her eyes down, not daring to look him in the face.

"What you did, you did for yourself and not for me. You were weak from the start. Any man who would surrender his honesty even for a woman is not a man. I see now that I ought not to have sent for you. I take back everything I have said." She paused, and then concluded with a little shake of the head:—

"I wouldn't marry you now if you were the last man on earth!"

Both rose to their feet. Habit, perhaps, rather than any regret for her words, induced her to dismiss him with a tender expression on her face. And Murgatroyd bowed low over the hand she offered him, pressed it and without a word of protest went out of the room. With his departure went out the last glimmer of hope that he would ever return to his better self. Nothing could stop him now. As for Shirley? The moment the door closed on him she sank with a moan into a chair.

＊　　　＊　　　＊　　　＊　　　＊

Thorne took an appeal from the verdict of conviction. He had been careful to take exception to each bit of questionable evidence.

"I think," he assured Mrs. Challoner, "that I have found more than one hook to hang a hat on. It looks to me like a reversal."

"I am sure it will be," she replied.

Her assurance was the same assurance that had sustained her in the trial. There was still that mysterious something that Thorne could not understand. She seemed the incarnation of hope.

"What do you think, chief?" asked McGrath of Murgatroyd, one day after the appeal had been argued.

Murgatroyd shrugged his shoulders.

"That verdict will stick," was his only comment.

"By the way," said McGrath, "Pemmican keeps mum up there in jail; but he's getting restless as thunder. He wants to know how soon you're going to try him on this gambling charge."

Murgatroyd smiled.

"In due course," he returned, "but you can tell Pemmican unofficially that the quickest way for him to get on trial—or in fact the quickest way for him to get off without trial—to get out of jail, is to let me know the name of the man higher up. I'm looking for John Doe, and I expect to keep Pemmican under lock and key until I get him. You understand?"

"He sure does kick," laughed McGrath.

Shirley and Miriam and even Challoner watched the course of events with great interest. Miriam's mouth was sealed upon the question of the bribe, but Challoner absorbed what he had heard in the court-room, and hazy though it had been, he noted that Miriam's manner was still hopeful, in fact, certain. Shirley,

too, felt, rather than knew, that Murgatroyd had removed from himself not the taint of bribery, but the
violation of his compact. She felt the thing was cut
and dried.

One day the Clerk of the Court of Errors and Appeals placed in the hands of a special messenger a
document some five pages long. It was a carbon copy.

"Take that to the prosecutor of the pleas," he commanded, "and tell him it's advance. The original,"
he added, "will be on file to-morrow."

Murgatroyd received and read it with inward satisfaction. As he was perusing it, Mixley rushed into
his private room, and yelled in alarm:—

"Chief! Chief! Look at this!" He, too, held in his
hand a document composed of several sheets of yellow
paper, scribbled over with a soft, black, lead-pencil.
"It's from the warden—" he whispered.

Murgatroyd laid down his carbon copy and took
Mixley's yellow sheets. He read the first page and
rose to his feet.

"When did all this happen, Mixley?" he asked in a
tense voice, with difficulty restraining his excitement.

"About an hour ago."

"Who was the keeper that took this down?"

"Jennings."

Murgatroyd tapped the yellow sheets impatiently,
and asked:—

"How did he kill himself?"

"Cyanide! Smuggled in somehow, nobody knows."

Murgatroyd read the yellow sheets again.

"Great Cæsar!" he exclaimed.

Mixley, still lingering, now asked:—

"Any news from the Court of Errors and Appeals?"

Murgatroyd nodded.

"Here's their opinion—just handed down."

"Reversal?"

Murgatroyd shook his head.

"No. Affirmed. By the way, Mixley," he added, "take this carbon copy over to Thorne, will you? He'll want to see it."

"Shall I tell him?" faltered Mixley.

"Tell him nothing," Murgatroyd replied. "Officially I know nothing of this other thing. I'll investigate it first, then I can talk to him."

That very day, Thorne, disappointed as he was, sent a copy of the opinion up to Mrs. Challoner, without comment. Later over the phone he told her:—

"There is no hope."

But Miriam Challoner was not downcast. She had doubted once; but now she held to her faith in Murgatroyd; she knew that Murgatroyd would keep his word. Shirley, though, shook her head. She felt that Challoner was doomed. But when Thorne told her,

she begged him not to tell Challoner until it was absolutely necessary.

And also on that same day Murgatroyd jumped into a cab and rode off on a tour of private inspection.
Entering a large building he asked:—

"I want to see Jennings, if you please."

The next day he sent for Thorne.

"Before making things public, Thorne," he said, "I
wanted you to read that."

Thorne read with bulging eyes the yellow sheets that
were thrust before him. Over and over again he read
them; then he leaned over and touched Murgatroyd
on the arm, saying:—

"Don't make it public."

"Why not?"

"There are political reasons—many of them,"
pleaded Thorne.

"But it's bound to leak out——"

"Never mind. I don't want it made public." Thorne
seemed terribly uneasy.

But again Murgatroyd persisted:—

"What of Mrs. Challoner?"

"I'll take care of Mrs. Challoner," responded Thorne.
"Just leave the whole thing to me. I'll see that everything is done."

"I'll go with you before the Court at any time you
please," said Murgatroyd.

And that very day they did go before the Court. The Court opened its eyes and heard what they had to say.

"Well, well!" exclaimed the Court.

A little while afterward Broderick and Thorne sat closeted. Every crisis found them with their heads together.

"Broderick," said the lawyer, "this is going to hurt Cradlebaugh's more than ever. The Challoner case has jumped from the frying pan into the fire." His grip tightened on Broderick. "This thing has got to be hushed up."

"If it's got to be, it can be," declared the politician.

"But there's the Court order?"

Broderick grinned as he said:—

"There's men has got to file it—men that know how to file papers so blamed far in the pigeon-holes that even a newspaper man can't crawl in after 'em. They'll do just as I say."

"Somebody's bound to find it out."

"Not if I stretch out this hand," answered Broderick. "That there hand has covered a multitude of sins." He squinted at Thorne. "But there's just one person I'm afraid of in this thing."

Thorne's nod seemed to say:

"Murgatroyd."

Broderick shook his head.

"No, not a bit of it. You take my word for it, Mur-

gatroyd will never open his mouth again on the subject of the Challoner case. He took that cash—he
can't fool me!"

Thorne sighed:—

"You think we're safe with him?"

Broderick dismissed the subject of the prosecutor
with a wave of the hand.

"Mrs. Challoner is the fly in the ointment."

Thorne, in turn, quite as vigorously dissented:—

"You're wrong there. I'll handle Mrs. Challoner. If
she ever asks questions, I'll answer her with the right
kind of answers. Don't worry, Broderick," and looking at his watch, added: "You'd better be about it
and do your little part."

"I'll do mine as soon as you do yours."

"What's mine now?"

Broderick held out his hand, and said:—

"A little cheque, counsellor."

And again on that very day the doors of the big
building that Murgatroyd had visited opened wide.
From them there stepped forth a man—no, four men
—four men laden heavily. With these four men was
a fifth, but he was unseen. Between them, in the full
light of day, the four men carried a long, oak box,
carried it quietly but swiftly, and swung it suddenly
into a battered-looking hearse.

"That's the end of him!" they said among themselves.

XII

Somewhere on the East Side, beyond Gramercy Park
and Irving Place, with their beautiful old houses; beyond Stuyvesant Square, once equally famous for the
princely hospitality of its residents; still further on
in that section which lies toward the river, where the
women and children as well as the men toil unceasingly
for the bare necessities of life, where evidences of poverty and suffering are all about, and which is com-
monly termed "the slums"; somewhere there, we say,
in one of the smaller tenement buildings, some months
later, Miriam Challoner, one time wealthy and fashionable woman of society, took refuge.

Within this new-found home—a nest consisting of
two rooms—everything was scrupulously neat; but
except for a small gilt chair that caught the rays of
the sunlight, and that seemed fully as incongruous to
its surroundings as was the woman herself, there was
nothing in its furnishings to remind one of former
prosperity. In a far corner of the adjoining room
was a stove on which a frugal meal was cooking, sending its odour throughout the small apartment—a meal
that in former days she would not have thought possible even for her servants. At the window of this
room,—which was bedroom and living-room com-

bined,—upon a small table was a typewriter, before which sat Miriam Challoner, clad in a sombre dress that was almost nun-like in its severity. She was pale, and on her face was the look of a woman acquainted with grief.

She read as she wrote:—

"Now this indenture witnesseth,— comma,— that the said party of the first part,— comma,— for the better securing the payment of the said sum of money mentioned in the condition of the said bond or obligation,— comma,— with interest thereon,— comma,— according to the true intent and meaning thereof,— semicolon,— and also for and in consideration of the sum of one dollar,— comma,— to him in hand well and duly paid——"

Suddenly she halted and fingered the copy lying on the table at her right.

"Twenty more pages—I can't do them now . . . " she muttered half-aloud, and crossing the room unsteadily, threw herself upon the bed—a cheap bed that groaned and creaked as if it felt her weight upon it.

" . . . tired—I'm so tired," she moaned, as she lay there supinely for some time. All of a sudden, she sat bolt upright in bed, for the sound of a timid knock on the door had reached her ears; but thinking, perhaps, that she had been dreaming, she waited until the knock was repeated, and only then did she cry out:—

"Well? What is it?"

There was no answer. A moment more, and she was at the door confronting a man and a woman, both gaily caparisoned. They stood hand in hand, sheepishly, smilingly, the woman looking more like some guilty child, who was being brought to task by an over-indulgent parent. For a brief second, that seemed interminably long to Mrs. Challoner waiting for them to speak, they stood thus; and it was not until they called her name that she recognised them.

"Mrs. Challoner—we thought—" they stammered in chorus.

"Why, it's Stevens," Mrs. Challoner broke in, at last, "and you too, Foster!" and the colour instantly went flying from her lips to her cheeks.

"Yes, ma'am," again came in chorus from Stevens and Foster, late butler and lady's maid to Mrs. Challoner, and still hand in hand.

"Oh, Mrs. Challoner," then spoke up Foster, "what do you think? We've gone and got married!"

"Married? Foster! Stevens! Why, yes, of course, you do look like bride and groom," said Mrs. Challoner, her heart for the moment sinking at all this happiness; and then: "Come in, and do tell me all about it."

"Mrs. Challoner," quickly put in Stevens, as they came into the room, "she pestered me 'till I had to marry her—there was no getting rid of her."

A faint smile crossed Miriam's face, and soon she found herself entering into the happiness of this couple, just as she would have done in the old days; and so well did they suceed in making her forget her present position, that she was actually trying to determine what would be a most appropriate and, at the same time, a most pleasing gift to them. Absorbed, therefore, in her laudable perplexities, it was quite a long time before she fully realised that there were but two chairs, a fact which had not escaped the eyes of these well-trained servants, who still remained standing in the centre of the room; and when, at last, the truth dawned upon her, it was with the greatest difficulty that she kept back the tears, as half-coaxingly, half-authoritatively she prevailed upon the terribly embarrassed pair to occupy them, while she seated herself on the edge of the bed.

"Yes, ma'am," resumed Foster, determined to tell all there was to tell, "there were about six men that I could have married as well as not—not like Stevens, but big, fine-looking men, every one of them. But Stevens here got in such a way about it, that I felt sorry for him, and I gave them all the go-by for him. But there's one thing certain," she concluded with a sigh, "I didn't marry for good looks, nor for money either, for that matter."

"You married for love, Foster, and that is so much

better," commented Mrs. Challoner, revelling in their joy.

"I dare say," conceded Foster, "that I'll come to love him in time."

"Yes, ma'am," put in Stevens, eager to get in a word, "she bothered me until I finally succumbed, though my tastes were—well, ma'am, I must admit that I like 'em a little plumper."

To Miriam Challoner, it was indeed a treat to hear their good-natured banter. Presently she asked with interest:—

"What are you doing now, Stevens?"

"He's a *shof*er, ma'am," spoke up Foster quickly with pride.

"A what?" inquired Mrs. Challoner.

"A show*fure*, ma'am," corrected Stevens with dignity. "She'll learn in time . . . I'm working for Bernhardt, the brewer—a hundred dollars a month, ma'am."

"Indeed! So you're a chauffeur, and earning one hundred dollars a month!" exclaimed Miriam Challoner. "Why that's fine!" And a hundred dollars never seemed larger to any one's eyes.

Stevens shrugged his shoulders as he answered in an offhand manner:—

"What's a hundred——"

"A hundred dollars a month!" again sighed Mrs.

Challoner; and fell to planning what that sum would
do for her.

Suddenly, Stevens broke in upon her thoughts,
with:—

"What a cosy little place you have, ma'am!" And
turning to Foster: "I hope we can have just such a
little place as this some day. It's great!"

"I'd know in a minute, ma'am, that you had arranged things," said Foster, falling in readily with
her husband's enthusiasm.

For an instant Mrs. Challoner shaded her eyes with
her hand. The room, she knew only too well, was the
very last expression of poverty, yet these two had
shown a delicacy and kindness that she had supposed
to be far beyond them.

"But where's your manners, Foster?" suddenly demanded Stevens. "Surely you might put your hands
to fixing up that supper on the stove! Do now, like a
good girl . . . "

"Indeed, she must not—and in that lovely gown, too
—besides, there is really nothing to do," Miriam Challoner quickly returned, for she could not bear to have
Foster see what was cooking there.

"Oh, I'll be very careful, besides, it will seem natural
to be doing things for you," persisted her former maid.

"Yes, take a look at the roast baking there in the
oven, anyway," said Stevens; and no sooner had his

wife turned her steps toward the kitchen, than he quickly leaned over to Mrs. Challoner, and thrusting something in her hand, he said in an undertone:—

"She's treasurer, ma'am, and I have to account for every penny; but this she knows nothing about. It's for you—please take it."

In an instant Mrs. Challoner was on her feet, and putting the money back in his hand, she exclaimed:—

"Why, Stevens, I can't take this! Really, I have money . . . "

For a moment Stevens's eyes wandered about the poorly furnished room, betraying his thoughts to the contrary. This was not lost on Mrs. Challoner, who immediately went on to explain:—

"Yes, Stevens, and I earn it, too." And she pointed to the typewriter with a certain pride.

"I beg your pardon, ma'am," said her former butler contritely, returning the money quickly to his pocket. "Only, don't let her know . . . "

When Foster came back into the room, they were standing over the typewriter, Mrs. Challoner explaining its mechanism.

"Oh, what a fine thing it is to have an education!" exclaimed the young wife, looking sharply at her husband; but her penetrating glance was too much for Stevens, and turning quickly on his heel, he proceeded to rearrange the chairs.

"Hey, there!" suddenly called out Foster. "Why aren't you more of a gentleman—where's your manners? Run along there, like a good fellow, and put some water in the tea-kettle!" Stevens lost no time in obeying; then drawing close to Mrs. Challoner, Foster whispered:—

"This is for you, ma'am, but don't let Stevens know, for he's as tight as a drum-head."

"But," protested Mrs. Challoner, looking at the other in astonishment.

"Please, I saved it just for you," insisted Foster, with a look of disappointment on her face.

"Really, Foster, I don't need it," declared Mrs. Challoner stoutly but kindly. "I can't take it. Some day, perhaps, I may need money, and then I'll send for you." And then quietly changing the subject: "How fresh you look, Foster! And what a man you've married! There is no need to ask if you are happy, for——"

"Well," said Stevens, approaching them, "we must be going now, for Bernhardt will be waiting for us."

"It was good of you to see us, ma'am," said Foster, putting out her hand, just as she had seen the ladies do in the old days at the big Challoner house on the Avenue.

"So you married for love," said Miriam Challoner, as they started to go.

"Well, *he* did," conceded Foster.

"*She* did, ma'am," corrected Stevens; and presently they were sailing down the street like a pair of lovers "walking out" on a Sunday afternoon.

"One hundred dollars a month!" sighed Miriam, re-seating herself at the typewriter. "And they were going to give me twenty-five dollars—the faithful dears!"

Once more engrossed in her work, she did not hear the door-bell, which had been ringing persistently. At the end of a page she paused and bent her head low over her work.

" . . . for love," she mused, half-aloud.

Meanwhile, her caller, determined to be admitted, had stolen softly into the room, though it was not until she stood beside her that she attracted Miriam's attention. For a moment Miriam glared hard at her; she could not believe her own eyes; then, suddenly rising to her feet, she cried half-joyfully, half-regretfully:—

"Why, it's Shirley Bloodgood! Oh, why did you come! You must not stay, you must not see . . . "

"Why did you hide from me?" quickly returned Shirley. "I have searched for you for months, and it was only yesterday that I learned from Stevens where you were, who, by the way, had orders not to reveal your whereabouts. You might as well have moved a thousand miles away, as everybody thinks you have."

Miriam sighed weakly.

"It takes money to move a thousand miles away," she protested feebly.

"You are like a needle in a hay stack over here," continued Shirley.

"But why did you come?" Miriam kept on protesting. "Why, Shirley . . ."

Shirley stretched forth her arms, saying:—

"And you didn't want to see me!"

"Yes, yes," cried Miriam, suddenly catching Shirley and clinging to her affectionately. "Yes, I have wanted you to come so much, but I hoped you never would see this!" And she spread out her arms as though to exhibit the room.

"What a poor opinion you have of me! Why, Miriam, if I wanted to see handsome apartments, I need not have taken all this trouble to find you. No, indeed, I value your friendship too highly to desert you on account of this."

And now the two women fell to talking about things past and present. After a while, it was Shirley who delicately broached the subject of Laurie.

"And Laurie—how is he?" she asked.

Miriam's eyes kindled for an instant, but its fire soon died out.

"Poor boy," she answered, "he's under such a strain. It's a wonder he doesn't break down. He's so good and kind through it all, too. He's a fine fellow, now," she went on with great enthusiasm.

"Let me see," said Shirley, reminiscently, "his conviction was reversed on appeal, wasn't it?"

"Why, no; don't you remember that it was affirmed —affirmed . . . "

"I do remember now. And it was that day or the next one that you ran away from me, you bad girl, and I've never seen you since. Affirmed—affirmed," she mused; and then suddenly leaned forward and inquired eagerly:—

"Then how did he get off?"

Miriam shrugged her shoulders.

"I don't know," she said, "nobody knows; not even Laurie knows that. One day after the affirmance, the jail doors were opened, and he was free—that's all— and he came back to me."

"Surely Murgatroyd knows," said Shirley.

"Oh, yes, of course he knows; but we have never asked any questions. Why should we? I shall never forget Murgatroyd though—I remember him in my prayers. He was honest; he kept his word——"

Shirley smiled a grim smile.

"Murgatroyd, the man with a *price!* Well, I sup-

pose it's just as well that there are people in this world
who can be bought now and then."

"I have never forgiven myself," sighed Miriam.

Shirley looked up at her questioningly.

"You? What for, pray?"

"For blurting out in the court-room what I did when
the jury found Laurie guilty. Why, it was abomi-
nable! it was treachery! I had promised, don't you
see?"

"That was clever in Murgatroyd," admitted Shirley. "He would have been a fool to acquit Laurie on
that trial. Oh, yes," she added, with a sneer, "he's
clever, all right!"

Mrs. Challoner straightened up.

"Fortunately my outbreak did no great harm; nobody believed me."

"Except myself," observed Shirley, "and Murgatroyd!"

"Even Laurie didn't believe me," went on Miriam,
"until—well, I don't know whether he's quite sure
about it to-day. We never discuss the subject, anyway. It's barely possible," she said, flushing, "that he
thinks we spent the money long ago."

There was a pause that was a trifle embarrassing to
both women. Miriam was the first to speak.

"Murgatroyd is making a name for himself, isn't
he?"

Shirley threw up her hands in indignation.

"Who wouldn't, with that stolen money to back him!" she exclaimed fiercely.

Miriam shook her head.

"He's doing good work with it. He's breaking up the organisation—the inside ring. I'm sure that the effect of his work is felt even over here." And then she added vehemently: "But his best work will be over when he has succeeded in breaking Cradlebaugh's. When he does that——"

"After he downs Cradlebaugh's," interrupted Shirley, "if he ever does, I hope he'll down himself. That's my wish for Billy Murgatroyd!"

"Murgatroyd is honest," protested Miriam.

Shirley smiled a hard smile.

"You mistake his motive, Miriam. He's ambitious —frightfully ambitious. Why even now he's planning to go to the Senate," declared Shirley; but she did not add that it was she who had put the idea into his head. "Think of Billy Murgatroyd's being Senator! He'll ask a billion the next time he's bought, instead of a million!" she wound up, scornfully.

"You forget," quietly but forcibly reminded Miriam, "that I stand up for Murgatroyd."

"Poor Miriam," sighed Shirley to herself, "she always was easily fooled." A moment later, she exclaimed: "A typewriter!"

"I don't wonder at your surprise," said Miriam.
"But it is easy work and I like it immensely. I work
for different people in the neighbourhood," she went
on to explain. "A real estate dealer, one or two
lawyers, it's——"

She broke off abruptly, for they were interrupted by
a faint whistle.

"It's the speaking tube," said Miriam, tremblingly;
but the next instant she was in a little dark alcove
calling down the tube.

Meanwhile, Shirley allowed her gaze to wander about
the apartment; nothing had escaped her notice, not
even the cooking that was going on in the kitchen.

"Somebody whistled up the tube," said Miriam, returning, "but I couldn't get an answer. I can't
imagine who it is."

Then suddenly for the third time that afternoon, the
outer door opened; but this time it was thrust open with
great violence, and James Lawrence Challoner came
into the room with the stamp of the gutter upon
him.

Shirley was dumbfounded. Quickly her mind went
back to that afternoon, long ago it seemed, when he
had come home after the tragedy. Then, it is true,
he was unkempt, soiled, but now . . . and she
asked herself whether it were possible that Miriam
could not see the man as he really was. The answer

was immediately forthcoming, for Miriam went over and caught him in her embrace.

"Poor Laurie, tired, aren't you, dear?" she said fondly; and then turning toward the girl: "Here's an old friend of ours—Shirley Bloodgood!"

"So I see," he growled; and without more ado he turned to Miriam and demanded gruffly:—

"Well, where's your money? I've got to have some money right away."

Miriam fumbled for an instant at her waist. She did this more for appearance' sake than anything else, for she well knew that she had none to give him. Every day she had given him about everything she made.

"Yes, Laurie," she faltered, "yes, of course." And turning to Shirley, added by way of apology for him: "Such an ordeal as Laurie has been through—such a strain."

Shirley was in a panic. What she had seen was enough to make her heart-sick.

"Oh," she suddenly exclaimed, "I have forgotten all about father! I left him alone—I simply must go now. You don't know how glad . . . " And turning to Challoner, she held out her hand to him. But ignoring her completely, he again said to his wife:—

"Miriam, where is that money?"

"Laurie is such a business man now, Shirley," said Miriam, smiling bravely at the girl.

But the contempt which Shirley felt for the man before her was too great for words; and she merely repeated:—

"Yes, I must be going now!"

Half way across the room she halted, hesitated for a moment, and then finally opening her purse, took from it a fifty dollar bill.

"There, Miriam," she said with a note of relief, "I have been meaning for a long time to pay back that fifty dollars I borrowed from you a few years ago—when I was so hard up for money. I'm ashamed not to have returned it before; and it's just like you not to remind me. There, dear, I've put it on the chiffonier; and now, good-bye!" And she was gone before Miriam could even protest against her action.

For Miriam knew quite as well as did Shirley that there never had been such a loan between them; and rushing out into the hall, she called to the other to come back; but Shirley by this time was well out of hearing.

"She's gone!" Miriam declared forlornly, panting from her fruitless chase.

Shirley's flight did not worry Challoner. He took advantage of Miriam's temporary absence to steal to the chiffonier and to seize the fifty dollar bill. Miriam entered the room in time to see him thrusting it into his pocket, and cried out angrily:—

"Laurie, I wish you to put that back! We are not thieves; it does not belong to us; and I'm going to send it back to Shirley."

Challoner grinned.

"What do you think I am?" he finally asked. "A fool?"

He tried to pass her; she blocked his way, and repeated:—

"I want you to put that back!"

"I have got to have some money," he maintained sulkily, stowing it still further in his trousers pocket.

"Give me that fifty dollar bill, I say!" went on Miriam, clutching at him.

"No, I will not!" returned her husband, stubbornly, and sought to escape; but she caught him by the arm and pulled him back. He tried to wrench himself away; but for once her strength was superior to his. She was beside herself with sudden anger, with shame, with ignominy, with agony.

"You give that bill to me!" she said through her closed teeth.

"You let me go!" he growled, almost jerking himself out of her grasp. Then followed a struggle that was short, sharp but decisive, inasmuch as he finally succeeded in wrenching himself free from her. And now, turning quickly, he smote her with his clenched hand full in the face.

Miriam staggered back; her eyes opened wide in humiliated astonishment.

"Oh! Laurie!" she cried, not with physical pain, although there upon her face, now red, now white, was a broad, blotched mark—the bruise that the brute had left there.

He made a movement to go; but again she was in time to prevent him; for quick as a flash she had darted to the chiffonier, opened the top drawer and drawn forth a weapon.

"Stop!" she cried in a hard voice. "Don't you dare to leave this room with that money!"

Challoner blinked at her stupidly.

"What are you going to do?" he demanded.

Miriam laughed hysterically.

"What am I going to do? I know what you're going to do! You're going to bring that fifty dollars back here to me!"

"Indeed? Well I'm not!" reiterated Challoner.

Miriam tapped the pistol in her hand.

"Do you see this?"

He grunted fearlessly.

"Well, what of it?"

"Give me that money," she insisted, approaching him. As yet she had not levelled the weapon; and Challoner, seeing his opportunity, started once more.

"*Stop!*" It was a new voice that spoke now: the blow that had struck her face had suddenly transformed her into a desperate woman.

Challoner stopped; for he saw the weapon trained upon him. Again, without affecting her aim, she tapped it.

"Listen to me!" she cried, her voice growing hoarser as she went on, "this thing has been responsible for one murder, and now, Lawrence Challoner, I'm going to kill you with it. It's the last straw that breaks the camel's back. I hate you! I despise you!" she raged. "I loved you once, I have always loved you until now; you loved me once, too, I know—though other people thought that you had married me for my money. But I knew different—you couldn't fool me about that! And it was because of that love that I have lived for you and nothing else. You have been everything in the world to me—my god, almost. But it is all over now! I'm through with you, and I'm going to have you thrown like some soiled rag into the gutters of humanity—where you belong!"

She paused for breath, but not once did her weapon falter.

"There are two things," she resumed, "that stand out in my memory just now. The first is the night when you did not come home! Do you remember that night?— No—there were too many of them later on!

But I have never forgotten that night I spent in the torture chamber! It was a white night for me."

Again she paused, and her voice deepened as she said:—

"Lawrence Challoner, the time will come when you will wail and whine and wonder why I don't come to you—why it is not my footsteps that you hear! But you will wait for me through a long, long night, and I shall never come . . .

"Oh, it does me good when I recall the day that Prosecutor Murgatroyd told those twelve men the kind of a man you were," she declared scornfully. "It does me good, too, to recall how you writhed under the lash and quivered when he cut you to the quick. But now I'm going to do more to you than you ever did to me —more than Murgatroyd did to you . . . "

She stopped, and then went on mercilessly:—

"I'm going to tear your soul out—yes, you've got a soul, or I would never have gone down into the depths with you! But now I'm through serving you without receiving so much as a smile," she continued fiercely, her body swaying, but her aim still true. "I don't ask for my rights or my just dues; a smile and a kind word now and then is all I ask. My pride is not all gone; I'd like to be proud of you just once. I lie about you to my friends—to my dearest friends

—and you convict me with the miserable truth! I
clung to you through all your vices, I clung to you
even when you killed, I clung to you because I knew
that somewhere within you there was something that
clamoured for me, that clung to my affection. But
feeble as it was, it is dead now. And you are the shell,
the ugly hulk, a thing without the soul that I cared
for! But I'm through with you—I'm going to kill you
—don't you move—I'm through with you—
through—" The next moment she dropped the
weapon, and it fell clattering to the floor.

"No, no," she cried, apparently calm now. "I won't
kill you—I wouldn't be guilty of such a thing. You're
not worth it," she burst out into a wild laugh.
"You're not worth it—no—no—no—" she cried,
trailing off into hysteria.

At that instant Shirley Bloodgood once more entered the room. Some instinct had brought her back
again.

"Miriam!" she exclaimed.

Miriam burst forth into another wild laugh, and
then threw herself into the arms of the girl, where she
lay unconscious for some moments.

"She's fainted," said Shirley, glancing at Challoner,
accusingly.

Challoner stood stupidly where he was for an instant.
Then he thrust his hand into his trousers pocket and

pulled out a fifty dollar bill, saying in a new strange tone:—

"Shirley, I took this fifty dollar bill from the drawer over there—you'd better take it—it belongs to you."

The girl took it wonderingly.

"I'll take care of her," Challoner went on, gently taking the form of his young wife from Shirley and holding her in his arms.

It was thus that Shirley Bloodgood left them; and as the door closed on her, Challoner leaned over Miriam and stroked her face and kissed her affectionately while the tears rolled down his cheeks. That same night she was taken to a hospital with a raging fever.

XIII

THE following morning, James Lawrence Challoner
did that which he had never done since his marriage:
he started out to look for a job. Something, which
he could not explain, was forcing him to try to get
work; but had he been given to self-analysis, he would
have known that it was Miriam's wrath in her ad-
versity that had kindled into flame the flickering, dying spark of his manhood.

Until now, Challoner had assumed that work was to
be had by any man for the mere asking of it; but he
was surprised, startled, shocked, to find that it was
not; that is to say, the clerkships and such work as he
thought would be to his liking; and each night he returned to his cheerless, lonely room in the tenement,
sore, leg-weary, after a long unsuccessful quest.
Work? Little by little he was learning that there was
no work "lying round loose" for the James Lawrence
Challoners of this world! And yet he persevered.

"I must find something to do," he kept saying over
and over again to himself.

And then one day at the end of two weeks he found
himself at the end of a long line of Italian labourers
who were seeking employment.

When the foreman came to Challoner, he called out in surprise:—

"What do you want?"

"Work!" replied the man inside the shell of Challoner.

"With the 'ginneys'?"

"With the 'ginneys,'" assented Challoner.

The foreman stared.

"All right," he said, after thinking a bit, "let's have your name."

For a brief second Challoner hesitated; there was a new light in his eyes when he said:—

"Challoner—J. L."

And all that day he worked—worked with his hands, and with his feet—worked with the gang tamping concrete. It is a simple enough process when one stands aside and looks at it; but after two hours of it, Challoner thought he would drop in his tracks.

It so happened that his work was on a new department store going up in town. Concrete suddenly had come into prominence as a building material. Challoner and the gang stood inside a wooden mould some two or three feet wide and as long as the wall which they were building; another gang poured in about them a mixture of sand, cement, and stone. Sand, cement, and stone meant nothing to Challoner, except that when those three things were mixed with water and dumped down into his trench, he had to lift up his tamper and pound, pound, pound the mixture into solidity, in order to fill the crevices, and to make the wall hard and smooth. Meanwhile, his feet were soaked; his boots were caked with cement; his hands were blistered frightfully; and his face was burned by the sun. Nevertheless, Challoner sweated, toiled on.

For days after this first day of labour he was stiff, lame, and sore all over. In his soul he wanted to die; but he lived on. And then, much to his amazement, he found that the harder he worked, the better he felt: the poison of his dissolute living was working toward the surface.

At last the day came when the doctors allowed him to visit Miriam in the hospital.

"I've got a job, dear," he whispered to her. That was all he told her then; but those five words were a history to Miriam.

Another day when again visiting her at the hospital, he told her how they mixed the stuff, how they made the wooden moulds, and about the crowds that gathered around them, for the process was a new one.

"People don't believe in it, don't think it will stand," he said, watching her closely.

On her face came the interested look that he so desired, and she asked:—

"Will it, Laurie?"

"Like a rock," he assured her.

But Challoner was ignorant of the danger then, for he had not reckoned with the human element in the character of construction. All he knew was that he worked from morning until night at the cheapest of all cheap, unskilled labour.

After a little while Miriam put out a thin hand and let it rest in his, saying:—

"How much do they give you, dear?"

Not without a suggestion of pride in his voice, the man answered:—

"A dollar and a half a day."

A dollar and a half a day! Surely a mere pittance; and yet the woman's face was radiant with joy.

It was not long before Challoner found that his arms and back and shoulders were perceptibly enlarging. At first it was merely at his physical strength that he rejoiced; but this, in turn, soon made way for a greater joy: he realised that his soul was surging back into his body; he had driven it out, but it would not stay away.

From time to time, Challoner noted that the tamping was developing him too much on one side. With the long broom handle, the weight down at the end, his downward stroke had been a right-handed one. So now he tried using force from the left side. And with that Challoner made a discovery!

After many experiments it had been gradually borne in upon him that light but incessant and vigorous tamping in one spot was more effective than the heavy, battering strokes employed by the Italians. The stuff was smooth and slippery when it first came in, and, consequently, all that was necessary was something to induce the stones to slip gently into solidity.

"If the tampers were only light enough," he argued to himself, "a fellow could almost use two of them, one in each hand."

And so he tried it with the two tampers that were on the work; but they proved to be too heavy. Then, one night, he made a pair of lighter ones and experimented with them. It was too much of a strain; he could not handle them satisfactorily. Somehow, the work needed the concentrated effort of two arms.

All one night he sat up trying to figure it out. "And yet," he assured himself repeatedly, "I'm on the right track." And so it proved. For at four o'clock in the morning the idea came.

"I've got it!" he exclaimed, jumping to his feet. "A pump handle!"

A week later, Challoner rigged up a simple contrivance depending upon strong leverage—one that would do the work of a man much more easily.

"It will do the work of *two*," he told himself.

But when Challoner had taken it to the works, the authorities refused him permission to use it.

"This here is a real job. We haven't time to monkey with things like that!" they told him with a sneer.

But Challoner was not to be turned aside so easily; and still he persisted:—

"It will do the work of two."

Now it must not be supposed that Challoner was of a particularly inventive nature; not a bit of it. Simply, he was a man of average intelligence, working at a dollar and a half a day. His intelligence, however, was superior to that of the men about him. Moreover, his brain was independently busy, while his hands worked.

So now he rigged himself up a small trial mould, bought some sand and cement and rock, and demonstrated the superiority of his pump-handle contrivance with its strong leverage, its regularity and its strong, steady beat, beat, beat, with two light tampers upon adjacent spots. When they knocked off the mould, these same authorities found that Challoner was right: this bit of concrete wall was as solid as if it had been cut out of smooth azoic rock. So they called out:—

"All right, Challoner—try it on!"

Challoner tried it on the big wall. It worked like a charm.

At the pay-window, at the end of the week Challoner
said:—

"I want two dollars and a half—two dollars and a
half a day, now."

"What for?" came from the voice inside.

Challoner replied firmly:—

"Because I've done the work of more than two men."
The next day he was paid at the rate of two dollars a
day.

Now he was allowed to have one of the corners all to
himself for his contrivance. The week after that they
laid off two men: Challoner now was doing the work
of three men. In fact, from that time he and his machine were made the pace-makers for the entire line of
workmen.

The boss was jubilant.

"Gee! I guess we'll get this job done on time after
all!" he was heard to say. "I thought for a while the
old man was in for a few fines sure."

Nobody else tried Challoner's device; nobody else
knew how to use it. In a way, that was a satisfaction
to him. It was a toy, something that he had created
to lighten his labours. On the other hand, he found
that in his eagerness he laboured three times as hard
as before; besides, he was even better at the work than
the Italians who knew it, had become accustomed to it,
and who were better fitted for it. And yet, there was

nothing wonderful in this contrivance of his. But
Challoner was convinced that if, sometime, he could induce the boss to put it into constant operation, it
would save that gentleman a great deal of money.
Nor did it ever enter Challoner's head to have it
patented. Its principle was that of the lever, and,
of course, even if he had tried, he could not have obtained a patent. In no way was there a dollar in
it.

"But," he told himself, "if ever I go into this concrete business, I shall insist upon its use. As a business," he went on, "what can be more profitable than
concrete? It produces a wall as solid as a rock and
as indestructible as brick. Bricklayers receive five and
six dollars a day,—and brick costs money. But this
sand, cement, stone and *unskilled* labour . . . "
Challoner could see millions in it!

Meanwhile, he was useful at two and a half dollars
a day. As we have seen, they had made him a pace-
maker; now, they determined to put his brain to work
for them: it became his duty to direct the mixing-
gang at his end of the new store.

"Don't forget, now, watch out," said the superintendent, taking him aside. "So many barrels of cement, so many barrels of sand, and so much stone.
Now say it as I told you."

'And Challoner repeated for him: so many barrels of

cement, so many barrels of sand, and so much stone. But when he was again alone, he said half aloud:—
"So, that's all there is to the concrete business!"
Challoner little knew.

The very first day that he watched the mixing process, he discovered that the mixer had put in too much rock and too much sand—and too little cement.

"Look here!" cried Challoner, "you've made a mistake! Two more barrels of cement go in there—do you understand?"

But the mixer merely grinned.

"Two more barrels of cement, I told you," persisted Challoner. The head-superintendent had given him his instructions, and Challoner meant to see that they were properly carried out.

Another grin from the mixer was all the satisfaction that he received. Instantly, Challoner leaped up on the platform and stood over the mixer. At that, the man waved his arm; his signal brought not the head-superintendent, but the general foreman of the work, who demanded gruffly:—

"What's the trouble here?"

Challoner explained in a few words.

"You blamed idiot!" burst out the raging foreman. "You leave the man alone! Do you think that he don't know how to mix concrete? Leave him alone, I say!"

But Challoner, now, was not a man to be so easily turned from his orders; and again he insisted:—

"Two more barrels of cement, I told you!"

And he kept on insisting so strenuously, that a little knot of labourers gathered around them to await the result. Finally, the foreman saw that the head-superintendent was coming toward them from far down the street.

"All right, then," he conceded reluctantly, "make it two more barrels of cement."

But that same afternoon, the foreman singled Challoner out and paid him. Then he lunged out, and striking Challoner on the shoulder lightly, he exclaimed:—

"There, you infernal jackass! You're discharged!"

"Discharged!" The exclamation fell from his lips before Challoner could check it; and notwithstanding his great disappointment, he made no further comment, but turned on his heel and left. The next day, however, he brought his case before the head-superintendent, who said:—

"If Perkins discharged you, I can't help it. I won't interfere."

"But what was I discharged for?"

"Oh, come now!" cried the superintendent; "you must know that you were discharged for stealing cement!"

Stunned for a moment, Challoner said not a word. Then slowly he began to understand. Graft! Yes, that was the solution of the matter. Cement was worth money in any market; and in the concrete business, nobody could tell,—until it was too late,—just how many barrels went into the mixture. With *bricks* —there was no doubt about bricks. A brick was good or bad; you could tell that by a trowel. But concrete was bound to be a problem henceforth to the end of time.

So it turned out that Challoner was discharged for doing the thing the foreman was guilty of doing. At the time he had little thought of resentment. It is true that he might have "peached" on the foreman, complained to the head-superintendent, and got them to test the walls with a testing-hammer. But it was too late, besides, he knew now that the head-superintendent was tarred with the same stick.

After this incident, Challoner cultivated a habit of strolling into the offices of the various dealers in the city.

"What are the proper concrete proportions?" was his request in all of them.

Charts were taken out and consulted. There was no difference of opinion: all agreed that the head-super-intendent's figures were out of the way, and by one barrel of cement.

Graft! There was no doubt about it in his mind; and
he proceeded to figure out just where the trouble lay.
On that department-store job there were several
mixers. On every mixing the head-superintendent made
one barrel of cement. There were several foremen. On
every individual mixing, the foremen, severally, made
two barrels of cement. In every mixing three barrels
of cement were left out.

"But what about the *wall?*" Challoner asked himself
when once more alone.

And so it came about that he found that in this business, of all businesses, there was a chance for an honest
man. After a little while, he found another job—
still at two dollars a day. It was beginning once more
at the bottom, and working up, yet he did it. But
the instant he had worked up, he was again confronted
with a similar situation. It was a question of "shut
up or get out!" Gradually, it is true, the burden of
the song of these men shifted slightly, and became,
"Come in with us, or keep silent."

A few more experiences of this sort, and it was given
to Challoner to perceive that he had knowledge of
these things in advance of the general public. People
looked upon concrete as something marvellous. The
agitation among the construction men, the newspaper accounts about its cheapness, together with
the wonderful results obtained by its use in

other cities, all combined to dazzle owners about to
build.

From day to day, Challoner could see the demand for
concrete increasing. He saw, too, that the price of
brick was falling off, because concrete had awakened
a new interest in the minds of the people, had aroused
their enthusiasm. Plainly, Challoner was excited. He
could see, could talk of nothing else. While Miriam
was in the hospital he had begun to talk concrete with
her; when she was convalescing and had returned to
their rooms,—they had three now,—figuratively
speaking, they had cement for breakfast and for supper. But it was his business now, and his whole mind
was concentrated upon it.

And in all this there was a singular and valuable
fact: Challoner was the only man in town,—literally
the only man, because of the circumstances of the
case,—outside of the contractors, who knew the business, and yet who had intelligence enough to understand the danger in concrete. Naturally, the contractors did not tell owners about graft. They did not
warn their customers; they took chances; and need-
less to say, the owners themselves did not know.

Challoner was quick to seize his opportunity; besides,
he was conscious that a duty rested upon him. Day
and night he scanned the papers, and when he found
a concrete contract recorded, he looked up the owner,

saw him personally and told him facts. Of course, most of this was done at night and on holidays.

"You don't say so," the owner would respond, opening wide his eyes.

But Challoner mentioned no names; he merely outlined conditions. Some contractors, he acknowledged, were honest, perhaps most of them, but many were careless. And then the foremen on these jobs unquestionably were poorly paid. Surely the temptations were great.

"You don't say so," the owner would repeat.

And when the job started, this owner would put a competent man on to oversee it. Frequently it happened that this man was J. L. Challoner. The time came when he made five dollars a day. Moreover, the time came when many of the good concrete walls in town owed their strength to him.

But even though his time was full, and money was plentiful, it did not interfere with Challoner's interest in the evolution of concrete and concrete graft; nor was he slow to recognise its value to politicians; and so when the "ring"—for there was still a "ring" in spite of the efforts of Murgatroyd—sprang its little surprise, Challoner knew what was coming.

"A new concrete hospital," said the "ring," and saw in it the thin edge of the wedge, for they foresaw a new concrete jail. Possibly they could go still further:

if they could educate the people up to it, they might
have more new concrete city buildings.

However, the new concrete hospital came first. It
was one-third finished when J. L. Challoner applied
for, and secured a job as foreman of the mixing-gang
on the east wing. The men who employed him did not
know him; if they had, they would have dismissed him
at once.

"Great Scott! The graft in cement is appalling!"
Challoner exclaimed before he had been on the work
twenty minutes. He voiced his protest; he would not
stop voicing it: for he found that the hospital was
being built chiefly of sand and broken stone.

And so it was that the superintendent said:—

"I'll have to *see* him, boys. We must have him in
with us on this."

But Challoner could not be "seen."

The superintendent shook his head, and later to the
contractors he remarked:—

"Challoner is a dangerous man, I'm afraid."

The contractors laughed.

"Oh, he'll come around, all right!" they assured him.
"They all do, after a bit."

But in this case, the superintendent happened to be
right. And the "ring,"—the inner circle of the political organisation,—descended upon Challoner like a
thousand of brick.

"Come, come," they said, "what's your game? What's your price? Name it and shut up. How many barrels of cement a day? Come, come now——"

Challoner still shook his head.

"Hang it!" they exclaimed; "he's too noisy."

Then they reasoned with him; but it did no good.

"It's a case of using force," they told each other. "To-morrow night——"

But to-morrow night never came for Challoner. The game of graft had sickened him.

"I have got to tell somebody about this," he assured himself. And then an inspiration came to him. "I know, I'll go to Murgatroyd!"

"Murgatroyd!" He shuddered as he repeated the name, for the prosecutor had been connected with the thing that had become to Challoner and his wife a subject forbidden and unmentioned.

But, nevertheless, he went to Murgatroyd.

XIV

IT is, of course, not given us to know what dreams of fame were in Murgatroyd's heart when he determined to throw down the gage at the feet of Cradlebaugh's; but, at all events, it took the best kind of courage and mettle; and certainly from the hour that he had sent for Pemmican and placed him on the rack in a vain attempt to get evidence, not to speak of the time when Mrs. Challoner exposed him in the court-room, he had never ceased his investigations of the secrets of the big gambling-house. But no sooner had he come to the conclusion that he had penetrated the mystery than he found himself in the centre of a vast maelstrom of his own creation: Cradlebaugh's was but a patch in a wilderness of riot and corruption, an incident in a series of big events; and Murgatroyd discovered that he was battling not only with a single institution, but with a huge political principle—he was at war with a big city.

Another man might have been discouraged, for millionaires, large property owners, reputable tax-payers, statesmen of the highest order, and even his best friends came to him and begged him to call off his crusade; but he only shook his head. As he proceeded, he made the discovery that a political organisation is not an organisation—it is a man; that crime is personified; and that corruption is concrete. And as the battle waged, he found himself constantly seeking his old stamping-ground—Cradlebaugh's. That, somehow, seemed to be the keystone of the edifice that he assaulted.

Then, one day, agitated, breathless but triumphant, Mixley and McGrath burst into the prosecutor's office.

"Chief," spoke out Mixley joyously, "we followed your instructions to the letter." And beckoning to his partner, "McGrath and me has got the goods!" McGrath pulled from his pocket a bulky document made up of depositions, and said:—

"This here is the report, sir."

While Murgatroyd read the document, his subordinates stood watching him with anxious eyes. Long before he had concluded they saw in his face the expression that they had waited for.

"By George, you don't mean it!" exclaimed Murgatroyd, suddenly rising to his feet and smiting his desk with terrific force.

"You can bet your bottom dollar that we do!" returned Mixley.

Murgatroyd clenched his teeth with inward satisfaction. Presently he said:—

"I've waited for this for many months."

After re-reading the report he ordered his men to go to Broderick and Thorne with the request that they come to him immediately.

An hour later Graham Thorne made his appearance, Broderick waddling in after him. Murgatroyd passed over a box of cigars.

Broderick lighted, and after puffing contentedly for a time, commented:—

"Good cigars, these. Strikes me that they're your first contribution to the campaign fund, eh?" And helping himself to three more out of the box, he tucked them away in his pocket with a wink at Murgatroyd, and asked:—

"Any Challoner money in these?"

Murgatroyd smiled grimly.

"You seem ready enough to burn it, anyhow," he answered. And puffing also on his cigar he said, "I wanted to have a little confidential talk with you gentlemen."

Broderick nudged Thorne and remarked:—

"Perhaps the prosecutor's goin' to divvy with us, Thorne!"

Murgatroyd smiled and laughed; but somehow the smile and laugh did not include Thorne.

"I'm not going to divvy up, as you call it, just yet —not *just* yet," he replied, pointedly.

Broderick shut his eyes and digested the glance and

the reply. Both seemed to satisfy him, for he nodded genially.

Rising now, and sitting lazily across one corner of his desk, Murgatroyd turned his attention to Thorne.

"I wanted to have a talk," he said casually, "with the man who owns Cradlebaugh's."

Thorne looked about the room, then he inquired innocently:—

"He doesn't seem to have arrived as yet—where is he?"

Murgatroyd blew a cloud of smoke toward the ceiling, and answered:—

"Oh, yes he has—his name is Graham Thorne." Murgatroyd could see the pallor of Thorne's face turn to a deeper white; he could feel that the ruddiness upon the countenance of Broderick had deepened into scarlet.

There was a pause. After a moment, Thorne rose and said indignantly:—

"Say that again!"

"With pleasure," returned Murgatroyd, "I say that you are the hitherto unknown owner of the most notorious gambling-house within the State."

There was another pause in which Thorne looked at Broderick and Broderick looked at Thorne.

"This is preposterous!" exclaimed Thorne.

Murgatroyd made no answer. Then he proceeded
with assertions.

"And with the earnings of that gambling-house,"
he said evenly, "you have stopped the mouths, closed
the eyes and ears, and paralysed the hands of the
authorities. With the earnings of that gambling-
house, you have bought the influence of Chairman
Peter Broderick, who lives upon those earnings—
grows fat upon them."

Broderick's eyes bulged; he, too, rose and started
toward the prosecutor.

"Say," he yelled, "I'll open up my anatomy to you!
Pick out any ounce o' fat and tell me Cradlebaugh's
put it there! Come on—my fat is my own—I earned
it by the sweat of my brow!"

With perfect coolness, Murgatroyd continued:—

"Thorne, ever since you sprang into prominence
here, you have posed in this community as a self-made
man—boasted of carving your success by industry,
integrity and brains. And yet—" pointing a finger
of accusation toward him—"you have bought every
item of your reputation, every iota of your respectability!" He stopped for an instant, and then: "Every
inch of your political progress, you've bought with
this tainted money, and with the same kind of money
you'd buy the United States Senatorship—if you
could."

"Lies—all deliberate lies!" Thorne ejaculated.

"Worse than slanderin' my fat!" added Peter Broderick.

Before Murgatroyd could speak again, Thorne took another tack.

"What evidence have you, I should like to know?" he said; "you can't prove these things, Murgatroyd."

"That," returned Murgatroyd, "is for me to worry about—not you. I'm going on, and when I'm through, you can stake your last dollar that I'll know all about this rotten system that you call your organisation—from the most insignificant ward politician up to Peter Broderick!"

The accusing forefinger shifted from Thorne to the County Chairman; under it the avoirdupois of that gentleman seemed to shrivel and grow less. In all his career no man had ever honoured Broderick with this kind of talk, and he wasn't used to it. All at once, he felt that his courage was slipping from him.

"I've got to see a man—" he began, looking nervously at his watch; then hunching his shoulders, he stole softly and almost on tiptoe to the door.

"*Broderick!*" sung out the prosecutor sharply.

Broderick stopped, but did not look back.

"Broderick!" thundered Murgatroyd, "I want you in this office to-morrow afternoon at four o'clock—

I want to have a talk with you—alone. If you don't
come, I'll—send for you. Do you understand?"

Broderick did not answer; he opened the door, and
slipping through it, disappeared.

Murgatroyd laughed, and turning to Thorne, he
went on:—

"Thorne, I sent for you to tell you to close up
Cradlebaugh's—to close it up at once. If you
don't——"

But Thorne's self-possession had come back, and he
demanded fearlessly:—

"And what about you, Murgatroyd? Are your
hands clean?"

The tiger leaped into Murgatroyd's face; his eyes
flashed fire; the accuser became the fighter.

"I can take care of myself!" he answered quickly.
"I'm talking about you, now. You are sworn as a
counsellor to uphold the law; you have lined your
pockets and built up your career with the coin of sui-
cides, profligates, drunkards, like Challoner, for instance.

"Yes," he went on, "and there is something more between you and me than this, Thorne." His voice now
dropped almost to a whisper: "You have the effrontery to pay attentions to——"

Thorne interrupted him, his tone, his glance, his
manner leaping at once into insolence.

"So that's how the land lies, is it? Well, let me tell you something that possibly you already know. All my life I have had the things I wanted—all my desires have been fulfilled. I wanted money—I got it. I wanted power, social and political—I got it. I have never stopped; I have always progressed. You have already said that I would be Senator of the United States—if I could. I tell you that I shall! Again, you have hinted at a woman who is worth while. . . . Well, I'm going on and on and *on*, in spite of you——"

"You are going on to your finish," returned Murgatroyd. "I have only just begun with you. Before I go further, it may be just as well for you to relinquish the last two of your desires. I don't demand it—I advise it."

Thorne glanced uncertainly at the prosecutor, who had spoken with complete assurance. Thorne recognised the danger. Murgatroyd had been getting indictments lately, and for every indictment, a conviction. Thorne did not know what proof Murgatroyd had in his possession, and he knew of no way that he could find out. Besides, the people liked Murgatroyd. Thorne believed in compromise, therefore he extended his hand.

"Look here, Murgatroyd," he said, "you know neither of us can afford to have things like these

talked about. Don't let us sling mud—let's fight in
the open. A fair fight and no favour—let's be decent."

"Why don't you get your ammunition in the open,
then?" asked the prosecutor.

Thorne flared up.

"Why didn't you?"

Murgatroyd smiled and said:—

"You'll find my ammunition in the open, Thorne, the
next time the legislature meets to choose a Senator!"

Thorne's insolence had returned as he demanded:—

"Do you mean to tell me that your name will be presented in the caucus?"

"That's precisely what I mean."

"Of course you'll try to buy votes with the Challoner
money you have."

"I'll get the votes—never fear."

"Try it, then—I'll match you dollar for dollar."

"Not with dollars coined from Cradlebaugh's, nor
from corruptions," declared Murgatroyd.

Thorne's eyes narrowed.

"Murgatroyd," said he, "you reckon without your
host—no matter who owns Cradlebaugh's—or runs it.
The organisation has its finger on every Grand Jury,
every petit jury, every judge. You can't accomplish
the impossible until you've beaten Peter Broderick
and the organisation, and until you do this you can't

beat me—you can't prove your assertions—your hands are tied. The organisation backs me up."

"If your name," retorted Murgatroyd deliberately, "is presented for Senator, it will be withdrawn; and mine will be presented in its place."

"Who'll present it?" sneered Thorne.

"That," smiled Murgatroyd, mysteriously, "is my business and not yours. But inasmuch as you told me your story, Thorne," he went on, "let me tell you mine now. All my life I've struggled like the devil to get the things I wanted; and I failed. But a big change is about to take place—here and now. You stop right here; and where you stop, I begin. It's my turn! The things you want—I want. Your surest and your best desires are my desires. If you've got them in your hand, as you think you have, why then—" he clenched his hands—"I'll take them away from you. The time has come, Thorne, when you are going to get the things that you don't want,—and you are going to get them hard. I'm going to get the things you want, yes, and by George, I'll get you too! That's all I've——"

Murgatroyd did not finish; Thorne had departed.

The next day at four o'clock there was a resounding rap on the prosecutor's private office door.

"Come in!" said Murgatroyd.

The door opened, and Peter Broderick came puffing

into the room with perfect nonchalance. He had had
a day to think things over, and he had made up his
mind that the outburst of the prosecutor had been
all bluster. Seizing a chair, he drew it up to the desk
and sat down, saying:—

"I never refuse an invitation to see a man alone; and
now that we are alone, I don't mind telling you that
I'm ready for another one of them good cigars."

The prosecutor passed a box, from which Broderick
helped himself to a cigar, lit it, and after sending a
few clouds of smoke in the air, went on:—

"Do you know, Murgatroyd, that I haven't had a
good chance to talk to you since the Challoner case—
you've been so blamed offish all the time. But now,
here I am sittin' here with you,—you, the only mug-
wump in the town that I ever used to be afraid of,—
and you know I can say any blamed thing I please to
you, and you got to take it and say nothin'. Do you
know that I'm one of the few that believe the truth
about that bribe?"

Murgatroyd smiled.

"In other words, you think we're both in the same
boat—is that it?"

"Not a bit of it!" returned Broderick. "I'm in a
coal barge; you're in a motor boat. Why, Murgatroyd, there's many a man been in honest politics all
his life, like me, for instance, and who's never pulled

out three quarters of a million! Not much! And out
of one deal, too! Why, look at me?" he went on
glibly, "I've been in a lot of deals; but that gets me!
Three quarters of a million and more on just one
deal! Confound it, man, do you know the most I ever
made out of any one deal?"

Murgatroyd lit a cigar, leaned back in his chair and
inquired in an offhand manner:—

"How much?"

Broderick shook his finger at him.

"Foxy, foxy boy! Do you think I'd give up to you
so easy? This particular deal I'm tellin' you about,
is away back outside the statute of limitations. You
couldn't get me on it if you would. It was the Ter-
williger tract—I was chairman of the common coun-
cil, finance committee, you remember? Bought the
tract for twenty-five hundred and sold it to the city
for two hundred and eighty thousand. That's me!"

"Good work!" said Murgatroyd, with genuine admiration. "I didn't know that you were in on that."

"In on it?" snorted Broderick. "I was the whole
show! That's where I'm coy, my dear boy; it takes
Broderick to do these things; but it takes a bigger
man than Broderick to find 'em out."

Murgatroyd shook his head.

"They found *me* out, all right," he said.

Broderick waved his hand, and answered:—

"Not a bit of it! It's all blown over, and if it hasn't, it will. All they'll remember, after a while, is that you've got a wad of money. They'll forget how you got it, and they won't care." He puffed away and purred contentedly.

"You're a giant," he went on, "an intellectual giant to bag six figures." Then he waved his hand about the room and said: "You take this old court-house, for instance; I was on the buildin' committee, but to save my life—hold on a minute—" he pulled himself up with a round turn, "that was outside the statute, of course it was. Well, to save my life I couldn't pull more 'n a hundred and twenty-three thousand out of it. I came near gettin' caught, too," he admitted, laughing.

"But you weren't," commented Murgatroyd.

"No, sir!" said Broderick. "I don't do jobs that way. You could have gone through the thing with a microscope, and you wouldn't have found hair nor hide of Broderick."

Murgatroyd lazily closed his eyes, and murmured:—

"Tell me about the new hospital—that little concrete job."

Broderick leaned forward, his face growing crimson as he did so, and peered into the face of Murgatroyd.

"What are you gettin' at?"

Murgatroyd opened a drawer within his desk and took out a bulky batch of papers.

"Broderick," he said severely, "do you know that I've got you implicated in more than thirty different violations of the law right here in town?"

"Me?" Broderick looked incredulous.

"Yes, you!" answered Murgatroyd, evenly.

Broderick held out his hand, and asked with a show of interest:—

"What are they, anyway?"

"See for yourself," returned Murgatroyd; and leaning back in his chair comfortably, he gave himself up to watching the changes in the countenance of the other, who proceeded to scan the batch of papers with marked interest. And, although Broderick made no comments, he did a lot of thinking. Finally eyeing Murgatroyd with suspicion, he asked:—

"Without prejudice to anybody's rights, I'd like to know how you got all this?"

"It's easy when you know how," returned Murgatroyd, smiling; "and I've learned how."

Broderick's face broke into a confused, distorted smile.

"Now, without making any damaging admissions," he conceded, "do you know it would be blamed uncomfortable for me if I were dealing with any other prosecutor than you?"

The prosecutor smiled again.

"How do you know it won't be uncomfortable for you as it is?"

Broderick burst into a laugh.

"You an' me is two of a kind—grafters together, tarred with the same stick. That's why."

Murgatroyd nodded, took back the list and laid it down.

"That's all right, Broderick," he assented, "I didn't send for you about these things. I've got a little job for you to do."

"Out with it!" said Broderick.

Murgatroyd leaned forward and told him in a low voice:—

"Broderick, I want to sit in the Senate of the United States."

Broderick jumped to his feet, exclaiming:—

"What!"

"Yes, I want to sit in the Senate," repeated Murgatroyd.

Broderick burst into a peal of laughter that wellnigh shook the building.

"And you want me to help you?" roared Broderick.

"Yes, of course," persisted Murgatroyd.

Once more Broderick laughed immoderately.

"You'll be the death of me," he said, sinking into his chair.

"You laugh too soon," remarked Murgatroyd.

"Is there more comin'?" questioned Broderick, with a howl. "You know the valvular workin's of my heart ain't over strong. You're crazy, man!" he added; "the whole organisation is against you!"

"The whole organisation," repeated Murgatroyd, "except *you.*"

"You blamed idiot!" roared Broderick. "The organisation's against you because I am."

"I've got to be the next Senator," persisted Murgatroyd; "and you've got to put me there."

"I can't put you there."

Murgatroyd cast an appealing glance at the other.

"But—you want to, don't you?"

"Indeed I do not!" returned Broderick, indignantly.

Murgatroyd rose to his feet, saying, as though speaking to a spoiled child:—

"I don't like to see that spirit; it looks as though you were opposed to me."

"Have I ever been anythin' else?" returned Broderick. "Will I ever be anythin' else?"

Murgatroyd continued to reprove him.

"I prefer to see a man do with a good grace that which he has to do."

"And who has got to do?" queried Broderick, also rising.

"I have just told you," went on Murgatroyd, looking him full in the face, "that you've got to put me in the Senate."

Instantly Broderick became doggedly belligerent.

"I'll spend my last dollar to keep you out of it—I'll work against you till I drop in my tracks!"

Murgatroyd seized a small thick book and leafed it over.

"You'll do both," he remarked, "and when you drop in your tracks, Broderick, it will be with hard labour. Sit down, and take that pencil and piece of paper—I want you to do some figuring."

Broderick, wondering, seated himself; Murgatroyd peered over the little book.

"Seven and seven are fourteen," he mused, "and six are twenty, and eleven——"

"What have you got there?" Broderick asked with mild interest.

"The Penal Code," answered Murgatroyd, lightly.

"Look under B. for Bribe," suggested Broderick, with an accusing glance.

Murgatroyd shook his head.

"I'm just figuring up the number of years you'd have to serve——"

"But I'm not goin' to the Senate," protested the politician.

"No, but I am," retorted the prosecutor. "Four times six are twenty-four; besides the amount of fines you'll have to pay. Take the first on the list, Broderick. You'll get seven years on that, and seven thousand dollars fine. Put that down."

"I'll put nothin' down—I never was a hand at figures."

"Then I'll do it. Twenty indictments for corrupting voters—I've got the goods on that; twenty years and twenty thousand dollars fines. Hold on a minute, we won't add up just yet. There's your interest in Cradlebaugh's; there's the hospital; there's your pool-rooms; log-rolling with police-headquarters— Why, say, Broderick," he exclaimed suddenly, gasping with surprise, "it will cost you in the neighbourhood of one hundred thousand cash in fines!"

"You don't say!" sarcastically returned the chairman.

"And," continued Murgatroyd, suavely, "about one hundred and thirty-five years to serve in sentences."

"I'm booked for a ripe old age," returned Broderick, still with sarcasm in his voice.

"So that eliminates you from the Senate," facetiously continued the prosecutor; "you'll go up for the rest of your unnatural life." He paused and shot at Broderick a glance that went home—one that meant business.

Broderick squirmed.

"You don't mean to tell me, prosecutor," he exclaimed, "that you're going to prosecute me for these things?"

The other shrugged his shoulders.

"How can I help it?"

"You don't dare prosecute me! You blamed idiot!" screamed Broderick. "If you do, I'll send you up myself—you with three-quarters of a million dirty money in your clothes."

Murgatroyd thought over his words and weighed them. Presently, he said:—

"I would get out in five years; you would be there for a hundred and thirty more."

Broderick snorted with rage.

"What are you driving at, anyway?"

The prosecutor was silent for a moment, then he said:—

"Broderick, since I've been prosecutor, I have achieved a reputation for just three things: first, whenever I have tried to induce the Grand Jury to indict, I've succeeded; second, whenever they indicted, I have secured a verdict of conviction; third, my verdicts of conviction are always affirmed upon appeal." He stood over Broderick, threateningly, and finally declared:—

"Now, you put me in the United States Senate, or I'll put you where the penal code provides! What are you going to do about it?"

Broderick swelled with anger.

"I'm going to call your bluff, Murgatroyd!" he yelled. "You can't work me! And you don't dare touch me, either! Why, there ain't a man in this whole State who dares to lay a hand on me! By George, I call your bluff!"

Murgatroyd sat at his desk and pressed a button; the door opened and two men entered.

"Mixley, McGrath," said Murgatroyd, picking up some rectangular slips of paper from his desk and passing them over to them, "Chairman Peter Broderick is going to leave this room inside of thirty seconds——"

"You bet I am!" Broderick interposed.

"There are ten warrants for his arrest," went on the prosecutor; "take him into custody the instant he leaves this room."

" 'Right, Chief!" the men replied in chorus, and, facing about, left the room.

"Now, Broderick," said Murgatroyd, "you called my bluff—you may go."

The politician strode to the door angrily, blustering, but with his hand on the knob, he paused. A new situation was confronting him—a thing imminent, concrete. To cross the threshhold meant a blow; Broderick crept back to Murgatroyd.

"Do you mean this, Murgatroyd?" he queried.

Murgatroyd was busy at his desk and did not look up as he remarked:—

"This interview is over."

Rebuffed once more, Broderick crept to the door, but again he came back, and whispered uncertainly:—

"So you want to be United States Senator, eh? The best job that we've got?" He hesitated for an instant before asking:—

"Can I be of any help?"

Murgatroyd laid down his pen and looked up, smiling.

"Now you are talking sense, Broderick. Yes, you and Thorne can help me."

"Thorne! Great Scott! I never thought of him! Why, he's the organisation nominee, and I'm tied up with him! Say, honest, Murgatroyd, I can't go back on him—Murgatroyd, you can't make it—for even I can't undo all that's been done. Thorne has been slated for that job for months."

"You've got to sponge him off the slate, then," returned the prosecutor.

"I'll be everlastingly confounded if I do!" returned Broderick.

Murgatroyd pressed a button; Mixley came in on the jump.

"Mixley," began Murgatroyd.

"Hold on!" said Broderick, "I'll help you——"

Murgatroyd nodded.

"Warmly, energetically, enthusiastically——"

"Oh, all that," interrupted Broderick.

"Mixley," said the chief, "you can hold those warrants—until after the next Senatorial election."

Broderick gasped; Mixley's nod as he left the room spoke volumes.

"Broderick," said Murgatroyd, looking him in the eye, "you mean business—you're going to back me straight?"

"Not because I want to, but because I've got to," returned the politician. "It seems I must . . ."

He paused and returned Murgatroyd's glance significantly. After a moment, he said:—

"Well, fork over, then . . ."

Murgatroyd smiled.

"How much? . . ."

"Thorne will spend and has spent a lot of money," answered Broderick; "and you've got to——"

"How much will it take?" asked Murgatroyd.

"How much have you got left?" responded Broderick.

XV

ONE afternoon, many, many months after the interview just described, a few keen observers among the passengers on an incoming Southwestern Express—pulling with final, smooth, exhaustive effort into its eastern terminal—noted with considerable amusement that the pulses of one of their number had quickened to such a degree, that evidently their owner found it quite impossible to resist the temptation to leave her seat and politely push foward to the vestibule of the car, where she waited until the train came to a full stop. And so it happened that Shirley Bloodgood led the first flight of men who were hurrying up the long lanes of the station toward a roped-off space where groups of people waited expectantly for relatives and friends. Not that Shirley looked forward to seeing a familiar face among them; on the contrary she was fully aware,—since she had neglected to telegraph to any one the time of her arrival,—that there was not one chance in a thousand of any of her acquaintances being there; it was merely that she had fallen under the spell of that subtle spirit of unrest and haste, which all travellers, however phlegmatic, recognise the moment they breathe the air of the metropolis. One quick, scrutinising glance, it is true, the girl threw

around and about her, as she passed through the
crowd, but there was no disappointment on her face
as now, looking neither to the right nor to the left,
she brushed past what seemed to her a hundred cab-
bies each intent on making her their legitimate human
prey.

Once clear of the exit she turned to the porter who
was carrying her bag, tipped him, and directing his
attention to an urchin in the centre of a howling
mob of youthful street Arabs ready to pounce upon
her bag the instant the porter dropped it, she cried:—

"Give it to him—him!"

It was a chubby, little, Russian Jew with red cheeks
and glistening eyes whom she selected, and, with a
howl of disappointment, the other ragamuffins opened
up a lane to let the victor get his spoils, stood while
Shirley and her escort marched off, and then swooped
down upon another victim.

"Come with me," said Shirley to the boy; and suit-
ing her pace to his running stride, she turned her face
toward the west.

As Shirley walked rapidly along, the even pavement
felt resilient to her well-shod feet. The keen air
brought new vigour into her face, into her body, and
in it—partial stranger as she was—she detected that
which the metropolitan never scents: the salt vapour
of the sea. Thousands of men and women passed her,

and to one and all, figuratively speaking, she opened
wide her arms. The glitter of a thousand lights
found an answering sparkle in her eyes.

"There is nothing in the world like it! It will ever
be home—the real home to me!" cried Shirley, half-
aloud. "The noise, the bustle, the crowds, the life—
Oh, how I do love it all!"

For a considerable time Shirley had been living on
the heights of Arizona—a wilderness crowded with
space, dotted here and there with human beings.
Leaving her mother out there until, under new and
altered circumstances, she could arrange their home
in the big city that belonged to her,—and to-day,
more than ever, she knew that she belonged to the big
city, that in truth she was one of its people,—she
had come all the way through without stopping, rea-
soning that in that way just so much less time would
elapse before she could return and fetch her. In the
West—a land where men stood out in bold relief, because they were few, they had pointed out to her
rugged specimens noted for their physical prowess,
their dare-devil recklessness of life. And viewing
these swaggering heroes, with the sense of personal
achievement, however remote, strong upon them, a
vague longing had crept into her inner consciousness.

"Oh, if I were only a man!" she had said to herself.
But now, as she swept along on the right side of the

sidewalk, facing the crowd that passed her on the
left, she knew and felt that here was the place of the
real struggle, the battle-ground, the fiery furnace that
men were tested in.   Out in Arizona, it had been man
to man; but here in New York, it was one man against
a million.   And yet, woman-like, she thought that
were she unsexed, she could meet this struggle with
tireless energy, could strike where men had failed,
could crowd her way up, inch by inch, to the top.   And
thus communing with herself, Shirley walked on and
on, feeling that she could walk on forever through
this rush of home-going-folk—people who had done
something that day with their hands—people who
had unconsciously pushed the earth another twenty-
four hours upon his journey.

All of a sudden there came a strong tug at her skirts
followed by a youthful voice that called:—

"Say, lady,"—setting down Shirley's bag in mild
protest—"youse don't belong so far away! Ain't we
got too far?"

After an instant of confusion, Shirley conceded the
fact with a frank laugh.

"What am I thinking of!" she cried, "I want to go
to the Bellerophon."

"This way then, lady," returned her small guide;
and picking up her bag he turned southwards.

At sight of the unpretentious hostelry, which re-

joiced in the distinction of possessing such a resounding name, Shirley was conscious of a variety of emotions. For a time, in the old days, it had been the
fashion to patronise the Bellerophon, and Murgatroyd
had been the first to take her there. On more than one
occasion she had lunched with him and he had always
been most enthusiastic over the respectful service, the
wonderful cuisine and the quiet of the place. It was
infinitely nicer, he had said, to have their luncheon
there than to go to any of the huge, noisy caravan-
saries like the skyscraping, five-acre, concrete Mono-
lith on the avenue. And she had agreed with him.
Another time, he had explained to her that he was a
one-club man; a man with few friends; and that,
when tired out after a long, hard day's work, he
greatly preferred a corner, all to himself, in the Bellerophon to dining with half-formed acquaintances at
the club. In this, likewise, she had sympathised thoroughly with his point of view. And so, not unnaturally, it came about that Shirley had had little difficulty, on her long journey east, in convincing herself
that it was merely her liking for the Bellerophon, and
not at all anything more subtle that had caused her
to decide upon this quaint, old hotel for her lonely
stay in the metropolis. Besides, Miriam and she had
often been there together, and for that matter, had
grown to regard it as their own especial discovery.

But, now, when she had crossed the portal, when the boy had dropped her bag at the feet of the Bellerophon porter,—charging her quite double, as the price of her unpardonable absentmindedness,—a flood of memories swept over her, and her face flushed and she laughed in an irritated sort of way on realising that all the time she had been thinking solely of Murgatroyd.

Murgatroyd! Would the man's name never be out of her thoughts! For a time, out west, it is true, she had been so engrossed in the cares and griefs of her almost hermit-like existence, that she had been able to look back upon the old scenes as chapters in some pathetic story book; but now, the odd, little prints on the walls all about her, the slender old gentlemen— aristocrats—who strolled to and fro, everything about the place recalled vividly the man who, not so very long ago, had been a part and parcel of her existence.

They showed her to her room—a wonderfully old-fashioned room without a particle of brass or glitter in it. Even the bedstead was of wood —a good, solid invitation to home-like rest and slumber.

"Get me an evening paper, please," she said to the bell-boy.

"Which one?" he asked.

"All of them," she replied with a beaming smile; after that the boy was not long in bringing them.

In Arizona Shirley had been reading news which was, generally, three, four days—frequently a week old. Out there her home papers had straggled in, stale and unprofitable. But these—of even date; why, they were damp from the press. Indeed, it was good to have them!

"Home, home," she whispered to herself as she sank into a chair. She decided that she would not dine until much later, for she wanted to think, wanted to classify the emotions which had rushed in upon her so suddenly. The easy chair responded to her mood; and with a sigh, and placing her hands behind her head, she leaned back contentedly, little knowing that she looked wonderfully pretty in that old room—a goddess in a travelling gown. All the care and sorrow that she had passed through in these last months had made a woman of the girl, had deepened her beauty. Time had rounded her gently. Travel-stained and feverish with the glow of a new experience upon her, she was more inviting, more human, more beautiful than she could possibly be in the latest Paris creation. And yet one of the fittest mates in a great metropolis was alone. East and west, everywhere she had wandered, men, great men, wonderful men had held out their hands to her beseechingly—drawn by a

certain undefinable magnetism and attractiveness
which she possessed—a charm of manner which few
could resist. And Shirley had passed on, and had
given no sign.

But now in the silence of her room, her loneliness appalled her. The insistent memories closed in around
her. And suddenly she knew that she wanted to live
as other women lived—with a man of her own choos-
ing. But where could she find the man in whom she
could put her faith?

After a while, Shirley picked up one of the papers
lying on the table. At the first glance she started and
laughed guiltily. There at the head of the third
column, a word, a name had caught her eye: Murgatroyd! Paper after paper she now scanned, and all
mentioned his name: some on the first page, others on
the second; and with it invariably was coupled another
name: Thorne! Finally, she rejected all but one, the
Pillar,—the most conservative evening paper in the
city,—and concentrated her attention upon it. At a
glance, Shirley could see that with all its conservatism,
the *Pillar* was holding up its hands in reverential
hero-worship. In a two-column article it reviewed
Murgatroyd's record from its invariably impartial
viewpoint. "Murgatroyd had been clean," it said,
"his reputation was unsullied." It even referred to
the Challoner incident as a pitiful piece of falsehood

which had strengthened Murgatroyd in his position. Shirley laid down the paper with a cry:—

"Oh, what a hypocrite he is!"

So Murgatroyd was still playing a game! The root of his record was dishonesty! Shirley was thoroughly sincere in her indignation. And yet after a little while she began to wonder whether his conscience troubled him—whether it had cost him anything? Oh, if only she could be sure of that! For she well knew, and a little sigh of shame escaped her, that if only he had abandoned all pose, shown himself in true colours, even become a machine politician, she could have forgiven him everything. Not a little distressed, therefore, she read on and on, marvelling at the *Pillar's* devotion, but soon it became apparent to her that its editor was picturing Murgatroyd more in the light of a losing martyr than as a successful saint. For the article pointed out the strength of the railroads, of Wall Street, of the brewers, of the machine, and predicted mournfully that Murgatroyd was bound to fall before all his powerful enemies, concluding with: "More the pity, more the pity."

Presently she read the other papers; all contained more or less adverse criticism of him. One thing, however, stood out: fanatic though some of them called him, they were unanimous as to his honesty of purpose —a man who could not be bought, who could not be

swerved from the straight and narrow path. Moreover, in none of them was there any reference to the
existence of Challoner. The Challoners had been forgotten—had dropped completely out of sight.

It was after eight o'clock when Shirley was reminded
of a sudden that she was desperately hungry. Once
in the dining-room, she directed her steps to the small
alcove—the corner which Miriam and she had always
occupied, after the first of those memorable occasions when she had lunched there with Murgatroyd.
Taking her place at the table with a sigh of satisfaction, Shirley threw a glance around the room. Palms
screened her table, making it impossible for her to be
seen, although it was perfectly easy for her to see
every one in the room. There were few dining at that
hour, and so after ordering her meal, she was thrown
back once more on her reflections—reflections of Murgatroyd; and she fell to wondering in what way had
the possession of almost a million dollars changed him.
Had he grown stout? Was he full-faced, or possibly
a bit insolent, overbearing and aggressively genial
with a wide laugh? In any event, she was quite positive that he was prosperous-looking—too prosperous-
looking; and, all in all, it was anything but a pleas-
ant picture which she mentally drew of him.

The waiter brought the chosen viands and withdrew.
Shirley ate eagerly. The air of the city was full of

life and body; it gave her an appetite. Being quite
a material personage, she enjoyed her dinner thoroughly. Things tasted deliciously to her, and yet
her thoughts wandered.

"If only Billy had been different . . . " she kept
saying to herself.

Suddenly the palms were parted, and a fat man approached her table. On seeing it occupied, he
mumbled his surprise and backed out again. But
while pushing his way through the palms he extended
a short arm and said:—

"That table over there, then."

The remark was made to a companion, whom as yet
Shirley could not see. An answer, however, came in
a man's voice; both men seemed disappointed: evidently, this corner was a favourite with others
as well as herself. And the fat man—his face was
strangely familiar. Who might he be? Shirley was
sure . . .

Broderick. That was the man: the funny, vulgar
politician who had been pointed out to her at the Challoner trial. Shirley wondered what a man of his
stamp was doing in the quietude of the Bellerophon.
Somehow, he did not seem to belong there; she laughed
silently to herself as through the palms she watched
him settle himself laboriously at a table in another
corner. The seat he had taken faced away from her,

and she noted how broad, how terribly broad was his back.

"But a power in politics—the real thing!" she cried half-aloud. It was not surprising, she told herself, that men of refinement hesitated a long time before going into politics, if this were a type of the men they had to compete with. Her thoughts running on in this strain, she determined out of curiosity to get a glimpse of Broderick's companion. It was not difficult to get a good look at him, as the man sat facing her.

At the first glance, Shirley had a faint suspicion that likewise she knew that face; then she looked again and for a moment she was startled. "No, it can't be possible that—" At that instant the stranger looked up and dispelled her doubts. She was face to face with the man who had filled her thoughts for the last two hours.

"And so that is Billy Murgatroyd!" she murmured to herself. He was the same Murgatroyd she had known, but different from the man she had pictured. And she would have gone on indefinitely criticising his looks, but she was suddenly interrupted by the sound of voices. It was Broderick talking, his big voice filling the room. Shirley listened attentively.

"Blamed good place to get away from the gang,"

he was saying; and there was a satisfied look on his face as he glanced about the room.

While Broderick ordered the dinner, Murgatroyd leaned forward and made some remark. Instantly something in the tone of his voice, or it may have been his manner, told the girl that the relations between the two men were, in a degree, confidential. The back of Broderick assumed the attitude of a political adviser. Shirley observed that he gesticulated a great deal and often wiped his brow with a handkerchief which, even at a distance, she could see was over-embroidered, but in none of his movements so far was there the slightest suggestion of hostility.

"And this is the use that Murgatroyd has made of poor Miriam's money!" she cried to herself. "He's bribing the enemy!"

Shirley bowed her head in shame.

Presently she lifted it again, for before their dinner had arrived and while Broderick talked on, Murgatroyd rose and walked for a brief while up and down behind the table; and, unseen herself, she scrutinised him closely.

The first thing that her woman's eye noted was that Murgatroyd was not in evening clothes; he wore a business suit, not altogether new, which to her thinking, needed pressing; it looked as if he had lived in it from daybreak to daybreak. He was no stouter

than when she had last seen him; if anything he appeared to have lost flesh, yet his figure still retained
its strong but fine lines. And Shirley was forced to
acknowledge to herself that it had lost none of its
grace. But on his face was the dull flush that results
from the strain of enthusiasm, of excitement, of over-
work. He looked fagged out, and his eyes were restless, though they glowed with steadiness of purpose.
From time to time he glanced quickly about him,
taking in every detail of the room, studying the people in it, and even peering through the palms that
hid the girl, as though he wondered what interloper
had had the temerity to rob him of his lair. One
thing, however, impressed her more than anything
else: his demeanour toward Broderick. There was
within it not a particle of that confidential concession
that Broderick seemed ever ready to offer; on the
contrary, it suggested a suspicious watchfulness.
Murgatroyd had every appearance of being a zealous,
jealous taskmaster who had set himself over a paid
but uncertain servant.

And Broderick,—only once did Broderick turn his
head so that Shirley might see his face; but in that
one instant the girl divined what she believed to be
the situation, the true force of the drama that was
being played by the two men. Broderick's face,
glance, his whole being, indicated the cunning of the

man; he was treachery personified, at least, so he appeared to Shirley; and she told herself, as she sat there and studied him, that any one with half an eye could see that he was hoodwinking the man opposite him.

"Murgatroyd was being fooled!" There was no doubt about it. The attitude of both men expressed it; but, more than anything else, Murgatroyd's air of feverish endeavour, of expenditure of energy, confirmed it. With Miriam's thousands he had paid for something that had not been delivered. Broderick had taken the money—every dollar of it, of that Shirley was thoroughly convinced,—and had given nothing in return. In the girl's mind there was no accounting otherwise for Broderick's leer; in no other way was it possible to explain the desperate effort that Murgatroyd seemed to be making. But, at last, the lawyer grew angry; he hit the table repeatedly with his fist and glared at Broderick. And the huge politician pretended to cower and tried to propitiate him.

"Yes, they are fooling him!" she repeated to herself. Miriam's money had been of no avail; Murgatroyd had failed to accomplish his purpose.

After a while this feeling of contempt for his failure gave way to a wave of pity. What right had she to judge him at all; what manner of woman was she, that she should set herself up to determine whether his lesson was deservedly bitter or not; and what should be his punishment. "Money so gotten will never do him any good," Miriam had said after the scene in the court-room; and how true her words had proved! Why, the papers, even though they believed in his honesty, had as much as said that he was going down to defeat. And then, in turn, her feeling of compassion was succeeded by one of gladness. She was not a little surprised to find herself fervently wishing that Broderick had robbed him of every dollar; but, later on, her cheeks burned furiously when an honest introspection disclosed to her the real motive of this desire. For, after all, what if Murgatroyd would come to her and say:—

"I have sinned, and I have lost; be merciful to me, a miserable sinner."

What if some day he should come to her free of all hypocrisy, stripped of all save truth, a beaten man, what then? Well, she felt unutterably lonely, she wanted to be loved, and after all, he had helped her friend by setting her husband free.

XVI

A few days later, dressed in light mourning, Shirley Bloodgood for the second time in her life wended her way to a certain tenement house not far from the East River.

"Surely I cannot be mistaken,—this must be the place," she told herself, groaning in spirit.

In reply to her timid knock and inquiry for Mrs. Challoner, a little girl directed her to the apartment above, the door of which was presently opened by a woman with full rounded face; and entering a neat, well-furnished, five-room flat, Shirley was soon seated at the window chatting with happy eagerness.

The young woman with the full, fresh, rounded face, it can readily be imagined, was Miriam Challoner.

"You've been away more than three years, Shirley," she sighed, as she bent over a bit of fancy work. "It seems a century almost."

"It hasn't seemed so long to me," returned Shirley. "Though when we first went west, I thought it would be nothing short of a nightmare—waiting for an old man to die."

"It must have been," assented Miriam.

Shirley held up her head proudly, and answered:—

"No, it wasn't, because for the first time in my life

I really came to know my father. I thought I had known him long before, but I made a mistake. I never knew him until these last three years in Arizona—I found out almost too late."

"I always liked your father, Shirley, and I think he always liked me," was Miriam's remark.

"Yes, he did. But did you ever stop to think," went on Shirley hastily, "why, my father never wronged anybody! My father was good—my father was honest! Oh, I could scourge myself," she declared sadly, "for the things I used to think about father. I even told Murgatroyd, once, that though I loved my father, I could never admire him, respect him."

Miriam raised her eyebrows and protested mildly:—

"You never told me that, Shirley."

"No!" exclaimed the girl; "my friends don't know the worst side of me! My father a failure! Fortunately in these three years I have come to look upon things differently—have come to know that he was a success, simply because he was real. Money! What is money? My father was a man!"

Miriam rose suddenly and went over to her and kissed her.

"I'm glad, Shirley," she said with feeling, "that you found it out. I knew it always."

All this time, Shirley had been watching with grow-

ing curiosity, the fancy work on which Miriam sewed
so industriously. At last, she ventured:—

"Miriam, I'm a regular old maid. I haven't
been one hour in your house, and already I'm burning up with curiosity to know just what you're
making."

Miriam glanced a moment out of the window, then
she answered somewhat evasively:—

"Why, it's just a bit of embroidery . . . "

But Shirley was not yet satisfied, and went on to
protest:—

"But what is it? Miriam, I must know . . . "

Miriam Challoner hesitated for an instant, then holding up in the air a tiny infant's dress, she said
softly:—

"Well, if you must know, why, you must."

There was a long pause. At last, Shirley exclaimed:—

"Isn't it dainty! Who is it for, Miriam?"

Miriam raised her head and looked squarely into the
eyes of her friend; the next moment Shirley had her
arms about Miriam, and drawing her close to her, she
cried joyfully:—

"You precious thing! I'm so glad, oh, so glad!
But why didn't you say so before?"

Miriam smiled softly.

"I'm just a bit old-fashioned, I'm afraid," she murmured. "Nowadays, it's the thing to make such an-

nouncements through a megaphone from the house-tops."

For some time, she continued to sew in silence, Shirley watching her the while. All of a sudden Shirley drew a long breath and said:—

"Miriam, I wish I were happily married. It's the only life for a woman."

"Yes, you are right," assented Miriam joyously, from whom had fled the recollection of all but the last few years.

"I have always taken the keenest interest in the romances of others, but I want something more than a mere vicarious interest in romances—marriage. I'm a marrying woman," declared the girl, "and I dread the thought of being an old maid."

Miriam laughed.

"And yet they say that they're the happiest women . . . ."

"Oh, but a real woman is one who has a husband and children—" Shirley stretched forth her arms, as though to grasp all life within them,—"children to bring up; to wipe their noses and dress them for school, and to hear them say their prayers at night. That's life! It isn't pride with me; it's instinct."

Miriam thought a moment. Finally she ventured:—

"But you've had chances. There was Murgatroyd . . . ."

"Murgatroyd," broke in the girl, "is not my ideal.
No, indeed, not after what he did . . . "

"Then, there was Thorne," persisted Miriam, "and
Thorne may be United States Senator, too—he's
forged ahead."

Shirley laughed and flushed in turn. Presently, she
said:—

"I'll tell you a secret, Miriam."

Miriam smiled.

"We seem to be full of secrets to-day."

"Yes," returned Shirley, "only yours is a respectable
married woman's secret; mine mustn't be told . . .
Well," she confessed at last, "I've seen Thorne since I
came back, and——"

"No!" Miriam ejaculated.

"Yes! He proposed to me once more, and——"

Miriam leaned forward eagerly.

"You accepted him?"

Shirley frowned.

"No—if I had accepted him, it wouldn't be a
secret."

Miriam looked at her blankly.

"Why did you refuse him?"

Shirley seemed puzzled.

"That's just what I want to know myself. I don't
know why . . . Somehow, I couldn't marry
Thorne."

"Well, for some unexplainable reason, I'm glad of that," assented Miriam.

"Tell me about Murgatroyd," said Shirley suddenly, reseating herself. "I haven't seen him——"

"There isn't much to tell," answered Miriam. "As a reformer, he's been a success. He's serving his second term as prosecutor, you know. It seems he wanted to finish his work there."

Shirley tossed her head.

"Who couldn't, with all that money!"

"He and Thorne," went on Miriam, "are rivals for the United States Senatorship. Things are growing warm, too, I hear; but it's only a question of a day or two now . . . "

Shirley laughed, but her voice was hard when she spoke:—

"He told me once that it cost over half a million dollars in this state to be chosen Senator. Well, he's got the money, anyway——"

Miriam raised her eyebrows.

"He told you that?"

"Yes—before he got the money."

Mrs. Challoner deprecated.

"Shirley, aren't you hard on Murgatroyd? He's a man of character in the city," and she poised her needle in the air and glanced at the girl in a quizzical way. "I think," she went on slowly, "that I understand Murgatroyd. I think he's a man who could go wrong once, and only once."

Shirley shrugged her shoulders. But whatever may have been her opinion to the contrary, she was prevented from expressing it by the sound of approaching footsteps on the stairs.

"Not a word of Murgatroyd," whispered Miriam quickly.

"It must be Laurie," thought the girl to herself, and sprang up like a frightened hare. The next moment the door opened, and Lawrence Challoner came into the room.

Dressed in rough, clean, business clothes, he was as different from the Challoner of five years before as she could imagine. This man was strong, healthy, with a ruddy flush upon his face. He had the appearance of being a bit heavier, but better set up. He looked solid, respectable. In fact, he looked so good that it was a willing hand that went out to him in greeting.

"Well, this is a pleasure that is a pleasure," said Shirley, smiling. "I need not ask how you are, Laurie, for you're the picture of health."

"And you, Shirley—why, you never looked better," and he looked at his wife for a confirmation of his words. "What have you been doing with yourself all these years . . . " The tide of his words receded

there, leaving his eyes stranded upon hers. The same
thought came simultaneously to them both.

Miriam's happiness at their spontaneous greeting
was good to see.

"If I dared, I'd kiss you," Laurie went on, laughing
good-naturedly; but he compromised on his wife, who
had been holding, all this time, the bit of fancy work
on which she sewed. Suddenly she glanced down at it.

"Oh," she said, conscience stricken, and running
across the room, hurriedly thrust it into a closet.
Challoner watched her in surprise; and when she returned, he put his arm about her and kissed her once
again.

"So much happiness," commented Shirley, with a
pretty little pout, "and poor me . . . . "

Challoner laughed.

"Oh, we'll have to look after you, Shirley! I've got
a dozen likely chaps down at the works—Americans,
too. Real men, every one of them—men who work
with their hands."

"The works?" Shirley looked in astonishment, first
at one, and then the other. "Oh, the selfish jades
we've been—Miriam and I have talked about every
man in creation but you! Aren't you ashamed, Miriam? I am!" She drew up her chair, and settling herself back comfortably into it, turned to Challoner and
went on excitedly:— "Now tell me about yourself."

"We've saved five hundred dollars," began Miriam, answering for him. "And——"

"Five hundred dollars!" interrupted Shirley, entering completely into the spirit of things. "How did you ever do it?"

Miriam turned to Challoner, and said with a smile:—

"Laurie, do you remember the day when we had saved our first ten dollars?"

"Shall I ever forget it," returned her husband, devoutly; and turning to Shirley: "The fact is, somehow or other I've made good—and done it in five years, too! But you don't know what it means to me, to us . . . When Miriam went to the hospital that day, I started in—one dollar and a half a day——"

"Yes?" said Shirley eagerly. "What kind of work?"

"Tell her about your invention, Laurie," suggested his young wife with pride.

Not waiting for a second invitation, Challoner immediately launched forth on his favourite topic, Shirley listening with great interest. But toward the close, he said something about concrete and frauds which instantly caused her to interrupt him.

"Frauds? What frauds?"

"Why, where have you been that you haven't seen the papers?" he inquired. "The papers the world over, almost, have had something to say about this political exposé. I was at work on the hospital job at the time, and it was I who made the discovery that everybody connected with the job was stealing cement: bosses, superintendents, inspectors, politicians, why, even I was invited into the ring. There was money in it," he continued, "money for me—hundreds, thousands . . . " He paused, and then wound up with: "But, what good would that do me when the hospital fell down?"

"Think what would have happened," interposed Miriam, "if it had been full of patients. It was good they found it out in time! It has to be rebuilt."

"But I wouldn't stand for the steal," Challoner went on, in his legitimate pride. "Maybe you know the rest?" He looked up questioningly; and convinced that she did not, he proceeded: "I went to Murgatroyd; he did the rest. I helped him, of course, by testifying, and all that sort of thing; in other words, I had to make good my accusations. But perhaps Murgatroyd didn't smite those chaps hip and thigh! You know what it meant, don't you? It well-nigh smashed the ring! Anyhow, it has crippled the organisation, and Murgatroyd did it!"

"Good for Murgatroyd!" ejaculated Shirley; and then added quickly with a blush: "Good for *you!*"

"Laurie's in business for himself," Miriam presently informed her.

"No!" exclaimed Shirley. "Concrete?"

"Yes," answered Challoner enthusiastically. "I've

got a bit of a reputation for honesty, now. People
that want an honest job done come to me. Of course,
for a time, the hospital scandal killed concrete to some
extent 'round here; but there's going to be a quick
recover. The trouble is not with concrete, but with
men . . . " Challoner sighed longingly. "I could
swing that hospital job," he said wistfully, "if only I
could get the bonds and the cash with which to start
me. But I suppose I have got to stick to the small
work for a while. However, I'm getting there, Shirley, and I'm proud of it, too. You'll begin to think
I'm suffering from exaggerated Ego," he finished
with a smile.

"Well," said Miriam in justification, "any man who
saves five hundred dollars in so short a time has a
right to blow his own horn."

"I believe in giving praise where it is due," protested
her husband. "It was you, my dear, who saved it."

"I?" returned Miriam, who never seemed happier
than when sacrificing herself.

"Yes, by not buying hats like Shirley's, for instance," he answered, although he glanced at the girl
in admiration.

Miriam sighed with joy. It was good to be appre-
ciated—good to have some one to talk with who could
appreciate their struggle.

"I won't deny," presently she said with a smile, "that

it was rather trying at times; but it was a work of love, and we've succeeded."

Shirley sprang to her feet.

"Lawrence Challoner, I'm going to kiss you—you're the kind of a man I'm looking for!" And on the impulse of the moment she went over to him and made good her word. "I'm proud of you," she went on. "You're the real thing—you're a success!"

Challoner laughed as now he drew his wife closer to him.

"They are like a pair of doves," said Shirley to herself; and then aloud, as she started for the door: "Miriam, I'm going to fix up a bit for dinner. I hope we're going to have a dozen courses, for I'm starved."

When the door had closed behind her, Miriam rose and started for the kitchen.

"Miriam, girl," said Challoner, gently, "never mind about the dinner now—that can wait."

"I haven't much to do, anyway," answered his wife.

"What have you been hiding from me for the past few weeks, Miriam?" presently asked Challoner.

She looked quickly up at him and repeated:—

"Hiding——"

He pointed toward the closet.

"What have you been putting away there every night for the last few weeks? What is in that closet now?"

Miriam Challoner hesitated. When she found her voice, she asked tremblingly:—

"Do you really want to know?"

"Yes," he answered in the same tone.

Miriam stepped to the closet, fumbled there among some things, and returning thrust something into his hands.

"There," she said, blushing.

Challoner held it up, looked at it a moment, finally he said, with just a tinge of suspicion in his voice:—

"This tiny dress—what?" He looked at his wife stupidly, and after a time, he added: "Why, Miriam, you never told me. . . . A little child for you and me?"

"Yes, Laurie," she whispered softly.

Challoner was visibly affected. For an instant he held the infinitesimal garment up before him; then acting upon a sudden impulse, he cuddled it down into the crook of his arm and held it there.

"A child—for me," he mused, and suddenly passed the dress back to her, but as suddenly he held out his hands for it again, saying: "Give it back to me!" After a moment, he looked up and exclaimed: "I wonder if it is given to mere man to appreciate thoroughly the anticipation of motherhood—the hours that are given to fashioning little garments like this, for instance! And yet it seems to me now that I could work forever for—" he broke off abruptly, quite overcome.

Miriam was deeply touched.

"Never fear, dear, there will be plenty of responsibility for you later on."

At that moment Shirley poked her head in through the door, and called:—

"Miriam! Miriam, the potatoes are burning!"

Miriam left the room hastily, leaving her husband still nursing the small garment in the crook of his arm.

"A father of a child!" he mused. "It's good to be a father—a good father." Suddenly he seated himself at the table and buried his face in his arms. For some time he remained thus; but when he raised his head again there were tears in his eyes.

"A little child for me—and I shot Hargraves," he moaned.

Just then Miriam came back into the room. At a glance she realised what was going on in his mind; and going over to him, placed her hand affectionately on his shoulder and with great tenderness said:—

"Don't think any more about that, Laurie, it's past and gone. You're a new man, don't you see?"

"I haven't thought of it for five years!" cried Challoner, fiercely. "I haven't dared to think of it—I haven't had time to think of it. . . . ." He paused a moment to pull himself together, and then suddenly went on: "But now I have *got* to think about it, if I'm going to be a father." He sighed reminiscently. "Poor Hargraves, I can see him now, Miriam, as he put up his arm. . . ."

"Don't, Laurie!" she pleaded. "Don't! The forbidden subject—forget it, dear!"

"I can't forget it!" he returned. "It's all before me now." He glared into space, as a man might who witnessed before his very eyes some conflict. "I can see it now, just as it happened——"

He stopped suddenly, fiercely, caught her roughly by the arm, and cried in a loud voice:—

"Miriam, Miriam, thank Heaven I have thought about it! Listen, dear—I can see it now—just as it happened." He stopped and looked down at her. "Can you stand it, dear?"

"What is it?" asked his young wife, trembling with the horror of it all.

Challoner gripped her arm with painful force.

"I did not kill Richard Hargraves!" he cried in sudden joy. "No, I did *not* kill him!"

Miriam caught her husband about the neck and tried to soothe him.

"Laurie," she said gently, "you're beside yourself."

"No," he answered calmly enough, though evidently labouring under great excitement, "no, I know! I did not kill Hargraves! It's the first time I have thought about it. Five years ago everything was muddled—life was a muddle then; and on that night at Cradlebaugh's everything was hazy. But now, Miriam, it's as clear as day. I can see it—I do see it!" He lifted his arm, his forefinger crooked significantly, and declared:—

"I shot. . . ."

"Yes," she said eagerly, "you shot . . ."

"I shot at Hargraves, but I did not hit him. It's all come back; I can see it now!" And pointing toward the junction of the side wall and the ceiling, he went on to explain: "The bullet lodged in the panel of the wall. Hargraves put up his arm like this—I meant to kill him and I shot; but I didn't *hit* him. It was the last thing I remembered before I toppled over in the big chair—that, and his starting over toward the door. I remember that. It's all come back in a flash. But I never saw him after that."

"Yet," she protested, "you confessed . . ."

"Yes," he answered, "I tell you everything was muddled—life was hazy. I knew I shot at him—I knew I shot to kill. Of course I thought that I had done it; but it's not so. I tried to do it, and then——"

She caught him wildly about the body and cried hysterically:—

"Laurie—are you sure . . ."

"I know, I tell you," he answered, and hastened to add:—"Yes, and there's another man that knows—Pemmican, that's the chap!"

He stopped again and looked down at the small dress, which through all his excitement he had *held* tenderly in the crook of his arm.

"I'm going to be a father," he went on, "and it's well that I didn't kill Hargraves. But I have got to prove it—the world must know that I didn't kill him. I must prove it—Pemmican will prove it for me—he was there."

Miriam shook her head.

"You remember his testimony at the trial, Laurie; besides," she added softly, taking an old newspaper clipping from a small drawer of her desk, "Pemmican is dead."

"Dead!" His voice rang out in astonishment. "Dead! I didn't know it. Why didn't you tell me?"

For answer she placed her finger on her lips.

"Why, he died in the county jail, not long after I was tried!" exclaimed Challoner, who was now reading the newspaper clipping. "Poor chap, the confinement killed him, I imagine. Well, I never killed Hargraves, and I'm going to prove it, somehow." He leaned over and kissed a tiny bit of ruffle. "I'm going to prove it for you and the little one."

"Laurie," insisted Miriam, quivering, "are you sure?"

"I was never surer of anything in my life than this," replied Challoner. "I tell you, it has all come back to me like a flash. It was you, little one," he said, bending once more over something imaginary in his arm, "that brought it back to me."

Miriam had watched him closely.

"Yes, yes," she conceded, "it is true, I can see it— I know." And sobbing, dropped her head upon his shoulder.

"I've got to prove it," he repeated over and over again, patting her head affectionately.

"But—Murgatroyd—why, if you were innocent . . ." suddenly cried Miriam.

"Well?"

"He ought to know it."

"What do I care about Murgatroyd! What do I care about anybody but you and the little one that is coming—coming to you and to me!"

"Laurie," breathed Miriam softly, "I'm happy, oh, so happy! I knew—I felt, somehow, that things would come out right. I don't care whether you ever prove this—so long as we know. Happy?" she repeated as she nestled closer to him. "I should think so, with five hundred dollars in the bank and a small business, and after a while . . ."

"The most important thing, now, is that I'm certain I did not kill Hargraves. That makes it easy for the next important thing—for you—my baby—my little baby."

Reluctantly he yielded the lilliputian garment to Miriam. There was a knock on the inner door that Miriam had closed; it was followed by Shirley's entrance into the room.

"I hope," she said gaily, little knowing what had happened, "that we are going to eat pretty soon, for I never was more hungry in my life."

"The dinner will be an hour late," apologised her hostess, "but you won't mind, I'm sure, when I tell you *why.*"

XVII

In the prosecutor's office, to which they had access at all hours of the day, were Mixley and McGrath, the latter occupying a strategic position, in that he held in his hand the latest edition of the *Morning Mail*.

"How's the joint ballot?" called Mixley from across the room.

"Oh, it's hot, I tell you—both houses up all night!" returned the other from over his paper. "The hands of the clock moved back about ten times, and still going it. Still in session."

Again Mixley called:—

"Let's see the extra!"

McGrath tossed it over to him. Across its face, in huge letters, appeared the single significant word:

"DEADLOCK"

"Oh, but it's Murgatroyd that gives them the fight!" exclaimed Mixley, with enthusiasm.

McGrath smiled.

"Sure," he answered. "He's holdin' 'em, but that's all he's doin'. But what of that? He's got nothin' to hold 'em on. Why, everybody knows that he hasn't any money. It's my opinion," declared McGrath, "that the job goes to Thorne!"

Mixley read the first page of the *Morning Mail* with care. After a while he read:—

"I guess you're right. Thorne will be the next Senator, all right. Hang the luck!"

"How can it be helped?" reasoned McGrath. "Look at them brewers putting up maybe a quarter of a million to help Thorne out! I say, what do you think the votes of the 'wise' assemblymen were quoted at— on the market last night?"

"I don't know. I wish I was an assemblyman at that," sighed Mixley.

"Twenty-five thousand dollars apiece, and a rising market growing stronger every minute," answered McGrath. "And them brewers 'll pay it, too. One fellow wanted fifty thousand—an' he'll get it—see if he don't."

"I wish I was an assemblyman," repeated Mixley wistfully.

"If you were, and there was Thorne and twenty-five thousand on one side for you, and Murgatroyd without a dollar on the other, who would you vote for? Come, now, answer!"

Mixley waved his hand.

"You'd vote for Murgatroyd," yelled McGrath, "you know you would—you couldn't help yourself."

Mixley sighed again.

"But I ain't an assemblyman," he answered; and in

the next breath he added: "There's somebody at that there door."

McGrath crossed to the door and opened it; and Challoner, Mrs. Challoner and Shirley Bloodgood entered.

McGrath, who remembered them well, and who knew Challoner especially well since the hospital investigation, bowed low, and announced that the prosecutor was out.

Shirley stepped forward and said determinedly:—

"But we must see him."

"He's expected any moment," said Mixley from across the room.

"We'll wait," chorused the three visitors.

McGrath bowed again and went back to his seat near the window.

Presently Miriam turned to Shirley, and said regretfully:—

"You ought not to have come, Shirley. Perhaps you had better not stay."

Shirley looked narrowly at Challoner and at his wife. After a moment she inquired:—

"Don't you want me to stay?"

"Yes, yes, of course we do," Miriam assured her, "but you don't want to stay, do you?"

"Indeed I do," was the girl's quick answer.

"What good will it do," sighed Miriam; but, nevertheless, she found herself clinging to the girl as she did in every crisis when Shirley happened to be on hand.

"Do you suppose I'd miss being in at the death?" said Shirley after a moment.

"At the death?"

"Yes, I could see him hanged, drawn and quartered!" she exclaimed, with mock ferociousness.

Meanwhile, Mixley and McGrath were still holding their desultory conversation upon the situation of the day.

"They said," Mixley remarked to the other, "that the chief was politically dead after he had black-jacked the organisation; maybe he was—maybe he is, but he fights all right."

"He certainly cleaned things up," admitted Mc-Grath, feeling of his biceps. "We helped him, eh?"

"He didn't do a thing to Cradlebaugh's," mused Mixley.

"Nor to the machine," smiled McGrath.

"Well, anyhow," said Mixley, "if he hasn't got the machine and the brewers and the twenty-five-thousand-dollar assemblymen back of him, he's got the people, all right. They know he's honest."

"Oh, yes, he's honest, and they know it," assented the other. "But hang it! The people can't get him into the Senate. It takes more than the people—it takes good money to do that. At least," he added emphatically, "it always has, up to date."

Mixley shook his head.

"If he only had half a million behind him now . . ."

The other snorted.

"It's well he hasn't—well he never had. If he had half a million, he wouldn't be running for United States Senator! Just like as not, he'd be playin' golf or running a devil wagon."

"Gee, what a scorcher he'd be!"

"And he'd be so loaded with golf medals," added the other, "that he couldn't walk."

"Well, it's a man's fight he's got on hand, now, and no mistake—and with nothing but his honesty to back him."

The three visitors had been listeners to this conversation in silence; but Shirley could contain herself no longer; and turning to her companions, she said sneeringly:—

"Nothing but his honesty to back him! Why, lynching's too good for him!"

And as though her utterance of the phrase were the prosecutor's cue, Murgatroyd sauntered into the room. He looked as fresh and unconcerned as though he did not know that a bloodless battle was being fought for him down at the State Capitol—a close battle, at that.

Challoner rose at once, and said nervously:—

"Billy, I——"

At the sound of his name, Murgatroyd turned. He had not seen them sitting there, and now bowed impersonally to all three.

"Want to see me?" he inquired suavely.

"Yes," faltered Challoner; and with a quick glance in the direction of the prosecutor's men, he added: "and alone, please."

Murgatroyd turned to his men and queried:—

"Anything new?"

Mixley pointed to the *Morning Mail* and to an unopened telegram upon the desk.

"That, from the assembly," he returned.

Murgatroyd shook his head, saying:—

"No, I don't mean that. I mean in the Tannenbaum case."

McGrath gasped.

"Gee!" he exclaimed, "we was so excited about this here that we clean forgot about it."

Murgatroyd took from his drawer a bundle of papers and handed it to Mixley, saying:—

"Look up that excise violation—right away. And, McGrath," he continued, "there are three witnesses in the Tannenbaum case that we've got to have. It's up to you to get them. If you can't find them by two o'clock, let me know. You may go."

And now seating himself at his desk Murgatroyd turned to Challoner with:—

"Well, Challoner, what can I do for you?"

Challoner advanced quickly toward the desk.

"Prosecutor Murgatroyd," he began, gulping, "it's up to you to clear me of that Hargraves affair. I'm not the murderer of Hargraves!"

Miriam and Shirley had risen, but they did not move; they hung upon the prosecutor's answer.

Murgatroyd leaned back in his chair, and returned calmly:—

"I know it."

"You know it?" gasped the three visitors; and the next moment the women were grouped around the prosecutor's desk.

Murgatroyd proceeded to open his mail.

"Yes," he mused, "I have known it for almost five years—you must have known it, too."

"Not until a few hours ago," Challoner quickly informed him.

"You don't say so," was Murgatroyd's answer; and presently he added: "though perhaps it is not so very surprising."

Challoner's eyes narrowed; his pulse was beating fast. Suddenly he said:—

"But somebody killed Hargraves—who did it?"

The prosecutor looked at the man incredulously.

"Do you mean to tell me, that though you know now that you didn't kill Hargraves—that you don't know who *did* kill him?"

"I'm here to find out," was Challoner's determined answer.

"Why thunderation!" ejaculated Murgatroyd; and looking the other squarely in the eyes, went on: "I knew that everybody didn't know, but I thought you knew long ago that it was Pemmican of Cradlebaugh's who did it."

"Pemmican," repeated Challoner, as if to himself, "was the only man who knew, and he's dead."

"Yes," assented Murgatroyd, "he killed himself in jail. He confessed just before the Court of Appeals filed its opinion of affirmance in your case. It was a game on his part, that murder. He had stolen ten thousand dollars from the management' of Cradlebaugh's, and had been threatened with prosecution for it. It was necessary for him to replace the money. The opportunity came and he seized it. He knew that there was bad blood between you and Hargraves; knew that there was a motive on your part; knew that you shot and missed; knew that Hargraves had a lot of money on his person, and he set out to get it. It was safe—he got it, and Hargraves, too—shot him dead with another gun,—after you missed him,— and paid back the money to Cradlebaugh's."

Miriam could not restrain herself, and burst out:—
"And you have known this for years?"

"Yes," he told her quietly, his eyes wandering over
Miriam's face; "but it's plain to me now that you
haven't known it."

"How should we?" protested Challoner.

Murgatroyd frowned, then he answered:—

"How? Because I advised your counsel, Thorne,
and he was present when the order releasing you was
signed. It was his duty, not mine, to communicate
with you. I represented the people; he was the counsel for the defence."

"Thorne—Thorne knew . . ." cried Miriam.

"Yes, Thorne knew . . ." admitted Murgatroyd.

". . . and he never told us," came finally from
Challoner's lips.

"Possibly he didn't dare," explained Murgatroyd,
with an enigmatical smile. "Just at that time, Thorne
and Thorne's crowd held the public in the hollow of
their hands. So perhaps," he added sarcastically,
"the news about Pemmican was suppressed for the
public good."

"And you—" spoke up Shirley, her eyes flashing,
but got no further, for Murgatroyd went on addressing Challoner.

"I had no trouble, then, of course, in setting you
free."

Challoner blinked stupidly at the prosecutor, but Miriam's face at once was wreathed in smiles; for she knew that their future happiness was assured—that the name of Challoner would be cleared of its stain.

But Shirley was not yet satisfied. And her eyes were blazing as she exclaimed hotly:—

"It was not you who set him free! The law set him free! He was innocent, and——" She paused and drew a deep breath before going on: "You took a million dollars to set him free!"

Murgatroyd rose suddenly, and turning to Mrs. Challoner, he said with great earnestness:—

"This is the second time this charge has been made against me: once at the trial, and again here. You understand the nature of this charge?" he asked Shirley, looking her full in the eyes. "What proofs have you?"

Shirley pointed to Challoner's wife, and answered:—

"Mrs. Challoner is my proof."

Murgatroyd turned his gaze now on Miriam, whose expression of joy had not changed, and asked:—

"Mrs. Challoner, do you renew this charge?"

But before Mrs. Challoner could answer, Shirley broke in with:—

"Prosecutor Murgatroyd, a moment please!" And on the prosecutor's turning his gaze on her, she continued: "You know I am speaking the truth! Mrs.

Challoner has tried to convince me that this bribe was
not a crime, inasmuch as you had kept faith with her;
but she knows as well as you do what my opinion
is on the subject. I told you in the court-room
what I thought, and again on another occasion
—I have not changed. No, you are not honest,"
she concluded mercilessly; "you've stolen, you're
a———"

She balked at the word; the next moment there
came a loud knock upon the door.

"Come in!" called Murgatroyd.

"Sorry to interrupt you, Mr. Prosecutor," said Mixley, on entering, "but Mr. Thorne is outside———"

Murgatroyd shook his head.

"Tell Mr. Thorne I'm busy."

But no sooner had Mixley left the room than he was
back again.

"Counsellor Thorne says that he must see you—he
won't wait."

The prosecutor ordered his man to keep him out, ending with:—

"I can't see him!"

On Mixley's retreating, Shirley once more stepped
forward, and her lips were parted to speak when suddenly the door was thrust open violently and Thorne
stalked in. Behind him came Mixley, trying to hold
him back; but the other jerked himself free, and on

reaching the prosecutor's desk, he held out his hand, and called out loudly:—

"SENATOR MURGATROYD!"

"W-what!" exclaimed Murgatroyd, rising.

"I want to shake hands with you. Then I'm the first to announce it? Good!"

And he proceeded to tell Murgatroyd that the latter had just been chosen on joint ballot, majority in both houses, for the Senatorship, ending with:—

"Allow me—allow me to congratulate you!"

His voice rang true, even though he did not mean it; and Murgatroyd shook his hand, saying:—

"I thought it would be you, Thorne; you put up a good fight."

"We did, you mean," protested Thorne. "My crowd did, as usual. But you, Murgatroyd, deserve your honours—it was one man against the field, one man against illimitable backing. Senator," he declared, bowing, "I take off my hat to you! You have done what has never been done before, and you've done it without a dollar! You're the first man in the State," he went on frankly, "to be chosen by the people, literally by the people, and without a dollar behind you."

Still Murgatroyd shook his head, and repeated:—

"Thorne, it looked like you."

"No; and we've learned something by all this,"

Thorne went on; "we're beginning to find out that the people worship honesty above all things.—Oh, yes, I'm honest," he continued hastily; "I understand that. But you—your honesty is the real thing—and the people know it, too."

Turning to her friends, Shirley muttered satirically:—

"Honest!"

Now McGrath, as usual, had followed close on the footsteps of Mixley; and standing in the door, he yelled:—

"Three cheers for Senator Murgatroyd!"

And Mixley and Thorne,—born and bred to political meetings,—gave them with a will; while Shirley and the Challoners sat in the corner in deep silence.

Murgatroyd looked at his men in surprise.

"Where have you been all this time?" he queried.

"Outside," they answered sheepishly, "waiting for the news."

Murgatroyd strode down upon them and thundered out:—

"You get that evidence and have it here by two o'clock."

The men piled out in confusion. A moment later, Thorne took up his hat, and holding out his hand, repeated:—

"Accept my congratulations once more, Senator!"
He turned to go, and then for the first time he saw
the three people huddled together in the corner of the
room. "Well," he suddenly exclaimed, "I thought
we were alone. I didn't know . . . "

Challoner stepped out in front of him, and blurted
out:—

"Mr. Thorne, I wish to know if it is true——"

Thorne, still not seeing who it was, nodded.

"Yes," he said in reply, "the prosecutor has been
chosen—I'm down and out."

"You don't understand," returned Challoner; "is it
true, true——"

"True?" repeated Thorne.

"True that you have known all these years that I
was innocent of murder?" And Challoner squared his
shoulders and lifted his head while he waited for his
reply.

"Yes, of course it's true," answered Thorne, seeing,
at last, whom he faced.

"You never told me," fiercely returned Challoner.

Thorne apparently was dumbfounded.

"Never told you? Why I must have told you," he
stammered feebly.

"You never—" Challoner's voice suddenly broke.
"And I thought all these years—and because I
thought——"

He paused abruptly. Then Thorne, turning to Murgatroyd, boldly equivocated:

"It's preposterous! Of course I told him . . . "

Murgatroyd smiled grimly, and added gently to himself:—

"Never . . . 'till now."

Thorne now waved Challoner aside, saying:—

"You must be mistaken, Mr. Challoner; I certainly told you—" And picking up his hat, once more turned his attention to the prosecutor.

"Well, Senator, good-day!" At the door, he called back: "You've made a clean and honest fight—you deserve success! Good-day!"

But no sooner had the words passed his lips, than Shirley, almost beside herself, again broke forth:—

"A clean, honest fight! Oh!"

Murgatroyd resumed his seat, smiling.

"Yes," he said, as if wholly unconscious of the girl's irony, "it is hard work to be chosen Senator without half a millon or so behind you."

Up to this time, Shirley had held her indignation within bounds; but at this remark, she lost all control over herself.

"Why you—you're a thief!" she cried.

Instantly, Mrs. Challoner stepped forward, and raising a reproving hand, she said with great determination:—

"No, no, Shirley, I won't have you say such things!
You must leave the room! You and Laurie—I insist
upon it!"

Such an outburst from Miriam was so unusual that
for a moment both Shirley and Challoner were taken
aback. It was clear that unknown to them, Miriam
had made up her mind to some course of action;
in fact, so completely had she taken the situation
in hand, that it was easy to imagine that she had
forgotten that she was in the prosecutor's office and
not in her own home.

Fierce anger burned in Shirley's impulsive heart, as
glancing at Murgatroyd, she perceived that he was
as impassive as ever, apparently taking little interest
in the scene that was being enacted before him. A few
moments elapsed before she could bring herself to
agree to Miriam's demand.

"Very well," assented Shirley, "we'll wait outside,
but don't keep us waiting long." And, as reluctantly
she left the room with Challoner, she said in a loud
whisper so that Murgatroyd could hear it: "What on
earth can Miriam want to see him alone for?"

For answer, Challoner merely shook his head.

Left alone with the prosecutor, Miriam asked permission to lock the door; and although surprised at
such a request, Murgatroyd went over to the door and
locked it. Then, motioning politely for her to be

seated, he took a chair opposite to hers and asked severely:—

"Mrs. Challoner, what do you mean by this? Do you recall the compact made nearly six years ago?"

"Yes, yes," she answered, in a manner that showed plainly her desire to conciliate him.

"Your husband went free," Murgatroyd continued, "and when we made our compact, we did not know whether he was innocent or not, whether it was within the power of the law to hold him or to free him. But I kept my part of the compact in good faith—innocent or guilty, he finally went free."

"Yes, yes, I know," she returned eagerly.

"Your part of the compact was silence,—you promised to keep silent,—and yet, twice in this building you have broken your word, and Heaven knows how many times outside," he concluded solemnly.

"Yes, yes," she answered contritely, "I know. Don't think for a moment that I have any fault to find with you, Mr. Murgatroyd. None, whatever. I have always upheld you, always believed in you, I believe in you now . . ."

"That's more than Shirley does," and Murgatroyd smiled grimly, "for I heard her say that she would like to lynch me—she would, if you would let her," he added lightly.

"But she doesn't understand, Mr. Murgatroyd. She

is frightfully impulsive; you must not take her so seriously. Besides, what can a mere girl know of the troubles of—" She paused for a brief moment; and continuing, said in a changed tone: "But I'm glad, very glad that my money could help to put the right man in the right place, glad that my money has done so much good at last. Yes, I was wrong to speak——"

All the while she had been talking, Murgatroyd eyed her strangely.

"What do you want of me?" he broke in suddenly.

"Yes, yes, I must get to the point," she answered timidly, and then looked up at him as if searching for some expression on his face which would help her to go on; but she saw there only impatience, and it was with some trepidation that she proceeded: "Of course you know how splendidly Lawrence has done these last five years—what a man he has made of himself? Why certainly you know, because he helped you with that concrete affair, and—" She paused to see the effect of her words; but again they had been received with apparent indifference. Nevertheless, she said proudly: "Lawrence has gone in business for himself. Yes," she added quickly, nervously tapping the desk before her with her fingers, "and Lawrence can get that hospital job. He wants it—wants it badly, for he knows he would do it right. Mr. Murgatroyd, it would be the making of his business——"

She paused, while her mind struggled helplessly to find the fitting words with which to frame the difficult request that was to come.

"Lawrence needs a bondsman to get that job—a man with one hundred thousand dollars to go on his bond. And you know it is very hard, particularly hard for him to find a man who is worth that much to go on his bond—a bond that he'll do the work, and do it right. Oh, Mr. Murgatroyd, would it be asking too much of you to——"

Murgatroyd rose and gazed at her steadily.

"And you are asking me to go on a hundred-thousand-dollar bond for your husband?"

The tone of his voice told Miriam what she had to expect, and her heart grew chill, but she braced herself to go on:—

"Yes," she answered; and her voice was very gentle and very winning as she proceeded: "And if he could get a little money, just a little to buy materials. We have saved five hundred dollars, but that will not go far. Oh, he has worked so hard, and I don't want him to get discouraged! He wouldn't ask these things for himself— No, indeed! You'll go on his bond, won't you?" she asked with a wan smile. "And loan him a few thousand dollars to start the job?"

There was a long silence; finally Murgatroyd spoke
in an even voice:—

"You want me to go on his bond and loan him some
thousands of dollars, too?"

Mrs. Challoner inclined her head.

"Why, Mrs. Challoner," Murgatroyd exclaimed,
holding up his hands in amazement, "I haven't got
the money! I couldn't go on a bond for a hundred
thousand dollars; and as for lending him money!
Well . . ."

To Mrs. Challoner, the prosecutor in refusing was
acting merely within his rights. However, her feminine instinct had made her conscious of some inde-
finable change in him; so she persisted:—

"If only you could—"

Miriam ceased abruptly and watched him as he
sprang to his feet and for a long time paced up and
down the room, gazing at her face each time he passed
her. After a while, he came and stood over her, apparently trying to make up his mind whether or not
to take a certain course of action. Finally he said
with great feeling:—

"Mrs. Challoner, you are the bravest woman I have
ever known. Yes, perhaps I can arrange it for you.
But first, won't you please call Lawrence—call them
both back."

XVIII

MEANWHILE, outside in the waiting-room, Lawrence
Challoner walked dismally to and fro. For, notwithstanding, that in the last hour a great joy had come
to him, this room had awakened memories of that
other occasion, when, likewise, waiting for Murgatroyd, his life had hung in the balance. A wave of
pity took possession of him—pity for himself for his
then mistaken views of life, pity for the little wife,
who had stood so nobly by him; and, suddenly, he
quickened his steps, as if impatient for the time to
come when he could make amends for the great wrong
he had done her. In a measure, entering into his
thoughts, though her own were somewhat complex,
Shirley Bloodgood, from where she sat in a far corner
of the room, also waited nervously for the door to
open. And it was thus that Miriam Challoner came
upon them, her eyes glistening, a happy smile on her
face.

"Laurie, Shirley," she stammered, "Mr. Murgatroyd says—no, come, he'll tell you himself." And
taking their willing hands into hers, she led them
back into the prosecutor's private office, from which
they had been so unceremoniously evicted a little while
before.

Miriam Challoner's intimation that good news would be forthcoming was indeed rather vague; nevertheless, unconsciously, both were affected by her mood, and came into the room, smiling. Perhaps it affected Murgatroyd, too, for it was with his most genial manner that the hitherto imperturbable prosecutor, from where he sat on the edge of the table, his arms folded, singled out Shirley, and said:—

"Ready for the lynching, Miss Bloodgood?"

A look of surprise crossed Shirley's features, but she scorned to answer.

Murgatroyd was now standing, his back still to the table.

"Would you mind locking that door," he called to Challoner; and turning to the ladies: "Mrs. Challoner, take that chair, please," pointing to one nearest to him, "and, Miss Bloodgood, that," indicating one next to Miriam's.

Meantime, Challoner had returned, and was waiting, hesitatingly, near the door.

"Aren't you going to join the family circle, Laurie?" the prosecutor said lightly.

Challoner then came forward, and placed his chair between the two women.

Murgatroyd's manner suddenly became chilly, stern, in short, once more he was the prosecutor of the pleas.

Addressing Challoner, whom he looked well in the eye, he began:—

"Mrs. Challoner has asked me to go on a hundred thousand dollar construction-bond for you; also, to loan you considerable money."

There was a dramatic pause. And except for a questioning glance from Challoner and Shirley, which found a ready answer in the eyes of Miriam, his listeners did not move nor speak.

"There it is," announced Murgatroyd, in the same business-like tone; and stepping aside from the table, revealed two old, battered, dust-covered, sheet-iron boxes.

"Those boxes!" exclaimed Mrs. Challoner, who was visibly excited. "What is in them?" she asked in bewilderment.

"I don't know," returned Murgatroyd calmly.

There was no question in the minds of the prosecutor's visitors but that these boxes were the same that Miriam had brought to him so long ago, filled with negotiable securities, to the extent,—as Miriam was not likely to forget,—of eight hundred and sixty thousand dollars; but, as to their present contents, all, naturally, were at a loss to conjecture. So, no one spoke, but continued to wait expectantly for Murgatroyd to make the next move. Apparently, however, that was far from his in-

tention, and after a moment Shirley broke out
with:—

"Do you mean to say that you don't know what is in
them?"

"Miss Bloodgood, there's only one person in this
room who knows that," he replied quietly. Then
turning to Mrs. Challoner, he went on in the same
tone:—

"Do you see these seals?"

"Yes," she whispered.

"Unbroken, are they not?"

"Yes," again she assented faintly.

"Well, then, you know what is inside of them; I do
not."

"I?—" faltered Miriam. "Why——"

Then followed a moment of racking suspense for
all, except, perhaps, Murgatroyd.

"Mrs. Challoner," he resumed, "you told me once
that there were eight hundred and sixty thousand dollars in negotiable securities in these boxes. If what
you then said was true, there they are, coupons and
all."

"But, Mr. Murgatroyd," protested Mrs. Challoner,
"you said that you did not have any money . . ."

Murgatroyd smiled.

"I spoke the truth. But you . . ." And now,
to Challoner's great surprise, Murgatroyd fixed his

eyes on him, and said in a voice that impressed them all the more, inasmuch as it was filled with a kindly confidence rather than with distrust:—

"There's eight hundred and sixty thousand dollars in those boxes, Challoner, belonging to your wife. Can you stand having it back again?"

Challoner looked puzzled; for as Miriam had told Shirley, he had had no reason to believe that his wife's fortune had not all been spent by them. Slowly he began to understand, but he was too overcome to speak. Presently he found his voice and said:—

"Can I stand——"

"Yes," interrupted Murgatroyd, "you know what money did for you before—what it led to—" He broke off abruptly, and turning to Shirley he added: "I told you once, Miss Bloodgood, that there was but one way to cure a bad millionaire, but one way to reform him, and that was to take away his millions. Well, I took away his!"

All eyes now rested on Challoner, who, oblivious to his surroundings, seemed lost in thought,—and who can tell what dreams may come to one suddenly lifted from the depths of poverty back again to affluence. But in any event, looking the prosecutor straight in the face he said in an easy, determined voice:—

"Billy Murgatroyd, a little while ago you asked

whether I could stand having all this again; the past five years of my life is my answer to that."

This reply brought to his wife's face a look of pride, and unconsciously she straightened up in her chair; while Shirley sighed perceptibly.

"Laurie," went on Murgatroyd, still probing, but not unkindly, "what are you going to do with all this money?"

"You'll have to ask Miriam about that," he returned quickly; and then with a charming smile, he added: "I have learned that a man's mission is to make money, and a woman's . . . ."

Suddenly, Challoner grew thoughtful again.

"To think of the time," he said, half-aloud, "that it took Miriam and me to save five hundred dollars!"

"That five hundred that you saved," commented Murgatroyd solemnly, "is worth more to you than all this eight hundred and sixty thousand."

"There's no mistake about that either, Murgatroyd," spoke up Challoner promptly; but bending over his wife, he added with a fascinating smile:—

"Miriam, you're going to let me build that hospital, aren't you?"

Simultaneously with Miriam's monosyllabic answer, Murgatroyd glanced at Challoner sharply, not forgetting, quite naturally, how easy in the past it had been for the husband to get whatever he wanted from

his wife; his doubts, however, were only momentary,
for presently he pushed the boxes toward them, saying:—

"There it is—it all belongs to you."

But in all this Shirley had been strangely silent.

"Mr. Murgatroyd," she now said icily, "do you mean
to tell us that your only motive in taking this money
was to save Mr. Challoner?"

Murgatroyd took a few steps toward her and regarded her coolly.

"No—and you alone were right. I was bribed—I
was corrupt—I was a thief."

"No, no," cried out Shirley, relenting.

"Yes," he went on mercilessly, "it is true. It was
my ambition that did it. Besides, I was tempted by
a woman——"

"A woman——" faltered the girl.

"Like Adam, I'm blaming it on Eve. This woman
wanted me to be, well, really great——"

"You——"

"Yes," he persisted, "I was bribed. I took the money.
Oh, you don't know about me! You don't know what
I was five years ago! It seemed to me then that
money was the only thing that could make me really
great. I knelt at the shrine of money—loved it as a
dipsomaniac loves his bottle."

He paused; then he continued in a low voice:—

"Yes, I took money to acquit Challoner, and then I convicted him. Why? Because the instinct within me to do my duty was too strong to allow me to do otherwise. All the evidence was against him; he had confessed; I had to convict him."

"And the money—" ventured Shirley.

"Like a dipsomaniac,—a reformed dipsomaniac,—I put that money as he might have his bottle, on the shelf—corked. There it was—I could have it any time I wanted it." His face became more serious as he proceeded: "Then I kept on being a thief, for there was a new and overpowering motive that got the best of me. Like the reformed dipsomaniac I was determined to see what I could do without it. It became a passion with me. I knew that every move I made meant the expenditure of money. A hundred times, yes, a thousand times I have had my fingers on those seals about to break them, and then have crawled away—once more to do without the money. Somehow, I knew, that my time must come. Besides, there was that overwhelming ambition,—prompted by a woman."

Shirley hung her head.

"Yes," he went on fiercely, "a woman who must have her due; it was up to me to be something more than merely honest. Anybody could be honest, she told me, but not everybody could be great!"

Shirley ventured to look up at him, but meeting his gaze fixed on her face, she shifted her eyes instantly.

"Then there was the United States senatorship,—the fairest office in the State,—which I knew I could buy with the money for which I had sold my soul. Again and again I came into this office and went to that vault there, determined to break the seals of the covers on those boxes—to buy the United States senatorship. But I could not bring myself to do it. Something always said to me: 'YOU MUST DO WITHOUT IT! YOU MUST BE HONEST! YOU MUST MAKE A CLEAN FIGHT!' Yet, still, I was a thief: holding thousands that didn't belong to me. But always upon me was that all-absorbing passion,—a passion, not to use, but to do without the thing which was at my finger's ends,—an incentive without which I could not succeed. And so," he concluded, "I went in and won without it."

A tense silence followed the prosecutor's amazingly frank revelation of his temptation and the success which he extorted from it. Unconsciously, he assumed an attitude which it would not be unfair to describe as a defensive one, in readiness, as it were, for any possible strictures on his conduct. Nothing of the sort, however, was forthcoming. On the contrary, at least, as far as Mrs. Challoner was concerned, at no time, not even when his self-arraignment

had been the most severe, had his terrible words succeeded in driving the happy light from her eyes.
There were moments, it is true, when a dull pallour
had spread over her features, a pallour, however,
caused solely by sudden stings of agonising memories,
and those soft brown eyes had been raised to his questioningly; but his personality had ever been more or
less baffling and mysterious to her; and so, whether
semi-fascinated or not, they left him thoroughly satisfied with their scrutiny.

Probably better than any one present, Challoner realised to the full what Murgatroyd had suffered. Man-
like, however, he was more than willing to permit the
great work that Murgatroyd had done to overshadow
completely his questionable proceedings. Of course,
Challoner was quite well aware that the prosecutor's
actions viewed in the light of a successful campaign
wore an entirely different aspect than they would had
he failed to obtain the senatorship. In the latter case
it was inevitable, no matter what moral satisfaction he
could derive from the return of the money,—and in
fairness to Challoner be it said that he never once
questioned it,—that in addition to the humiliation of
a ruined career, the prosecutor would have to endure
the mortification of knowing that his loss of self-re-
spect was wholly futile. But in any event, Challoner
was too generous not to accept without reservation

Murgatroyd's contention that, at least in part, he was actuated by a praiseworthy desire to save his wife and him from the results of his dissipations. To a man, such as Challoner now was, it can easily be imagined, therefore, that he would regard that alone as sufficient reason to overlook everything else, and so rising, he grabbed impulsively Murgatroyd's hand, saying:—

"Not another word, old man! It's all right!"

Murgatroyd was visibly affected.

"Thank you," he said simply; and then added: "Only one thing more remains to be done. Mrs. Challoner, I must ask you to break these seals."

Miriam demurred.

"Oh, no, Mr. Murgatroyd!" she said. "Surely you must know that I believe you!"

But Murgatroyd insisted; and obeying him finally, Miriam broke the seals, and presently she showed to them the securities, undisturbed, just as Murgatroyd had taken them, dollar for dollar, bond and bond.

Suddenly Murgatroyd felt a touch on the arm.

"And I believe you, Billy," said Shirley contritely.

An enigmatical smile passed across the prosecutor's face.

"Do you, indeed?" he said dryly; and added: "That's, perhaps, more than I had any right to expect."

'A slight pucker showed on Miss Bloodgood's beautiful brow, but she replied, quite unruffled:—

"Why, of course, I do. After all, you were honest, weren't you?" And not waiting for his answer, added ingenuously: "You were not a thief!"

Instantly the expression on Murgatroyd's face became a very serious one.

"Yes, I was," he protested, "I was a thief." And with that he turned to Challoner and said in a voice of great feeling: "Challoner, this money is your wife's. Take it. And great God, man," he groaned, "don't, don't forget what it did to you—what it made you, years ago."

Mrs. Challoner shivered at the prosecutor's earnestness; but Challoner, hesitating for a moment only, advanced and said:—

"We'll take it. I'm not a bit afraid now, Murgatroyd—for I *know*." And then holding out his hand, he continued kindly: "Billy, if you hadn't taken it— where would I have been to-day?"

"Free—free as you are now," said the other man in a low, strained tone.

"Yes," assented Challoner, "out of prison, but——"

Mrs. Challoner quickly rose and put an end to the conversation going on between the men.

"Come, Laurie," she said abruptly; and holding out

her hand, "good-bye, Mr. Murgatroyd! I'm afraid
we have taken up altogether too much of your time."

Murgatroyd shook hands with the Challoners; but
on Shirley making her adieus, he said:—

"May I have a moment with you, Miss Bloodgood?
Won't you wait, please?"

Mrs. Challoner answered for the girl:—

"Shirley, don't be in any hurry. Laurie and I will
wait for you in the ante-room—" And as they
passed out Challoner called: "Wait until you see that
concrete hospital, Murgatroyd!"

For moments that seemed hours Shirley and Murgatroyd stood facing each other, neither having the
courage to speak, the girl filled with shame at the
great wrong she had done to the man she loved; while
he, feeling as if the burden that had rested upon his
soul had at last rolled away, was drawing deep breaths
—breathing like a man who has suddenly come out of
darkness into the daylight. Shirley was the first to
break the silence; and now looking up at Murgatroyd,
with a little shake of the head she asked:—

"Billy, do you care to know what I think of you?"

"Perhaps, if I had cared less, I——"

But not for a moment would Shirley listen now to his
censuring himself further, and quickly she cut him
off.

"I think it was a far finer thing to take the money

and not touch it," she declared with true feminine
logic, "than never to have taken it at all."

"But what if this habit should grow upon me," he
retorted smilingly. "Evidently Miss Bloodgood
doesn't know what graft awaits me in Washington?"

Shirley laughed softly.

"To think that you accomplished all this without
money," she said happily.

"But the worst is yet to come," he observed quickly.
"It means that one has to keep up the social game,
the club game, the political game, and the Lord knows
what other games on five thousand—or is it now sev-
enty-five hundred a year? It means that an unmar-
ried man must starve; and Heaven help the married
senator! For he and his family must live on a back
street in the capital and freeze. That's what it means
to a senator who lives on his salary."

"But doesn't poverty always travel hand in hand
with greatness," she remarked enthusiastically, and
with superb disdain for anything that she may have
said heretofore to the contrary.

Murgatroyd looked at her with admiration. Never
before had her eyes seemed to him so blue and so
lovely.

"There's one thing—one thing that I didn't tell
Challoner and his wife," he said, lowering his voice almost to a whisper. "Can you guess what that some-

thing was that always made me keep my hands off
those iron boxes?"

Shirley lifted her eyes to his in quick understanding.

"It was my love for the woman who wanted me to be
great," he went on in a voice so shaken with emotion,
that she scarcely recognised it as belonging to
him. "That was the motive that beat down all
others."

"And will you forgive the foolish lips that told you
to go wrong?"

For answer he held out his arms to her and she came
to them. Then he stooped down, and catching her
face between his hands, raised it slowly, and kissed the
lips tenderly, murmuring lovingly:—

"Her soul would not let me go wrong."

After a moment Shirley slowly drew herself out of
his arms and placing a hand on each of his shoulders,
asked laughingly, looking deep into his eyes:—

"And we'll go to Washington?"

"Yes, dear," he smiled back. "We're going to
Washington—to freeze and starve together on that
back street— Yes, my revenge is now complete."

Before he could kiss her a second time, Shirley darted
to the door, opened it and called:—

"Miriam, Laurie, come here—come back!"

One look at the face of the girl that she had left in
the office was sufficient to tell Miriam that she had

great news to communicate. Nevertheless, she asked innocently :—

"What for, my dear? Are you going to lynch him?"

Blushing furiously, Shirley waved her hand at the boxes on the table and said:—

"Billy says that you've gone off and forgotten all your money!"

THE END